AFTERGLOW

AFTERGLOW

Karsten Knight

SIMON & SCHUSTER BFYR

NEW YORK LONDON TORONTO SYDNEY NEW DELHI

SIMON & SCHUSTER BFYR

An imprint of Simon & Schuster Children's Publishing Division
1230 Avenue of the Americas, New York, New York 10020

SIMON & SCHUSTER BFYR is a trademark of Simon & Schuster, Inc.
For information about special discounts for bulk purchases, please contact
Simon & Schuster Special Sales at 1-866-506-1949
or business@simonandschuster.com.
The Simon & Schuster Speakers Bureau can bring authors to your live event. For
more information or to book an event, contact the Simon & Schuster Speakers
Bureau at 1-866-248-3049 or visit our website at www.simonspeakers.com.
Also available in a SIMON & SCHUSTER BFYR hardcover edition
Book design by Laurent Linn
The text for this book is set in Arrus BT.
Manufactured in the United States of America
First SIMON & SCHUSTER BFYR paperback edition November 2014
2 4 6 8 10 9 7 5 3 1
The Library of Congress has cataloged the hardcover edition as follows:
Knight, Karsten.
Afterglow / Karsten Knight. — First edition.
pages cm
Sequel to: Embers & echoes
Summary: Ashline Wilde, her sister Eve, and new boyfriend Wes set out to
stop Ash's trickster-god ex-boyfriend, Colt, once and for all when they learn
he plans to kill the Cloak, the benevolent beings that oversee the gods, and
merge Ash and her two sisters back into the too-powerful goddess, Pele.
ISBN 978-1-4424-5037-0
ISBN 978-1-4424-5039-4 (eBook)
[1. Supernatural—Fiction. 2. Sisters—Fiction. 3. Goddesses—Fiction.
4. Gods—Fiction. 5. Tricksters—Fiction.] I. Title.
PZ7.K7382Aft 2013
[Fic]—dc23
2012051443
ISBN 978-1-4424-5038-7 (pbk)

To Mom and Dad—
Four lines in the front of a book
can't repay twenty-eight years
of encouragement.

CONTENTS

NORWAY:
SIX MONTHS AGO

Colt's snowmobile picked up speed as he revved the engine, racing north across the vast glacier. Even with the Arctic wind stinging his cheeks and his cold fingers numb on the handlebars, he couldn't stop the excited smile that crept across his face.

After all, out of the hundreds of gods he'd hunted down throughout his many lifetimes, Mnemosyne was always his favorite goddess to kill.

Still, he couldn't help but gaze at the endless tundra around him and think, *This? This sparsely populated island, this barren wasteland is where she chose to hide from me?*

He'd hunted her down twice before in fact—once in 1829, and then again in 1924—but apparently this time Mnemosyne thought if she tucked herself away at the end of the world, he'd never find her. The goddess honestly believed she could outsmart him.

Well, she should have known better than to try to out-trick a trickster god.

The thrill of the hunt grew in him as he saw the lone structure appear on the horizon.

A church.

For nearly forty miles Colt had seen nothing but snow, rocky outcroppings, and the occasional silhouette of a reindeer darting through the polar night. Now, through the darkness, he could see the outline of the log walls, the acute triangles that made up the roof. Up this far north the winter night lasted for more than four months, but the golden cross atop the impressive steeple still glinted in the low twilight spilling over the horizon.

Colt was so transfixed on the church and the target lurking inside it that he never saw the ambush coming.

The first arrow slipped into his shoulder with a sickening *shick* sound. The second tore a bloody line along his jawbone, but it was the third that struck him dead-on in the heart.

He toppled off the back of the snowmobile and onto the unforgiving glacial ice. The snowmobile slid to a stop thirty feet ahead, where a figure in a fur-lined coat emerged from her hiding place—she'd been lying in wait for him beneath a special tarp that had camouflaged her amid the ice and stone. She tossed her crossbow to the side and advanced on the trickster with a serrated hunting knife, ready to finish the job.

Even with two arrows protruding from his body and blood pouring out of his chest, Colt sat up.

He climbed to his feet.

He wrapped his hands around the shaft of the arrow in his shoulder, and with a savage scream he jerked it out of his flesh.

With an even louder howl he ripped the second arrow out of his heart.

But then he smiled.

It was enough to make the huntress pause in her tracks.

Beneath his parka his regenerative abilities worked their magic, rapidly repairing muscle and arteries, and finally sealing the flesh over what should have been mortal wounds. When the process completed just seconds later, there wasn't even the faintest scar peeking through the holes in his parka.

Colt tossed the bloody arrows to the assassin's feet. Now that he could get a good look beneath her hood, he recognized her as Artemis, Greek goddess of the hunt. "So Mnemosyne hired you to protect her from me . . . without warning you that I can't be killed?"

Artemis circled around him, a lioness stalking her prey. "She told me all about your healing abilities. But she also told me that you're not as immortal as you pretend to be. That you have . . . a weakness."

When her eyes darted to his chest, he knew she was talking about his heart. The only way he could die—the only way he'd ever died—was to have his heart ripped right out of his chest or otherwise completely destroyed. Still, he would show her no fear. "Weakness? Was she talking about my fondness for chocolate?"

Artemis didn't take the bait. "I'm going to carve you up like a pumpkin, trickster. But don't worry—I'll keep your heart on ice for you."

Artemis lunged for him with superhuman agility, closing the space between them in a single bound. Her hunter's knife arced down, aiming for his heart.

But Colt, no stranger to battle, intercepted her in midair and held her by the wrist. Before she could break free, he withdrew the stun gun he'd been concealing in his pocket, pressed it to her exposed neck, and pulled the trigger. A heavy electric current racked her body for several seconds, until Colt let her drop to the ground.

He wasn't done with her yet, though. He dragged the convulsing huntress over the ice, and with quick work he tied her to the back end of his idling snowmobile. Using a second length of wire, he jammed up the throttle. The snowmobile's engine roared as it lurched forward, and Colt watched with unbridled glee as it took off, riderless, across the glacier, dragging Artemis behind it.

Five minutes later, when he pushed open the heavy teak doors to the church, he half-expected Mnemosyne to be in hiding. Instead she was kneeling at the altar with her back to him. Beyond her a small gap in the back wall must have either collapsed or never been finished, because the church simply opened out into the sharp cliffs of the fjord beyond. The polar twilight spilling through the opening and the chandelier overhead combined to give the church an eerie purple glow.

"Beautiful Mnemosyne," Colt called out in a lyrical, singsong voice. "Greek Titan of memory, and bane of my many existences."

Mnemosyne turned her head to the side and gazed at Colt over her shoulder. Between her shorn haircut and her dark robe, she had a monastic look to her. "So," she said calmly. "You've come for me again."

Colt rolled his eyes. Some gods always had a penchant for dramatically stating the obvious. "You know, last lifetime, when I told you that I'd hunt you down to the ends of the earth, I had no idea you were going to take me so literally." He toed the coal stove that she must have been using for cooking and warmth; it clearly didn't heat the room very well, thanks to the drafty hole in the rear of the church. "You could have at least lived out your short life in luxury—maybe a Manhattan penthouse, or a jungle loft. This is just . . . depressing."

"I wasn't hiding from you. I was waiting for you," Mnemosyne said. "Besides, I like it here." Mnemosyne turned back to the beautiful scene through the open wall. The sounds of the Arctic Ocean lapping at the ice and stone a hundred feet below were just barely audible. Finally she pointed to something on the eastern wall he hadn't noticed before. "They like it here too."

It was a painting, so crudely done it could have been some Paleolithic cave drawing. Rough as the artwork was, Colt recognized the image in the painting.

The dark, pitch-black body of a massive creature.

Its gray, bear-trap teeth.

Its single blue flame of an eye.

"The Cloak . . ." Of course the ancient, monstrous bastards liked it here. In their home netherworld they were hyper-intelligent and all-knowing. But they had a weakness: They were allergic to hate. It was like radiation to them—exposure to hatred and violence slowly devolved them into something vicious, bloodthirsty, and wild. Enough exposure could actually kill them altogether.

It was a fatal flaw that Colt planned on exploiting soon enough.

"They were right, you know," Mnemosyne said. She was on her feet now, leaning against one of the wooden pillars. "When they took our memories from us. Being able to remember lifetime after lifetime, accumulating centuries of history and wisdom—it should have made us wiser, more compassionate, more capable of creating a better world for humans and gods alike to share. Instead the weight of all those memories created monsters like you."

Colt used his fingernail to scratch a big *X* through the Cloak's blue flame eye in the painting. "Funny you should say that, since when you think about it, it's their fault I have to keep killing you in the first place." From

Mnemosyne's crestfallen expression, Colt knew she realized that in a twisted way, he was right. When the Cloak had tinkered with the brains of the gods to deny them access to their old memories—to give the gods a fresh start every time they were reborn—the procedure had only failed on two of them: the goddess of memory and the Hopi trickster whose regenerative abilities healed the amnesia.

The two of them alone had full, unfettered access to their former lifetimes.

And that's exactly why Mnemosyne had to die. Only she knew all about Colt's millennia's worth of deception and manipulation and murder. Only she could warn the other gods and goddesses of the webs this trickster was spinning. Without her, his monopoly on the old ways was complete.

A lifetime spent in hiding and isolation had clearly taken its toll on Mnemosyne. Her eyes had sunk in, and her body looked so frail from malnutrition that a strong Arctic wind probably could have blown her off the edge of a fjord. Still, her gaze remained resolute. "You've got all the gods on your payroll convinced that if they help you exterminate the Cloak, it will bring their old memories back. . . . But it's just the opposite, isn't it? If the Cloak die, they can't undo the brain damage, and the amnesia will be rendered permanent forever."

Colt just smiled. "Part of being a good trickster means telling people exactly what they want to hear. A few false promises and they eat right out of my hand. Hell, some of them are so stupid that I could take an apple from the supermarket and convince them that it was the forbidden fruit of knowledge if I wanted to."

"Knowing you," Mnemosyne said, "it would more likely be a poisoned apple."

"You know," Colt went on, "I might have found it in my heart to let you live your cold, sad existence here a little while longer . . . but then you had to try to warn Ashline Wilde that I was coming. If I hadn't intercepted your messenger before he got to her, you could have put a real damper on my love life."

"You leave that girl alone," Mnemosyne snarled, her caved-in cheeks drawing taut against her high cheek-bones. It was the first time she'd shown any real emotion since he had arrived at the church.

"You know I can't do that." Colt bent down, opened the door to the stove, and plucked a hot, burning coal right out of the furnace. He held it out to Mnemosyne, and even as much as she hated the trickster, she still flinched as she watched his palm blister under the smol-dering stone. "I crave her fiery touch," he said, closing his eyes and tightening his hand into a fist around the stone. As the odor of smoke and burning flesh hit his nostrils, he was momentarily lost in reverie, fantasizing about the volcano goddess, Pele, who had first captured his heart five hundred years ago. He'd loved her when she was an outlaw in 1920s New Orleans; he'd loved her when she was a protectress of the Hawaiian islands a hundred years before that.

"The volcano goddess that you once loved is gone," Mnemosyne said.

His eyes snapped open. "Because they took her from me!" Colt raged, stabbing a finger at the painting of the Cloak. "They had no right to break her the way that they did." Two lifetimes ago, after deciding that she was too powerful and too volatile, the Cloak had split Pele's soul into three pieces, three goddesses: a conjurer of fire, a summoner of storms, a wielder of explosions. Colt had pledged to put the pieces of her soul back together at all costs, and then he would be reunited with his beloved once more.

Ashline Wilde was one of those pieces—his favorite one—and soon she would love him again.

Colt finally dropped the hot coal to the floor and then held up his hand for Mnemosyne to see. The deep burns and festering blisters all vanished before her eyes, replaced with smooth skin. "All I want is to heal her. To make her whole again. Do you know what it's like to love someone so intensely that you'd tear the heavens down just to find her again?"

Mnemosyne just shook her head, and the look of borderline pity she gave Colt made him feverishly angry. "You've confused love with obsession. If you truly cared for Ashline Wilde, you would let her go, let her blaze a new life for herself, with no memory of you. Instead you see her as a toy that keeps being taken from you. And you dare to call that love?" She pointed to his chest. "No, there's no love left in that heart of yours. Just the faintest, crippled shadows of it."

Colt quaked with seething anger. "I'm going to enjoy hanging you from the rafters." He unslung the length of rope that he'd coiled around his shoulder; his trembling fingers struggled impatiently to tie a hangman's knot.

With a resigned sigh, Mnemosyne wandered over to the opening in the back wall and clasped her hands behind her back. There was nowhere for her to run, so Colt allowed her to take in the scenic view of the fjord and the frozen bay one last time.

"There's a lot that you can learn from the Arctic, Kokopelli," she said, using his true godly name—the one his people had given him thousands of years ago, before he'd forsaken them. "Up here the polar night lasts all winter. Suddenly the constant darkness makes the days bleed together until time loses all meaning. After weeks of this, months of this, you start to honestly believe that you'll never see the sun again." She tilted her head toward the horizon. "But then one morning, when you've lost all faith, you look out to sea, and there it is—a sliver of gold peeking its head over the eastern waters."

In response Colt started to stalk slowly toward her, holding out the noose.

Mnemosyne turned bravely to face him as her

executioner marched forward. "Even the longest darkness has an end," she said, "and yours is almost over, Colt Halliday. You just don't know it yet."

With that, before Colt could dart the last few steps to secure the noose around her neck, Mnemosyne dropped backward through the gap in the church wall, down the steep cliff face of the fjord. Colt rushed forward just in time to watch the Greek goddess of memory leave a crimson smear on the ice and rocks below, before the Arctic waters swallowed her body.

"Always a dramatic exit," he muttered.

In her stockpile of equipment to forge a living up in the bitter north he found a torch, which he ignited in the coal furnace. Then he wandered over to the painting of the Cloak and held the burning end against the mural until the wall went up in flames.

As the inferno climbed into the rafters, and the firelight danced around him, Colt let the intense heat wash over his face, once again imagining that he was back with his fiery beloved. With Mnemosyne gone there would be no one to stop him from reuniting with her.

Together, trickster and volcano goddess, hand in hand, they'd light the fuse.

And they'd watch the world burn.

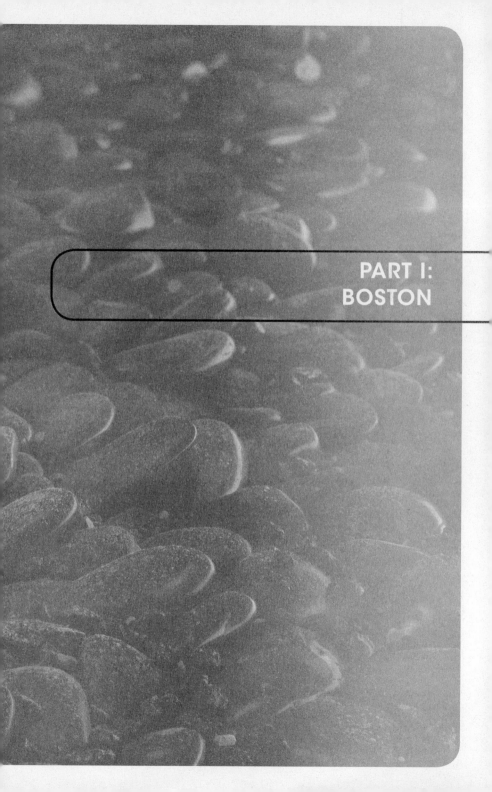

PART I:
BOSTON

The aromas from the Italian restaurants and bakeries were at war in the streets of Boston's North End, a hunger-inducing mix of fresh bread, marinara, and cannoli. At this time in the early afternoon the cafés of the old Italian neighborhood were nearly empty, the narrow lane just as desolate, except for a few cooks and bakers smoking cigarettes and leaning against the brick storefronts. Ash could feel their eyes keeping pace with her as she walked down the street, sensing the tourist among them.

Of course she couldn't blame them. With the way she had her cell phone and its GPS held out in front of her, she might as well have been clutching a big, wrinkled map. For the second time in as many weeks she'd traveled to a new city with absolutely no preparation or plan . . . and it showed.

That didn't stop her from pausing in one storefront to admire two big crimson awnings that read CAFFÉ POMPEII. A volcano goddess standing in front of a restaurant named after a town destroyed by a volcanic eruption? If Ash believed in signs, this one might have indicated that she was on the right path.

But Ash had no faith in signs anymore.

She had no faith in people anymore either. In the last few months she'd witnessed the grisly murders of three of her best friends—innocent gods whose lives had been snuffed before they'd even graduated high school. She'd watched power-hungry deities descend into madness, the worst offender being Colt Halliday, a villainous trickster who, unfortunately, also happened to be her ex-boyfriend. And worst of all, her two sisters, Eve and Rose—her own kin—had betrayed her and teamed up with the puppeteer.

Colt had charmed and deceived his way into her life, pretending to be human, when in fact he was a supernatural entity just like her. His ultimate agenda: to merge Ashline and her two sisters back into Pele, the destructive Polynesian volcano goddess that he'd supposedly loved for centuries, over many lifetimes. If he succeeded, then when Ash, Eve, and Rose were reincarnated in the next lifetime, they would all wake up in one mind, one body.

Ash knew she wasn't perfect, but she liked her soul just the way it was now.

And she'd do whatever it took to stop Colt from tampering with it.

After a five-minute walk down Hanover Street, the storefronts opened up onto a beautiful, tree-lined walkway—the Paul Revere Mall. A bronze sculpture of the famous patriot on the back of his horse loomed over Ash, but her attention was fixed on the tall monument in the not-too-distant background.

The Old North Church.

She made her way down the walkway toward the towering white steeple. As a lead, the nearly three-hundred-year-old church hadn't been much to go on, but she'd learned during her last encounter with Colt that he wanted something here. What could Colt so desperately need to acquire at a church? She couldn't imagine that Colt was after a Bible or a hymnbook, and he certainly wasn't going there for confession. And more importantly, why had both Eve and Rose willingly followed him here?

Ash jumped the short wrought iron gate behind the church and cut through the little garden. Against the shrub-lined wall was a statue of Saint Francis, who gazed back toward the street as though he were imploring her to turn around.

The front doors to the church were wide open to let in the crisp July air, but there were only a few people inside. A young man dressed in a shirt and tie stood near the altar, looking remarkably bored. His attention seemed divided between his cell phone and the few random tourists who were wandering around with cameras and camcorders. However, Ash noticed the well-dressed man straighten his posture and smile stupidly when he saw her.

Good, she thought. *He looks eager to please. . . . Sometimes being a girl really does have its advantages.*

Unfortunately, Ash had no idea who she was looking for, and the tour guide didn't exactly exude that "person of cosmic importance" vibe. It's not like she'd been expecting to walk through the front doors of the church and find Colt and her two sisters camping out in the white pews. Still, she'd hoped that someone—or something—would scream, "Colt was here."

Instead the place of worship looked just like an ordinary church. White walls and high ceilings. Tall windows to fill the room with light. An old pipe organ with its rigid metal fingers pointing to heaven.

Then Ash's attention drifted to the stairwell against the back wall, which was barricaded by a red fabric cord.

She tried her best to plaster a smile on her face, something she hadn't done a lot lately, and approached the man at the altar. As soon as he saw her coming, he stuffed his phone back into the pocket of his khakis and tried to look casual.

Nice try, Ash thought. It didn't help that she could still hear the tinny sound effects of the video game on his phone chirping through his pants.

Ash stopped just inside the man's personal bubble. "Do you work here?" she asked.

Unlike hers, the lopsided smile on his face was genuine, if slightly idiotic. "No," he said. "I just like to dress up and stand around in historic churches wearing a name tag." He angled the metallic pin up so she could read his name: Dave.

Someone has to teach this kid some game, Ash thought. She touched his elbow. "Well, Dave, I just wanted to tell you how adorable I think it is that you let those kids out in the garden make chalk drawings on the side of the church."

Dave, who had been glancing with anticipation at the hand on his elbow, suddenly blanched. "They're . . . they're drawing on the church?"

"Well," Ash said, "one of them is technically using finger paint, but I'm sure it will wash right off the brick. I especially like the kid who drew the devil and its two big red—"

Dave sprinted down the aisle toward the front door before she could even finish her sentence. Ash made sure the tourists were too engrossed in their filming to pay her any mind. Then she darted over to the stairwell, ducked under the red rope, and jogged up the stairs.

The second floor was just more of the same, but Ash found a door leading farther up into the church. Sixteen hours ago she'd watched her friend Raja fall to her death off the top of an apartment building—a fate that Ash had nearly shared herself, if her fiery abilities and some quick thinking hadn't saved her on the way down—so the last thing she wanted was to climb a series of rickety staircases and ladders to the bell tower of a hundred-and-ninety-foot tall church . . . but she was running out of options and clues. Colt and her sisters had reached Boston half a day ahead of Ash, after they'd jumped through one of Rose's portals, and there was no time to lose.

The musty stairwell, which was barely wider than her shoulders, led up into the dark, brick-lined interior of the steeple. Eight thick ropes descended from above. When Ash craned her neck to gaze up into the rafters, she saw that they were attached to a series of enormous bells. She grabbed one of the red grips but resisted the urge to tug on it.

Ash leaned beneath the little circular window and sighed. "What the hell were you looking for, Colt?" she whispered. Unless there was someone or something hiding up in one of the boulder-size bronze bells, she was faced with two possible realities:

Whatever Colt was looking for wasn't here, or worse—

Colt had already found it.

Ash dropped down into a sitting position on the dusty floorboards. She was overcome with defeat and out of leads, and her fatigue suddenly caught up with her. She buried her face in the crook of her elbow. She just needed to rest her eyes, just for a moment. . . .

Ash wasn't sure how long she'd been out when the telltale creak of the stairwell door woke her up. She scrambled to her feet just as a skinny college-aged boy popped into view. The moment he saw her, he froze in the doorway, his foot only beginning to come down. He had a bulky backpack slung over one shoulder and a pizza box in his hand.

Beneath his red and black baseball cap, there was something in his expression. . . .

Recognition.

And that's when he tried to run.

Disoriented as she was, Ash caught up to him before he could even make it to the second step. She looped her fingers around the handle of his backpack and pulled hard, sending the boy flying back into the bell tower. He landed in the dust beneath the bell ropes. Ash slammed the door shut to block his escape.

"Listen." He held up his hand. "I already told you people where you could find him. If he's not at the observatory, that's not my fault. I'm not his keeper."

"I'm not here to hurt you. I just have a few questions." Ash took a step forward, into the path of the light streaming through the window.

The boy visibly relaxed a little when the afternoon sun lit her face. "Your hair is longer than hers," he said. "But you two *must* be related."

"You saw my sister?" Ash asked. Must have been Eve, too, since Rose had longer hair than all of them. "And they were asking for someone?"

"I take it you're not with them, then." He sounded relieved and took off his Red Sox cap to wipe his brow. The hair over his ears turned up in wingtips from where the cap had probably made a home since his last haircut . . . whenever that was.

"Hell no," Ash said. "When were they here?"

The boy swept aside the heavy ropes and threw down his backpack in the corner. "The two of them came in before I left for lunch," he said. "The Native American guy and your sister, apparently."

So Rose hadn't been here . . . which explained why the church was still intact and not a pile of brick and wooden rubble down on Salem Street. Colt must have put Proteus, the shape-shifter, in charge of babysitting her somewhere—a weird image, since six-year-old Rose was now in the body of a sixteen-year-old.

The guy seemed to have decided that Ash wasn't a threat, because he popped a squat on the wooden stool that his pizza box had landed next to. The top had flipped open, but the pizza inside remained magically unscathed. "I'm Tom, by the way." The aroma of greasy cheese seemed to have distracted him, and he took a moment to inhale with his eyes closed. "Nobody makes pizza like the Italians do."

"Dude," Ash said. "I didn't come here for a Food Network episode."

Tom took a huge bite of pizza. "Sorry," he said, his voice muffled through cheese and crust. "Anyway, they were looking for my friend."

"What friend?"

"My classmate. At MIT." He kicked his backpack, which was so overstuffed with textbooks that it probably weighed as much as the bells above them. "We're both biomedical engineering majors—and Bellringers, too."

She pointed to his blue T-shirt that, sure enough, read

"Bellringer" across the front. "I just thought that was the name of some band I'd never heard of."

Tom laughed through another mouthful of pizza. "It sort of is. We're the guild in charge of making music with those things." He jabbed the slice of pizza crust up toward the rafters, then to the ropes. "Eight men, each to a rope, in charge of one bell, one note."

"Riveting," Ash muttered. "I bet all the girls throw their panties into the belfry when you guys give concerts."

"That's why I'm going to med school. Chicks dig doctors. Anyway, the Native American dude and your sister somehow found out that Modo and I do all our homework up here during the week—it's quieter than the library, you know?—but he's off preparing for his performance tonight."

Ash raised her eyebrow. "His name is Modo? My sister and her friend were looking for a guy named *Modo*?"

"You know, like short for Quasimodo?" For the first time since his arrival Tom actually looked a little embarrassed. "The guy has a crippled leg, walks with a limp, and hangs out in a bell tower. It would be a travesty of literary justice if we didn't nickname him that."

"You named your friend," Ash said slowly, "after the Hunchback of Notre Dame?"

"Oh come on. Even he calls himself Modo now."

Ash held up a hand to shut him up. "I just want to know where to find . . . Modo. Where did you send my sister and the douche bag with her?"

A slow grin trickled across Tom's face. "Where you'll

find Modo and where I said he is are two different things."

"You lied to them?" A peal of relieved laughter burst out of Ash. "Tom, I could kiss you right now!" When he lowered the slice of pizza in his hand and leaned in hopefully, Ash shook her head. "It's just an expression."

Tom shrugged and bit into the slice. "I sent them to an observatory on the other side of the state where Modo likes to go stargazing sometimes. . . . Only they won't find him there. He's working the fair tonight." Before Ash could ask, "Fair?" he reached into his backpack and pulled out a flier.

The one-page handbill was printed to look like it was on old, beige parchment, to match the headline across the top:

King Edward's Feast

It was an advertisement for a freaking Renaissance fair.

The pictures showed women in corsets and men in chain mail, with jousting and court jesters and medieval magic shows.

Tom leaned in, and at first Ash thought he was making another pass at her. Instead he put his greasy fingertip on a picture toward the bottom, of a boy with olive skin dressed in medieval garb. Ash guessed he was of Mediterranean descent, possibly Greek. His curly black hair fell to his shoulders, which were covered in chain mail. It wasn't that his face was unattractive, but there was something grizzled and timeworn about his skin that made him look much older than a college student. He sat on top of a horse, with a lance under one arm and a metal helmet cradled in the other.

"So that's Modo, huh?" Ash said. "How can I get to this dorky little festival?" Since she had arrived, she'd barely had time to drop the bag of clothes she'd thrown together at a cheap hotel, and she wasn't old enough to rent a car.

"It has a small fan base among the MIT kids, so they charter a bus to the fair. If you hustle to campus, you might make the four o'clock shuttle."

Ash stood up, already programming the engineering school into her cell phone's GPS. "I won't need a student ID to board the bus?"

"Nah, they don't check it." Tom smirked. "And even if they did, you could easily pass for an engineering student."

"Why's that?" When Ash realized what he was implying, she crossed her arms. "Do we need to have a discussion about cultural stereotypes? I'm Polynesian."

"Maybe we can discuss my ignorance over dinner?" he asked hopefully.

But Ash was already on her way out the door, heading for the subway. The fourteenth-century lords and ladies of the Renaissance fair were about to get a special visit from a twenty-first-century goddess.

Ash slept most of the bus ride, having pulled an all-nighter to catch her early morning flight out of Miami. The next thing she knew, her seat was being jostled as the students behind her stood up. She blinked away the thin veil of sleep and stepped down into the dirt parking lot with the others.

After paying the entry fee to get in, Ash's first thought as she entered the fairgrounds was: *I am completely under-dressed.*

She knew she'd been the only one on the bus wearing jeans, but this was ridiculous. As far as the eye could see across the wooded marketplace, people were dressed in tunics and trousers and dresses. Some of the women rocked elaborate braids, while the men donned feather-tipped caps and leather helmets.

So much for looking inconspicuous, Ash thought.

She wasn't quite ready to go flashing a picture of Modo around to random strangers, playing the "Have you seen this knight?" game, so she decided to take a walk around the compound. The fair basically consisted of a series of wooden storefronts and huts, each containing some type of medieval craftsman. Weaver. Corset maker. Even an artist painting the profile of a squirming schoolgirl who wouldn't stop giggling.

Ash took extra care to scan the lines at the archery and knife-throwing games, since she figured those would be the first logical places a typical twenty-year-old guy might go at a fair like this.

However, it wasn't until after she wandered past the sword-swallowing act in a circular amphitheater that she heard a suite of sounds that caught her attention.

Hammering.

The crackle of open flames.

Ash wasn't sure if it was the rhythmic *clank-clank-clank* of metal striking metal, or if the fire was somehow calling to her, but she felt herself magnetically drawn to the blacksmith's open-air hut. Even despite the shade of the roof and the tall oak trees surrounding it, the boy inside was sweating profusely, thanks to the furnace glowing in the back. Perspiration dripped off his curly ringlets and onto the anvil where he was stationed. He gripped a hammer in one hand, which he was using to repeatedly strike the blade of a glowing metal sword he held in the other.

Modo was wearing a sleeveless tunic, which revealed a detail his picture had not: Modo was ripped. His bicep bulged every time he brought the hammer down. From the size of his forearms, Ash guessed this whole blacksmith thing was more than just a part-time gig. He certainly didn't get those muscles from ringing church bells.

The word "blacksmith" triggered something in Ash's mind, and she experienced a tremble of excitement. There was little that Ash knew about her own Polynesian mythology, but she had retained a few random facts about Greek mythology from Mr. Carpenter's ancient history class.

The reason she was excited was because the Greeks had a god of metallurgy . . . one who was exceptionally good at weapon making and forge working.

One who was characterized by a wizened face and a lame foot.

"Hephaestus . . ." she whispered.

Just then, Modo looked up from his smith work. His

hammer was cocked back, ready for another strike. "Did you say something?" he asked in a faux English accent, with a historical lilt. He sounded like he'd stumbled out of one of the Lord of the Rings movies.

Ash cleared her throat and stepped under the straw roof. "I, uh, said 'how festive.' As in, the sword you're making is festive to the, uh . . . festival."

Modo gave her a once-over, from her T-shirt down to her jeans. "Well someone around here has to look festive. Can I presume that this is your first trip to our fair kingdom?" He smiled, just slightly baring his pointy teeth. "If you feel like slipping into something a little more comfortable, I can recommend a talented corset maker just a few huts away."

"I treasure my ability to breathe too much." *And my dignity,* she stopped herself from saying. "But I'll remember to bring a pair of pantaloons next time."

She was struggling with how to broach the "So you're a god too, huh?" topic, but Modo kept right on going in character. He pointed to her forearms. "Quite the sinewy arms for a maiden . . . This leads me to believe you're used to wielding a short-range weapon—a quarterstaff or an archer's bow, perchance?"

"Tennis racket," Ash replied.

"Ah, yes," he said musically. "Difficult to master, but deadly in the right hands." He hammered away at the sword a few more times and then held it up to the light to inspect the blade. "So, stranger—if you haven't come to King Edward's realm to fit your person with clothing befitting of a lady, and you're not here to engage in close-quarter combat like a man, then why have you come?"

"I came here to find you," Ash said, then added, "Modo."

At the sound of the name, Modo's arm once again paused on its way down to the blade. When he finally spoke, the medieval inflection to his voice faltered, and she could hear a distinctly Canadian accent. "Where did you hear that name?"

She stepped farther into the tent and put a hand on his arm. "Listen, we don't have much time, so just for the sake of efficiency, let's drop the whole Renaissance act and stop pretending like we're not gods."

"Gods?" Modo stared at her as though she were a complete lunatic. He tilted his head to the side. "Who put you up to this? Was it my frat brothers at Delta Psi? Or was it the Bellringers?"

"Nobody's putting me up to anything. You need to come with me." She tried to tug him away from the anvil.

He wouldn't budge. Instead he let out a short, husky laugh. "Wait a minute—it's my birthday tomorrow. Did the guys hire a stripper to come here and do some sort of weird, fantasy role play?"

Ash punched Modo in the arm, eliciting a whiny "ow" from him. "I am not," she enunciated, "a stripper. I am a god like you who has come here to save your ass from a group of other gods who are far less friendly." Every time she said the word "god," his confusion deepened, and it was then that she had an epiphany.

Modo honestly had no idea what the hell she was talking about.

"You seriously don't know?" Ash asked. "I figured it out within five seconds of seeing you, and you have no freakin' clue what you are? Who you are?"

He just stared blankly at her.

"Hephaestus?" she said, sounding less sure now. "You know, the Greek god of the forge and metallurgy?" Maybe the forward approach wasn't the brightest plan after all. Modo was starting to look like a rabbit that had been backed into a cave by a coyote.

He shrugged free of her grip, and his hand tightened around his hammer, as though he might need to defend himself. "Are you completely off your rocker?" he rasped. A group of boys chowing down on turkey legs gave them weird looks as they walked by, so Modo switched back into his theatrical voice. "I mean, what sort of strange sorcery is this, mage?"

Ash slapped him on the back of the head. "Modo, I know you're under the impression that I'm a nut job, but take a moment to connect the dots: You're a Greek boy . . . with a crippled leg . . . and despite the fact that it's well into the twenty-first century, you're a fucking blacksmith."

"Listen, cupcake," Modo said. "It's no secret that I like women who are into the whole fantasy role-playing thing, too. But even if I didn't have a girlfriend already, you are seriously starting to freak me out—and that's saying something."

Ash growled in frustration. It was never easy—but then again it had taken some convincing two months ago for Ash to finally accept the truth about her own identity.

Well, she'd just have to convince him, too.

She snatched the hammer out of his hand, grabbed him by the wrist, and forced his fingers down onto the flat of the blade. Then, with her free hand, she touched the other end of the sword.

He yelped and jerked his fingers away. Where the blade had almost completely cooled down before, Ash had heated it right back up so that the metal glowed orange against the anvil.

"If I'm not a goddess, then how the hell did I do that?" Ash ran her finger along the length of the sword, which whistled under her fingertip. "And if you're not a god, then why aren't you burned? I bet you've never been so much as singed a day in your life. You're just conditioned to associate heat with danger . . . when it holds no danger for you at all." She pointed to the smoldering furnace in the back. "You could probably stick your hands in those coals and be fine."

This seemed to give Modo pause. He was starting to look at least a little reflective. Maybe he was reviewing the last twenty years of his life, all his time spent around fire and forges, struggling—even hoping—to remember a time that the flames had left a mark upon his skin.

"I was where you are barely two months ago," she went on. "And unfortunately, just like me, you don't have the luxury of taking time to let it all sink in. Of sorting through the lunacy of what I'm telling you. Of wondering why the news that will change your life has to come from a complete stranger." She put her hand on his chest and let a swell of warmth pulse through the fabric of his tunic. "But when you start to realize how my crazy theory fills all the cracks that have been accumulating in your life, you'll be left with four words: I am a god."

For a moment, given the way he was staring into the embers crackling out of the furnace, Ash thought that her little speech had done the trick, that Modo would cave and come with her. This oblivious engineering student somehow factored into Colt's dark vendetta. If she could keep Modo out of Colt's hands, maybe she could prevent the trickster from putting Pele back together.

But Modo had other plans. He scooped up his sword, which was still glowing, limped across the tent, and submerged it in a trough of water. With a hiss, a thick curtain of steam billowed out of the trough as the sword rapidly cooled. "I have a choreographed duel to get to," he said, withdrawing the wet blade. "At least the cripple gets to be the hero—the audience loves cheering for the underdog." He waved his sword at her and turned his back as he hobbled out of the tent.

"Shit," Ash muttered. She'd gone the straight-up honesty route, and now Modo thought she was a total psycho.

She would have probably had better luck luring him away from the Renaissance fair by seducing him, then springing the whole "surprise—you're the reincarnation of a Greek god" concept on him.

She dropped onto the footstool next to the trough and sighed. *And to think most men would be flattered to be called a Greek god.*

She was stirring her finger in the trough, letting it burn hot and creating her own veil of mist, when she saw something that made her blood run cold, so cold that the flame on her finger instantly extinguished.

Through the wall of steam, shimmering like a desert mirage, a figure in a medieval cloak was jostling her way through the crowd. Ash might have just written her off as another costumed fairgoer had she not spotted the telltale jeans sticking out from under the knee-length cloak. And when she turned at just the right angle, Ash was able to see beneath the hood.

It was Eve, in the flesh.

The desire to punish Eve for her treachery urged Ash to leap over the trough and tackle her sister, but she stopped herself. So far Colt and Eve had no way of knowing Ash had followed them to Massachusetts. To reveal herself now would be to piss away any advantage of surprise she currently had. She hesitated just long enough that Eve disappeared into the milling crowd.

Well, two could play the chameleon game. Ash grabbed Modo's hooded brown cloak that was hanging from the roof and wrapped it around her shoulders. It was big on her, but that could prove useful, since it was long enough to cover her jeans. She popped up the hood and slipped into the marketplace.

The fairgoers were gathering in the outdoor amphitheater for the six o'clock sword-fighting demonstration. Eve had somehow stealthily blended in with the audience, and Ash was having a difficult time finding her again—the Wilde girls were on the shorter side, and the upcoming duel had drawn a brood of taller teenage boys. It was like trying to spot a shrub in a copse of redwoods.

Already the show was beginning. From what Ash could see between heads, a burly boy wearing lightweight armor and a red dragon crest had given Modo a rough shove across the stage. He leveled his finger at Modo. "You dare to block the path of the king's guard?"

Modo, who had rather ungracefully regained his footing, leaned on his sword like a crutch. "You? You're one of the king's knights?" He turned to address the audience. "It's so generous of King Edward to give his court jesters the opportunity for advancement."

The crowd rumbled with laughter. Meanwhile Ash elbowed her way closer to the stage. Still no sign of Eve.

The knight drew his sword. "Step aside, knave, or I shall skewer you like a swine upon a spit."

"Skewer me like a swine?" Modo echoed. "So you're a knight, a jester, and the king's cook. A true Renaissance man." He turned to the audience again. "Apparently good servants are exceptionally hard to come by these days. And to think with all that money the king spent on wanted posters for Robin Hood, he could have invested in a help-wanted ad."

More laughter from the audience. At this point Ash pushed her way through the last of the spectators to reach the front of the stage. She scanned the crowd for Eve, but with so many people in medieval garb Eve's cloak had effectively camouflaged her in the sea of browns and blacks.

"Your retorts are as lame as your foot, blacksmith," the knight said.

"And your face bears striking resemblance to a lady I frequent at the brothel," Modo replied. "What was your mother's name again?"

This time the crowd stepped forward to cheer on Modo, and as they pushed closer to the stage, the river of people parted just at the right time for Ash to spot Eve's cloak. The weather goddess wasn't watching the duel.

She had her face angled to the sky.

This wasn't good.

The knight leveled his sword at Modo, and two identically dressed swordsmen joined him on stage. "I'll give you one last chance to move aside before we cut you up and feed your remains to the king's pet pig."

"Pet pig? You mean the queen?" As the audience roared once more, Modo lifted his sword and brandished it at the three men. "In the words of a good wizard friend of mine: You shall not pass."

The cheers were deafening as the fairgoers prepared for the fight—the three knights had fanned out in a circle around Modo. But the cheering spectators were missing the little details that Ash was beginning to observe.

The way the air pressure around the amphitheater was rapidly plummeting.

The clicking in their ears.

The point of light gathering at the tip of Modo's sword.

The way his matted hair was slowly beginning to rise off his head from the static electricity.

Ash vaulted up onto the stage to the surprise of both the spectators and the nearest knight. Modo, however, was oblivious, with his back to Eve and his weapon raised, ready to strike the incoming swordsman.

Ash knocked aside one of the king's guards and tackled Modo around the waist, right as the clouds overhead crackled. She hit him just hard enough that he relinquished his tight hold on the prop sword and it went sailing into the air.

It didn't even land before the lightning snaked down from the sky and, in a blinding flash, zapped the makeshift lightning rod.

The lightning strike was about as loud as a high-speed car crash. The stage itself quaked where the lightning continued right through the sword and pounded an electrical fist into the wooden floorboards. Screams broke out in the audience, but even the shrieks couldn't drown out the ringing that had erupted in Ash's ears.

Ash could feel Modo—who was still crushed beneath her—staring at her in shock, but she had already locked eyes with her sister through the crowd. Eve had her hand outstretched and looked momentarily taken aback to see Ash protecting her target. Once the shock wore off, however, Eve seemed to be considering whether or not to send another bolt of lightning through the crowd to kill Modo . . . even if it had to pass through Ash first. Ash held out her own hand in warning. Even Eve wasn't immune to a fireball to the face.

The clouds overhead gave way to a monstrous typhoon. The sudden downpour was enough to send the spectators running for shelter. Ash shook her head. So the crowd had just stood there gawking when a lightning bolt nearly fried them all, but they fled for their lives as soon as it rained. Common sense at its best.

As soon as Ash had helped Modo to his feet, she stepped between him and Eve, who was sauntering unhurriedly toward the stage. "There are two of you?" Modo asked, his voice cracking.

"Remember that time I told you that there were evil gods after you," Ash snapped over her shoulder, "and that you needed to come with me . . . and you decided to have a fake sword fight in a public place instead?"

Modo started to lunge for his fallen sword, which was faintly smoking, the rain evaporating off the blade, but Ash grabbed him by the front of his chain mail and yanked him back. "Don't pick that up, idiot."

"Oh, please," Eve muttered, climbing up onto the platform. "Metal might speed up the process, but we both know that I can make a perfectly workable lightning rod out of a human being."

Ash shook off the mental image of Eve electrocuting the field hockey captain a year ago on the Wilde's roof. Even after all that time Ash could still smell the gruesome odor of burnt flesh.

"After all you've done, after all the people you've hurt," Ash said, "I still came to the Cloak Netherworld, risked my own life to get you down from that terrifying tree they'd plugged you into—and you repay me by coming here to electrocute another high schooler?"

"College student," Modo corrected her.

Eve slicked back her rain-drenched hair. "You don't know what you're doing, Ashline. If you knew who he is—what he is—you wouldn't be protecting him."

"All I know is that if Colt wants him dead, then I want him alive," Ash said. "I'll stand between you and him as long as—"

She cut off when she heard a splash behind her. Modo had hopped off the back of the stage and was fleeing out the rear of the amphitheater. Despite his impediment, he moved at a surprisingly quick gait.

"Courageous, isn't he?" Eve said. With that she held out both her arms, letting electricity crackle over them until a bright, white charge accumulated at her fingertips. She aimed her hands in Modo's direction, ready to take him out with a bolt before he could disappear behind the row of marketplace shops.

Before Eve could release the charge, Ash spun around and slammed a fireball into her sister's stomach. The detonation shot Eve backward like an arrow. She landed in the dirt of the amphitheater floor and carved a long line through the thick mud until friction brought her body to rest.

Ash stepped up next to Eve, who was groaning and trying to pull her wits together enough to stand up. Ash drove her heel into Eve's ribs and pushed her over so that she flopped onto her back. The mud splattered up around her.

"Do you know what my major motivation is for stopping Colt from melting you, me, and Rose back into one goddess?" Ash said. "It's the fact that if I were given the choice between waking up in the next lifetime sharing a brain with you and not waking up at all, I would choose eternal death in a heartbeat."

Eve started to say something, but Ash was too disgusted with her sister to listen to another word out of her. Using the supernatural strength that only came to her in times of true rage, Ash scooped her up by the waist and hurled her up and out, toward the nearest medieval workshop.

Eve landed on the slope of the roof, which yielded under her weight. She dropped through the roof and into the hut in a shower of straw, wood, and shingles, where she lay still.

By the time Ash caught up to Modo, he was already

staggering across the parking lot. He held up his keys, which he'd magically hidden somewhere in his pocketless trousers. When he pressed the button, a little green sport coupe nearby clucked twice, its lights flashing.

Ash didn't let him get to the car. She caught him by the arm and pushed him up against the side of a nearby van. "Look," she said to him, pinning him against the wet metal. "If this were just about you, I'd say screw it—the kid can try to survive on his own if he really wants. But it's not just about you."

Modo squirmed but Ash held tight. "I'm just an engineering student," he protested. "I build prosthetics for amputees, for God's sake. Fake feet, fake legs. What the hell could anyone possibly want from me?"

It was a valid question. But if Modo was truly Hephaestus, a god whose specialty was weapon making, and Colt had sent Eve to assassinate him . . . "It's probably about what they don't want from you, something they don't want you to build. Something worth killing you for." Her mind replayed watching Rolfe get skewered through the heart, watching the weeping willow tree crush Aurora, watching Raja get thrown off the side of a skyscraper. "Three of my friends are dead because of them. If you run away from me, if you won't let me protect you—if they find you and get what they want—then my friends died for nothing." Ash finally released him. "At least stay alive so they'll have died for something."

Modo surprised her by reaching out and tenderly

wiping the tears off her cheek. "It's just rain," she said.

Modo offered a sad, close-lipped smile. "Of course." He nodded back toward the Renaissance fair. "So these guys really want to hurt me? To kill me?"

"Modo," she said. "You were about two feet from being zapped with enough lightning to run Boston for a day."

"Then I guess we better clear out of here . . . and get the hell out from under these rain clouds." He cringed and ducked down, as though the lightning were coming for him again.

Once they'd climbed into his car, there was a moment when they both sat silently in the front seat. The car vibrated quietly beneath them. Modo's hands rested on the steering wheel as he blankly watched the windshield wipers bobbing back and forth. "What do we do now?" he whispered.

Ash's window had begun to fog up from the air conditioning. She drew a little flame in the condensation. "First we find out exactly what they don't want you to build. . . ." When she'd finished the flame drawing, a few beads of water dribbled down the glass. "And then we build the hell out of it."

THE DRIFTWOOD STRANGER

This beach is your favorite because the other gods avoid it.

The Council loathes it, in fact. Hundreds of islands in this archipelago, innumerable beaches to choose from . . . so why, they ask, would you willingly opt for the one covered in dark lava rocks over one with smooth, walkable sand?

To you this *is* walkable, comfortable. You love the way the coarse igneous stone feels beneath your bare feet. Those same dark stones protrude from the water, where the lava once pooled after cascading from the summit of Haleakalā and didn't let anything stop its path until the sea itself finally cooled it. *I made this,* you think proudly. Although on second thought, as you gaze back toward where the rising sun is illuminating the summit of Haleakalā, you think: *I made* all *this.* Every big island, every little one, all gifts of the volcanoes, of the magma rising up through the sea. You may not remember it—they were from a former incarnation of Pele, after all—but this beach and the archipelago in general are a point of major personal pride and accomplishment for you.

As you walk in the shallows, you're so busy watching the morning light play over the bay to the south that you don't see the corpse until you trip over it.

You nearly drop knees-first down onto the man's back, but catch your balance. He floats facedown in the shallows. He wears no shirt, and his waterlogged trousers are in tatters. Curiosity seizes you, so you bend down and roll the man over.

The first thing that you notice: He's not of your people. The deep tan of his skin leads you to believe that he's lived under a sun just as strong as the one that kisses these islands, but he is by no means an islander.

The second thing that you notice: He is beautiful.

It's an otherworldly beauty. You've long thought that Tangaroa, the sea god on the Council, was the summit of attractiveness, among gods and mortals alike. And he's shown no subtlety in the way that he looks at you.

But this dead man is something else altogether. His hair is cropped close to his head and bristly. Unlike Tangaroa and the others, his skin remains untouched by tattoos. He's muscular, from his thick neck down to his tapered torso. You can learn a lot from a man's skin, but this corpse's flesh is a blank canvas. No scars at all to suggest he'd ever been to war; no calluses on his open palms to suggest that he was a fisherman or, for that matter, had ever worked a day in his life.

It's not unusual for dead men to occasionally wash up on these shores, but their bodies are usually bloated, or rotting, or covered in sores from where they've been nibbled away by fish.

This stranger, however, must be newly dead, because he shows no sign of decay, or of being fish food. On a whim you lean over and press your ear to his bare chest.

You hear the beat of his heart at the same time he springs back to life.

The stranger bolts upright and throws up a mouthful of briny vomit that you barely dodge in time. His eyes are wild, and he flounders in the water, frantically patting around his body to make sure that he still has all his limbs and all his flesh. His crazed, wide pupils finally focus on you, crouched in a defensive position on a lava rock, and one word escapes his mouth, a word you've heard the missionaries use before:

"Angel?" he mutters.

Then his eyes roll back into his head. He collapses back onto the lava rocks and loses consciousness once more.

For a few moments you gaze down at him, expecting him to stir again. He remains unmoving, but his chest moves up and down with labored breaths.

You glance around the beach, as though you might not be truly alone. There is only the wind and the lapping tide.

The Council has a strict rule when it comes to outsiders: They are not welcome here. Many foreign explorers have sailed past these shores, tried to give their own new names to things that have had names for many years. Missionaries visit your islands to bring word of their god . . . without realizing that there are many gods already walking these shores, down among their people, where they belong. You've used your storm powers yourself to send lightning bolts down on unwelcome ships, ruffled the ocean with swells to ward off foreigners.

There's something magical about this one though. He'd somehow survived the elements, possibly drifted for days or weeks, from somewhere far beyond the horizon, and still arrived here unscathed.

So you make up your mind: You must hide him from the Council until you've had a chance to speak with him, to learn of his past.

You know just the place too. You scoop him up in your arms; he may be larger and heavier than you, but your strength is unparalleled on these islands. Then you carry him down the shore to the sea cave.

You often come to this cave to reflect. It's concealed under the shadow of a magnificent sea arch—a monument of stone carved away by the ocean that protrudes from the cliff face above like a sea giant's elbow. You've always loved the sound of the tide as it echoes down the tunnel; it's almost like a poem whispered to you by Tangaroa, the sea god . . . although Tangaroa is just a fleeting thought right now, with a strange man cradled in your arms.

You wade through the waist-high water until the tunnel ground rises up to a patch of sand that's safe even from high tide. You place the stranger down on the smoothest area you can find, far enough from the water that he won't accidentally roll in and drown while he's still unconscious.

His eyes flicker half-open for a few seconds. He looks delirious and as if slumber will drag him down again any moment, but there's a brief flash when he gazes up at your face with complete clarity. His hand touches the side of your cheek, and while instinct tells you to pull away, you let his smooth fingers cup your skin. A deep warmth flushes your face where his palm lingers.

Then he says five words to you, four of them in the language of the missionaries, but one of which is all too familiar and sucks the warmth right out of your cheeks.

"Thank you," he whispers, blinking twice. "Thank you, Pele . . ."

Before he can explain how he knew your name or that you were the legendary volcano goddess, he's dragged down into the murky dark of a feverish sleep.

You want so badly to wait beside him until he wakes again. However, it is the morning before the new moon, which means the monthly Council meeting will start shortly. You must not arouse the suspicion of the others if you're to keep this a secret for now.

So you reluctantly wade back down the tunnel. You

cast a final look at the sleeping stranger before you tear open the air and step through a portal into a forest not too far from this sea cave.

But suddenly, everything seems too far from the cave and the human heart beating within it.

You hate when you're not the last one to arrive. Life on the islands has bred patience in the other gods that you distinctly lack, and so you make a point of being a little late so you don't have to wait for anyone else to lazily straggle in. This time, though, everyone seems to be tardy—and there's no real excuse, since there are no clouds to block the sun's progress across the sky, marking the time of day.

You'd know because they're your clouds to put there.

Instead, when you emerge from the portal into the bamboo forest on the eastern end of Maui, at the base of Haleakalā, only Rangi—Father Sky—and Papa—Mother Earth—await you. Rangi and Papa are both older than you and the others. You call them the elders, even though they've only seen five more years than you have. Still, there's a sternness in the couple that the other three lack.

The bamboo shoots in the clearing rustle as the portal seals closed behind you. Both Rangi and Papa offer you a nod and an "Aloha kakahiaka." You nod back to Rangi, who has his arms crossed, and say, "Ka makani 'olu'olu," to thank him for the delicate wind that's threading through the trees. It's a refreshing breeze that certainly didn't come from you. He shrugs off the compliment and mutters, "He mea iki ia," as though anyone could change the fervor of the wind with a flick of their hand.

Tu, the god of war, is the next to arrive, on foot instead of through a portal like you. Just about every inch of his body is covered with intricately patterned tattoos. Strangely, no needle has ever touched his skin. He was born this way.

Soon after, the stealthy Tane slips out from between the bamboo shoots, which didn't even tremble as he moved through them like a wraith. He spends so much time among the leaves that his bare chest and arms always maintain a greenish stain, and his legs remain powdered with soil. Today he has an even wider smirk than usual on his face when he arrives, and he's chuckling the way he always does. You've never seen him in a bad mood.

"New missionaries came ashore on O'ahu," he explains without so much as an "aloha" first. "I found the highest branch that I could and perched there, making terrifying sounds. Then I woke all the bats to attack them from above. They thought I was some sort of forest spirit haunting them and warning them to turn back."

You snort. "But you *are* a forest spirit."

"Yes, but spirits to them are evil red creatures, enemies of their god." Tane reaches under his kapa loincloth and pulls out a green fruit with a furry coating. You don't want to know where in his malo he was storing that.

"Do those even grow here?" you ask.

He takes a big bite out of the fruit, and the juice dribbles down his chin. "They do now. I ask the trees, and the trees listen."

"With some help from the earth," Papa adds.

At the edge of the clearing, where the bamboo forest gives way to a short cliff and the ocean pools below, something hisses like water turning to steam. Tangaroa rises up from the pool below, supported by a geyser that carries him to the cliff top. Once he steps off, the plume collapses behind him.

His eyes usually regard you with warmth and affection, but there's something wrathful in them today. He didn't even look this furious when you out-wrestled him a year ago. "Who is he?" he barks at you the moment his feet hit solid ground.

You frown. So your secret, secluded beach isn't quite so secluded after all. "Have you been following me, Tangaroa? Have you been . . . watching me?"

Tangaroa purses his lips. *That's never bothered you before,* his eyes say. "I didn't need to follow you. Do you think an outlander could drift through *my* seas to *my* shores without me knowing about it? When it comes to the waters around these islands, my eyes see all."

The others are watching silently, but Tane lets out a giggle. "If that's the case," he says between bites of his fruit, "I hope you've looked the other way when I've gone swimming with a few certain girls on Oʻahu."

Tangaroa growls at Tane to silence him. Before he can

launch more accusations at you, Rangi speaks, his voice as deep and tremulous as thunder. "There is an elder on Kaua'i, a blind man who has achieved such stillness in body and soul that he can stand out in the water and snatch a fish from a passing school with his hands. He is also a seer. He has told me many stories, not all of which have come true . . . but there was one a few years ago that I never forgot: a prophecy about a Driftwood Stranger, a man from another land who would come and bring ruin to us all."

You tilt your head back to the sky in frustration. A cloud rolls in front of the sun. "I have met that blind man before. He also tells stories of a man-eating tortoise and a sea lion that steals babies from the arms of their sleeping mothers. And this Driftwood Stranger? He's probably thinking of that white man who tried to kidnap the king years ago—you know, the one they stabbed to death in the water? Some dangerous visitor he was."

"No," Rangi says, unmoved by your argument. "That man, Cook, came on a ship with many others. The Driftwood Stranger, the elder foretells, will come alone . . . and he'll come without a ship."

This makes even Tane pause mid-bite. You can't deny that the circumstances of the stranger's arrival make you uneasy. No shipwreck. No signs of starvation on his filled-out body. Not even a sunburn.

And he knew your name.

"He is my prisoner," you say sternly. Your eyes burn

red when your gaze finds Tangaroa's again. "No one touches him until I find out who he is and why he's here."

"And if he proves dangerous?" Tu, who had remained silent until now, asks. "How will you handle him then?"

"Then I'll drop him into a lava pool on Kīlauea," you reply, "and find out if the Driftwood Stranger burns like driftwood."

"And for those among us who don't spend our days lighting fires, Pele," Tane says, "how *does* driftwood burn?"

You try to sound as merciless and uncaring as possible when you say the next word, so that they'll trust you to handle the stranger on your own:

"Slowly."

The cove where you left the stranger isn't far from the bamboo forest, and ordinarily you'd run back after the Council meeting, drawing strength and energy from Haleakalā, the quiet volcano. But Tangaroa could be traveling by sea to "visit" the stranger himself, so you explosively gouge out a section of the air and pass through the narrow portal.

Only, when you step into the cave, the stranger is gone.

It hasn't been more than an hour since you left him for the tense meeting with the other gods, so he couldn't have gone far. You try not to panic, and you let your eyes take in the heat within the cave. As you concentrate, the color fades from the world around you until the cave and the light filtering through its opening have muted to mostly shades of gray and sepia.

However, the hollow depression in the stone glows a soft orange, where the stranger's body heat lingers on the pebbles. Unfortunately, the water cooled any heat trail he might have left on his way out, so you return to the mouth of the cave.

As you stand beneath the magnificent sea arch, you worry that you may have lost him for good. The sea and stone together are just a cool variety of grays, with only the sun lighting up in vivid red.

But when you turn around, back to the cliff, you catch just the slightest hint of color among the rocks. In fact there's a staggered trail of fading embers leading up the cliff face, where hands and bare feet have recently touched.

He must have scaled the nearly vertical stone wall.

You don't have the patience to climb it yourself, so you carve a new rift in the air and step out onto the top of the cliff above.

He's sitting close to the edge, with his knees bunched up against his chest. He flinches, momentarily startled, when you appear next to him and the sea water that leaked through the portal splashes into the grass, but he doesn't appear afraid of you. "Aloha," he greets you.

You skip the pleasantries. "Who are you, and where have you come from?" you ask him in his own language.

"You . . . speak English?" He actually looks more surprised by this than when you stepped out of a hole in the air moments before.

"It is the language of your missionaries," you say indignantly, "who flock to our islands like bats to a nest of moths."

"They are not *my* missionaries." He points toward the eastern horizon. "They came to my lands, unwelcome, the same way they did to yours . . . although," he adds with a smile, "my lands are so vast it will be some time before they've conquered them all."

Against your better judgment you sit down beside him, although an arm's length away, as though he might be rife with sickness. Out in the water a humpback whale surfaces, then another. They've always seemed just as fond of this bay as you have, though they never come close enough to admire the lava rocks.

"My name is Colt," he says.

You open your mouth and laugh deeply. The gathering thunderclouds chuckle with you. "They named you," you say once you've caught your breath, "after that strange four-legged creature that those *haoles* like to ride on?" You laugh some more.

Colt doesn't look offended. In fact, after a hesitation, he laughs along with you. "What? Colts are dependable, powerful, and fast, with an energetic, masculine spirit. They can travel for miles."

"As have you," you say, spreading your arms out to the ocean. The laughter stops. Neither of you is watching the whales anymore. As he studies your face, you're struggling with the sense of instant familiarity you feel with him. He *just* washed up on shore. You can tell he's holding back something, like he doesn't know how much to trust you, how much to share with you.

"I wish I could tell you how I got here," Colt says at last. "One moment I was falling asleep at the base of a dune, back on the mainland, letting the sound of the tide carry me into slumber. . . . When I woke up next the tide actually *was* carrying me away. I couldn't even see the shores the waters were so choppy with storm waves. The current dragged me under a few times." He shook his head. "I have no idea how long I was floating out at sea before I washed up here. Under the heavy sun, and without fresh water, I plunged into delirium for many days."

It was impossible. You know from the pesky missionaries who come here that the mainland is a long ways to the east. It's a far journey even for a boat with sails. . . .

It should be an impossible journey to survive for a man who simply *floated over*.

"What are you?" you ask him. "And how did you know my name?"

"I can't answer your first question," he says. "But as for the second . . ." He swallows and runs a hand over his short, cropped hair. "Pele, I've been seeing you in my dreams. Every night . . . for the last twenty years. Only . . ." This time he summons the courage to look back into your eyes, and you see your reflection in them. "Only I don't think they're really dreams at all."

Ash knew that Modo was supposedly the Greek god of the forge, but he snored like a thunder god.

After his near death by electrocution at the Renaissance fair, it had been pretty easy for Ash to convince him that her hotel room would prove a better safe haven than his frat house, since Colt and Eve probably knew where he lived. He had grumbled a little bit about how spending the night with a random girl in a Boston hotel room was going to be tough to explain to his girlfriend, but Ash just pinched him hard until he shut up.

Now it was nearly noon, with the sunlight peeking through the hotel room blinds. While Ash did research on her laptop, Modo was out cold on the scratchy twin-size bed, lying on his back with his chest rising and falling in bellowing snores. Still, it was the memories of the dream—the vision—she'd experienced last night that dominated her thoughts.

Memories from her previous lives had bled into her dreams before; it was a curse thrust upon her by Colt weeks ago. After nights spent dreaming of her last incarnation in the 1920s and 1930s, her restless brain had apparently moved on to the life before that one. It had been strange inhabiting the brain of Pele and knowing now that the volcano goddess wasn't just her, but a composite of all three Wilde sisters.

Still, the vision left Ash perplexed. Ash had trusted the Cloak, who insisted that they'd split Pele into three goddesses because she'd proven to be too volatile and dangerous as one entity . . . but the Pele in her dream didn't seem so bad, did she? A bit impetuous, a bit quick to anger, but she'd mostly been concerned with protecting Colt.

What could Pele have possibly done that would instigate the Cloak to take such an unthinkable, drastic measure: splitting a soul apart?

Then there was Colt. In her vision, Pele had truly believed the trickster's tale about being washed up on the Hawaiian shore merely by chance, but now Ash recognized it for what it was: another one of Colt's lies. Each lifetime since the Cloak had stripped the gods of their old memories, Colt had capitalized on her inability to remember him or their longstanding romantic history together, and he'd manipulated his way back into her life. He would always pretend that he was just meeting her for the first time, and usually pretended to be human as well. Perhaps he'd watched Pele walk that rocky beach for weeks before he finally faked washing ashore, unconscious and half-dead.

Strangely, despite all the lies he'd ever told her, Colt had always used his real name.

Ash was so involved in her thoughts that she didn't even notice that the snores had stopped until Modo's head was peering over her shoulder. The guy moved stealthily, considering he had a serious limp. "What are you doing?" he asked, far too wide-eyed and alert for someone who'd been passed out until just moments ago.

"Looking at porn," Ash said, gesturing to the laptop screen. "Also, searching Amber Alerts in the New England area over the last few months."

"Amber Alerts?" Modo echoed. "Like missing children?"

Ash nodded. "Before my little sister took Colt, Eve, and Proteus through a portal to Boston, Colt mentioned something about how Rose could only form portals to places she'd seen before. So unless my six-year-old sister has been jet-setting through Massachusetts on her own, there's a good chance that she may have originally been adopted by a family here . . . and I really doubt that her family willingly donated her to be some sort of lab experiment in the Central American jungles."

Modo flipped another chair around and dropped down next to Ash. "Maybe her adoptive parents thought they were sending her to summer camp?"

"Or maybe . . ." Ash double-clicked on one of the

Amber Alert listings . . . and after six lines of reading, she knew she'd found her match.

> Monterey, Massachusetts. April 23. Six-year-old Penny Wallace was forcibly taken from her home in Berkshire County at approximately 2:15 a.m. on Thursday morning. Penny is described as being of Polynesian descent, 4'1" and 65 lbs., frail, with waist-length black hair. No leads on the identity of her captor(s), but incendiaries were used in the forced entry of the Wallace household. Suspects should be considered armed and dangerous. If you have any information pertaining to Penny's whereabouts, call . . .

As if the description wasn't definitive enough, attached to the bottom was a school picture of Rose, stoic and unsmiling as ever, but still six years old. Now this little girl's mind was trapped in the body of a sixteen-year-old, and she was as lost and frightened as ever.

Ash realized that she had been unconsciously touching the laptop screen and let her hand fall away. She'd become so accustomed to calling her sister Rose that it was hard to imagine her by any other name . . . and even harder to imagine her fitting in with a nice family out in the Massachusetts countryside.

The strangest part: Monterey, Massachusetts, was only a hundred miles and a state border away from Scarsdale, New York, where Ash grew up.

All those years living a normal life, and not only did Ash never realize she had a younger sister—but that sister was living only a two-hour drive from her.

Modo squeezed her shoulder. "I guess that description of Rose is a little outdated now."

Ash shook her head. "Yeah, but I doubt they'll understand if we ask them to update it to, 'Five-foot-nine, one hundred forty pounds, supernaturally aged ten years by a goddess of death. Just follow the sound of devastating explosions.'"

"Not to be a downer," Modo said, "but what good will this do you now? I really doubt Colt, Eve, and Proteus are playing house with Rose at the same house where she grew up. Especially, you know, with her parents there."

"It's not Rose I'm expecting to find there," Ash said. "Rose might be in a sixteen-year-old body, but she still has the mind of a six-year-old. And children respond to things that remind them of safety and home. I'm hoping I can find out more about her, take a look around her old room, anything at all that might get her to trust me instead of Colt, especially since our last encounter concluded with Rose hammering me with an explosive blast." *And sending one of my best friends flying off the apartment building to her death.*

Modo snorted. "So you're going to lure your

sixteen-going-on-six-year-old sister away from a bunch of killers . . . using, like, a nursery rhyme or a teddy bear? Why do I feel like this can only end with the teddy bear—and the person holding it—getting blown up?"

Ash didn't have a retort for that. The plan was a crap-shoot, at best. But right now the odds were four against one (unless she counted Modo, in which case it was really just four against one and a half, considering he'd only found out that he was a god less than twenty-four hours ago and didn't yet know how to wield his powers). Any possible advantage she could get before facing Colt again was worth looking into.

After all, her soul was at stake.

Ash held out her hands. "I'm going to need the keys to the Modo-mobile." When Modo just gave her a funny look and didn't hand them over, she said, "Come on, Pop. I promise to return it with a full tank."

"I," Modo said definitively, "am coming with you. No one—I mean no one—drives Sir Revsalot but me."

Ash pinched the bridge of her nose. "Holding back so many comments right now. Look," she said, putting a hand on his shoulder. "I would very much welcome your company if we were just going sightseeing through Massachusetts. But I barely saved your life yesterday when you were out in the open, and that was against only one god. If the entire gang comes out and tries to go all *West Side Story* on the two of us on our way to Monterey, I won't be able to protect you."

Modo gazed at her for a long moment, then finally sighed. He limped over to his jeans, which were balled up beside the bed, and fished his keys out of the pocket. "If you return him with any scratches, or volcano goddess char marks for that matter, you're going to be in big trouble."

Ash caught the keys and curtsied to him medieval style. "I promise not to harm a hair on the head of your prized silvery steed, my liege."

"What the hell am I supposed to do in the meantime?" he asked. "Room service? Rent a movie?"

Ash's eyes lit up. "I'm so glad you asked." She pulled up a window on the laptop—a short little slide show presentation that she'd spent the morning putting together for him. "I've compiled all the information you need to know about Colt, Eve, Rose, and Proteus. Commit all this to memory like you're studying for a final exam at MIT."

Modo quickly tabbed through the pages. "You wrote out physical descriptions, but didn't include any pictures? Don't you think that would be helpful if I could, you know, recognize the gods that are trying to murder me?"

"Kind of hard to find pictures of homicidal gods when they tend not to have Facebook profiles," Ash explained. "And Proteus is a shape-shifter, so he'd probably look different in every picture anyway."

"Gods, shape-shifters, Native American tricksters trying to meld their past-life volcano goddess ex-girlfriends back into a single soul . . ." Modo rubbed his eyes. "If it turns out this is all some trippy hallucination from drinking bad mead at yesterday's Renaissance fair, I'm going to make a book out of this."

Ash paused on her way out the door, the car keys jangling in her hand. "Just pray that when this story is over, there will be someone left alive to read it."

As Ash pulled Sir Revsalot around the circular driveway in front of the large ranch in Monterey, she couldn't help but think: *This is where Rose grew up?*

The massive home was idyllic to say the least. Hidden toward the end of a narrow dirt road, the ranch had a front lawn that seemed to roll on for an acre and beautiful antique gas lights that lined the long driveway. Ash had admittedly grown up in luxury herself, but this was a different kind of wealth, more rustic and grounded. Of course, that "tethered to the earth" feeling was in part thanks to the horse stables off to the side and the unmistakable farmy smell wafting over from them.

Ash was plagued by all sorts of questions as she climbed out of the car. Had Rose really led the normal lifestyle of a suburban six-year-old here, under the unassuming name Penny Wallace? Climbing on a big yellow bus every morning, a brown-paper-bag lunch clutched tightly in her little hands? A cubby with her name on it waiting for her at school where she would tuck her galoshes and backpack before some patient, matronly kindergarten teacher wrote the alphabet on the chalkboard for her to mimic?

And then she'd come home to a loving family who'd ask about her school day over dinner, take her out for ice cream, and host a slumber party for her birthday?

Ash couldn't imagine that at all. The Rose she knew was a girl of few words, aloof and cerebral, who interacted with the people and the world around her like some alien beamed down to Earth.

But then there were her violent moments.

In the short time Ash had known about her little sister, she'd watched Rose tear out a man's throat with her bare hands, sink a battleship like it was a milk-carton sailboat using only her mind, and create deadly explosions that killed the guilty and the innocent alike. So to imagine her taking piano lessons and parading around a ranch on the back of a pony . . . it just didn't compute.

Ash paused in front of the grand double doors to the house, her finger hovering over the doorbell. What the hell was she supposed to say if the girl's parents came to the door? *Hi there. I'm your kidnapped adopted daughter's biological sister. Our unhinged third sister kidnapped her with a band of other mythological reincarnates, including a Hopi trickster who wants to meld us into one soul to relive the volatile romances of his previous lifetimes. Is there anything you could tell me about Rose that might help me lure her away from the crazy people, before she blows someone up again? P.S. She's sixteen now.*

Ash sighed and pressed the doorbell. "Maybe I'll just tell them I'm selling Girl Scout cookies."

After several minutes had passed, however, no one had answered the door. She shrugged and wandered past the gardens, around to the back of the house.

What she found there was enough to chill even the blood of a volcano goddess.

Beside the chimney, where there should have been pristine walls and picturesque windows like the front of the house, there was only a large, gaping hole. Parts of the void had been covered with clear plastic sheets to protect the inside of the house from the elements, but Ash could still see the charred portions where a large, fiery explosion had clearly chewed through the wooden frame.

Standing before the wreckage now, Ash could make an educated guess what had happened here. The kidnappers had come to take her sister away, and in the struggle, Rose must have panicked and let an explosion rip through the house. When Rose became scared, panicked, or angry, she had a nasty habit of self-detonating—unleashing a deadly blast that left her unscathed but did gruesome things to anyone unlucky enough to be standing nearby.

How many of her attackers the supernatural bomb had taken with it this time, Ash couldn't guess, but someone must have knocked the little one out or sedated her before she could finish the job.

You didn't want to mess with Rose when she was awake.

Ash pushed aside one of the plastic flaps on the bottom floor, making sure to watch her step in the rubble. There were some construction materials lying about the living room, and she could even see where work had been started to repair the house. Had the restoration just begun? Or had it been abandoned? The flat-screen TV smashed on the floor, the couches that had been singed by the fire, the oriental carpet littered with debris . . . Rose's kidnapping happened months before, but the family had left the house this way since the attack?

Then Ash had an even more sickening thought:

What if Rose's adoptive family hadn't survived the kidnapping?

And if they hadn't, was it because they died at the hands of the kidnappers . . .

. . . or in the explosion created by their own daughter?

Ash tried to let that thought go as she took the stairs two at a time to the top floor. It wasn't difficult to find Rose's old bedroom. The door was still ajar, and the first thing Ash noticed when she walked through was the lacy bedspread on the unmade bed, from where Rose had probably been snatched in her sleep. Her dolls had cascaded everywhere in the struggle.

Like the living room, the bedroom was now missing its entire back wall, and the floorboards ended abruptly in a jagged line. A pair of hummingbirds, which must have slipped through the protective plastic sheets, flitted around the room, and Ash spotted the nest they'd built on Rose's old dresser.

Only when Ash turned around did she discover the crimson splatter against the wall.

She'd been so fixated on the bed that she missed the bloodstain on the way in. It not only splattered the walls, but coated the decorative horse border that ran around the room as well and even speckled the ceiling fan. Granted, the bodies had clearly been carted away, but one thing was for sure: No one could lose that amount of blood and survive.

The awful odor of death suddenly found its way to Ash's nose, so she rushed out of the room. Nothing in the bedroom, not even the dolls, had given Ash that "this must be important to Rose" feeling . . . or maybe she was just looking for an excuse to escape the nausea that had overcome her.

Back outside Ash wasn't quite ready to give up. She eyed the stables across the way. Ash had only begun to explore the strange mental link the Wilde sisters seemed to share, but this time something told her the wooden building would have been important to Rose. The Cloak had told Ash during her visit to their Netherworld that the Wilde sisters were like a candelabra: separate flames from the same vessel. When they'd split Pele into three souls, some cerebral connection had clearly lingered, allowing Ash, Eve, and Rose to find each other, lifetime after lifetime.

The same way that Colt seemed to always find her no matter what. . . .

Inside the stables Ash immediately sensed that

something wasn't right. And not just in the sickening way that she could imagine the events that took place during the kidnapping.

Something here had been disturbed recently.

Very recently.

She crossed the hay-strewn floor to where she could hear the shuffling of a horse's hooves. Sure enough, there was a black stallion milling about in one of the enclosures. There was a wild, unbroken air about him—Ash didn't really know much about horses, but something about the stallion's demeanor made her think that this wasn't the kind of domesticated horse that a family with small children kept on its ranch. In fact, as she cautiously crossed toward the pen, her gaze never leaving the creature's volatile eyes, she thought: *If Rose's family really is dead or gone, then who the hell has been taking care of this horse?*

"He doesn't belong to you, you know."

Ash spun around. In the entryway to the horse stables a girl Ash's age stood with her hands planted on her hips. Her hair, which fell in ringlets nearly to her waist, was so red that with the afternoon sun backlighting it, it could have easily been made of fire. She was smiling at Ash, but not in a friendly way—there was barely restrained animosity simmering just below the surface, to the point that the girl was visibly trembling when Ash looked closely.

He doesn't belong to me . . . ? Ash repeated in her head. She pointed to the black stallion and raised her eyebrows. "I mean, the horse and I just met a minute ago, and I'm not sure the two of us are ready to put labels on anything this soon."

"You know who I'm talking about," the girl seethed. Her tattered long green skirt billowed behind her like a punctured sail as she took a few strides forward. Ash must have still looked perplexed because the girl scoffed. "Well, that shows how much Colt must mean to you."

"Colt?" Ash couldn't help it—she laughed, even though she was fully aware that there was a dangerous situation brewing. "Honey, I realize he's easy on the eyes, but believe me when I say that he leaves an aftertaste like battery acid. Where did you meet him anyway—online dating?"

The girl's hand tightened around one of the wooden beams holding up the stable roof, so tight that Ash was afraid the post would snap. "I met Colt Halliday many lifetimes ago. Long before even you knew him, before he adopted a human name . . . when he was still known across the continent as the trickster Kokopelli. He has been my lover for nearly eight lifetimes."

Another laugh had been perched on Ash's lips, but with that, it suddenly died. So this girl was a reincarnated goddess just like her. No wonder her danger sensors had gone through the roof when the girl walked into the stable. Worse, this fiery redhead's face was starting to tingle in the back of Ash's mind, where dormant memories of her previous lives slept—the memories that Colt had awakened as a means to manipulate her. No doubt he'd done the same to this girl, probably to use her for whatever pathetic bidding he required. "Wait, wait, wait . . . ," Ash said. "Your Colt's . . . mistress?"

The redhead stabbed a finger at Ash and snarled, *"You're* the mistress, Pele!" She turned the finger on herself. "I am his true love, his soul mate. You're just the temptress that pops up like a weed in the cracks every lifetime, strangling the happiness out of him. You're poisonous to him, but he's addicted to you like some sort of drug."

"Listen—" Ash stopped herself. "What's your name, by the way?"

The girl straightened up to her full height, nearly six feet tall and rail thin. Between her frame, her hair, and her freckled Irish paleness, she was the physical opposite of Ash. She guessed she couldn't blame Colt for wanting to diversify his lovers. "I am Epona," the girl announced proudly, "Celtic goddess of horses . . . and nightmares."

"Uh-huh," Ash replied without interest. "Well, Epona, I can totally respect the fact that you're . . ." Ash paused because she was really tempted to complete the sentence with *just another psycho who needs to let go of the past and learn to be an independent woman.* Instead she opted for the more diplomatic approach. ". . . a hopeless romantic. And I'd love nothing better than to let you and Colt ride off into the sunset together, if it meant I'd never have to hear from either of you again. Unfortunately, your boyfriend is like an annoying boomerang—no matter how hard I throw him away, he just keeps coming back, and some-one always ends up hurt."

For a moment Epona's face relaxed, and Ash thought she might actually listen to reason. Ash had been through her fair share of fights over teenage romance before, and it had always ended poorly. Lily, the disturbed blossom goddess, had killed Rolfe out of envy and died at Ash's hands for that same boiling hatred. Ash had needed to kill Rey, the Incan sun god, too, when he tried to avenge the death of his winter-goddess girlfriend. And who could forget what happened to field-hockey captain Lizzie Jacobs, Ash's old rival back in New York and the girl who stole her asshole ex-boyfriend. . . . Ash realized that the teenage years were when people were expected to be reck-less and stupid, but couldn't any of these people stand on their own two feet without making their universe revolve around a boyfriend or girlfriend? "Look, I've found myself in sticky situations because of guys who didn't treat me right before. But believe me when I say that the ones you want to fight over are never worth it."

Just like that Epona's expression rebounded right back into wrath. "If you won't die for someone—if you won't kill for them—then it's not love. You don't deserve Colt. He and I had been perfectly happy together for years this time around before I discovered that he was trying to track the three of you down again. To put you back together. He was confused and had forgotten who he really loved. Me," she added, as if Ash were a moron and hadn't caught the drift. "I knew Colt couldn't put your filthy soul back together without all the pieces, so I decided to send a piece of you away where I figured he'd never find you." She glanced back in the direction of the half-destroyed house with a knowing smile.

"You?" Ash whispered. "You're the one that convinced that Central American *junta* to kidnap Rose from the good life she was probably leading here?" Ash felt her own temper returning. "She's a six-year-old girl—not just some roadblock to your happiness, you stupid bitch."

Epona's smile fell. "Clearly it didn't work. I sent that mute little toddler halfway across the hemisphere, and Colt still found a way to bring her back. And he picked up you and your twisted older sister along the way." Epona ran her tongue over the top row of her immaculately white teeth. "Without all three Wildes, he can't put Pele back together. I tried to be humane. But even if I send you to the ends of the earth, Colt is too brilliant and resourceful not to find you. So if I can't hide one of the three puzzle pieces from him . . . then I guess I'll just have to destroy one."

Ash's incendiary rage continued to bubble up, a rage that she'd tried—but more often failed—to suppress since it got Lizzie Jacobs killed a year ago. She'd wanted so badly to leave the "old Ashline" behind when she left New York, but even when she thought she'd finally become a temperate and forgiving person, she could still feel her volcanic, impetuous instincts lurking under the surface. It was times like these when she realized that she still contained remnants of Pele, the destructive, earth-rending goddess whom the Cloak had deemed too dangerous to walk the planet.

Ash wanted to hurt Epona, really hurt her, for upturning Rose's life like she had.

But even as she pictured herself throwing down with this dangerous stranger, she remembered the terrible cold she'd felt when she killed Bleak, the Norse winter goddess. And Rey, the crazy Incan sun god. And even the wretched blossom goddess Lily, who deserved it most of all. They were all killers, yet Ash had felt no thrill of justice or vengeance as she'd stood over their bodies. A corpse was a corpse.

"Epona," Ash said, trying one last chance to reason with her. "Let me take a wild guess as to how this all played out. Colt came to you when you still had no memories of your previous lives. Wormed his way back into your heart, then used that persuasive voice of his to reconnect you with some of those old memories . . . but just the ones that he wanted you to see. Just the ones that would make you loyal to him again, make you love him again. Enough that you'd do anything for him." Ash swallowed. "I know, because that almost became my story too, before I saw through the illusion. Before I realized that there are most certainly memories he *didn't* let me see that would reveal him to be the monster that he really is. The truth is that you and I have both had the misfortune of falling for the world's most gifted liar. If you kill me now, then, yes, you'd rob Colt of the patchwork bride that he's so desperately after. Don't think that hasn't crossed my mind either. But whether you like it or not, I'm going to survive long enough to stop Colt Halliday. Because, with or without Pele, as long as he walks the earth, good people will keep dying." As she said that, she pictured her friend Aurora, the winged goddess of the dawn, being devoured and entombed by a weeping willow tree. She pictured Raja falling off the edge of the skyscraper and Rolfe taking a spear through his heart.

So many dead bodies, and that was only the result of two months of Colt's deadly scheming. Who knew what the bastard could accomplish in ten, or twenty, or forty years?

"You know what the difference is between a nightmare and me?" the Celtic goddess asked. "You get to wake up from a nightmare."

Ash had been so busy keeping her eyes fixed on Epona that she'd forgotten all about the horse. With a whinny it crashed through the gate, out of its pen. Ash twirled around only to see it rear back on two legs and then punish her with a hard kick to her chest. Her lungs instantly deflated, and she went flying back into another enclosure.

Before she could even pick herself up out of the hay, the horse was on her again. Ash never thought that a horse was the kind of animal that could look fierce, but this one came at her with its lips curled back, its big yellowed teeth exposed. It bucked up onto its hind legs again, and then attempted to bring its front hooves down on her ribs.

Ash rolled away as the hooves speared the stable ground where she'd been just a moment before. The horse reared up, ready to try for another killing blow, and Ash's first instinct was not to harm the creature. The beast was just doing Epona's telepathic bidding after all, but every second that Ash wasted here getting nearly trampled by a horse was one she could use to get her sister back.

So with that in mind she drew in a quick breath, aimed her finger at the horse's exposed tail, and fired a quick line of sparks at it.

The embers ignited the tip of the tail, and the horse let out a bellowing whinny. The "oh shit, my tail's on fire" realization must have severed whatever mind control Epona had over it. It hastily backed away from the stall and took off at a gallop out of the stables.

Ash started to rise to her feet. "That's what happens when you send Mr. Ed to do a crazy girl's job," she started to say, brushing the hay off her jeans, but a fierce scream interrupted her. Epona seized her by her shirt. The girl was tall and wiry, to be sure, but she was surprisingly strong, and of course had the gift of insanity on her side. She heaved Ash with all her might.

A hard pain shot up Ash's back as she connected with one of the wooden beams. The impact was enough to shake even the heavy bales of hay stored in the rafters overhead.

Epona sauntered over to her, wringing her hands. The

girl's killer instincts had gone into full force. Whereas Ash had thought before that Epona wouldn't follow through when push came to murder, now it looked like the Celtic goddess was just trying to decide which method she'd use to kill her.

While Ash writhed against the support beam, still rattled, Epona pressed one of her equestrian boots into Ash's chest. "With you out of the picture, Colt will finally see that I'm the true love of his life, the strong, devoted survivor. And you . . ." She shook her head. "You're just some soon-to-be-forgotten old flame."

Even though Ash's back was racked with pain, she managed a smile. "You should be more careful about using fire metaphors around a volcano goddess."

Ash let her arm harden into volcanic rock, with just the faintest flicker of fire throbbing between the plates. Then she snapped her elbow back into the wooden support beam with all her might.

The beam cracked in half, and the loft overhead caved in. Ash crab-walked backward, but Epona only had time to look up before the heavy bales of hay cascaded down on her.

When Ash finally pulled herself to her feet, Epona lay fully buried under hundreds of pounds of hay, with only her hand protruding from beneath the mountain. Ash leaned down and touched the girl's wrist. She still had a pulse, and just moments later she heard a frantic murmur from beneath one of the bales.

"I could easily torch this pile of hay," Ash said to the buried goddess. "One spark, one little ember, and I'd make a bonfire so big out of you that all the local kids would come running with marshmallows, sticks, and graham crackers." She took a deep breath. A dark voice was telling her, even then, to go through with it, that she needed to be sure that she was rid of Colt's mistress. But at the end of the day, Epona's warped mind had been Colt's doing. Even the healthiest brain couldn't process a thousand years' worth of complicated memories, not to mention Colt's mental manipulations, and still come away unscathed. In this the reincarnated gods and goddesses were more human than anything. "Fortunately for you," Ash continued. "I'm not Pele. Not anymore at least. And I'm going to make sure that she never comes back . . . even if that means killing Colt Halliday. Don't come looking for me again." She kicked at one of the bales and then started for the entrance to the stable, saying over her shoulder, "Oh, and if you really have to take this stupid vendetta out on someone, introduce yourself to my older sister instead."

Outside, Ash only made it a few feet into the yard before a splash of color caught her eye. Next to the stable doors lay a small ornamental box—a music box, she discovered as she opened it. It had been mostly hidden by the unkempt grass. Chillingly, there was a tiny bloody handprint on the mahogany and the gold crank on the outside. Ash could almost picture the scene: Rose, fleeing the house where she'd just detonated and killed some of her pursuers, running for the stables—a place of comfort for her—with her most prized possession still cradled in her hands. They must have caught her here, maybe sedated her before she could blow up anyone else.

But even if this little music box meant a lot to Rose, Ash wondered as she returned to the car, would it be enough to draw her away from Colt? Master manipulator that Colt was, he'd somehow already lured Rose into a sense of belonging, one that Ash, her own blood, had failed to establish with her.

Ash climbed into the driver's seat, and before she shifted the car into drive, she cast one last look at the music box, which she'd buckled in on the passenger side. "You better play one hell of a song," she said to it, then roared out of the long driveway.

On the drive back to Boston on the MassPike, Ash called the hotel room. Modo had been cooped up in there all day, so she was going to sweeten the deal by bringing him whatever takeout his heart desired.

The metallurgy god never picked up. Not on the first try. Nor on the fourth. Either he was taking the world's longest shower, or something was seriously wrong.

She made it back to the Hyatt in record time. When she found the hotel room—as she had feared—completely empty, her mind immediately went to a dark place. Of Eve kicking down the door, throwing Modo to the floor, sending a million volts through his body. Maybe she dragged him out onto the hotel balcony and held him up by the neck to let a real lightning strike finish him off, the bolt forking out of his mouth and into the heavens just as it had with Lizzie Jacobs that awful night a year ago.

No, Ash told herself. *They would have left his body.* And that much she believed—why kill him and transport his body somewhere else, when they could leave it here as a warning to her?

That's when Ash's eyes turned to the computer. There was a single yellow sticky note on the corner of the monitor. In a nearly illegible, predictably masculine scrawl, Modo had written only three words:

I HAD TO.

Ash frantically tapped the enter key until the laptop emerged from sleep mode, and the answer was sitting right on the screen. Modo had left his e-mail account logged in, with two messages still open, as though he wanted Ashline to find them. The first was an invitation to a frat party—thrown by Modo's fraternity—in Cambridge, not far from the MIT campus. The theme was *A Midsummer Night's Dream,* and the invite encouraged the fraternity brothers to "bring lots of chicks so it doesn't turn into a sausagefest like last time."

When Ash closed that window to look at the e-mail behind it, her breath caught. It was a picture of a very beautiful girl, whose flaxen hair and penetratingly blue eyes would have given her an almost fairy-tale quality . . . that is, if there hadn't been tears carving channels through her mascara.

If there hadn't been a gag threaded into her mouth.

If she hadn't worn a terrified and resigned look in her eyes that said: *The person taking this picture is going to kill me.*

Below the picture a brief message addressed to Modo said: "Come to the party tonight, alone, or there will be one less 'chick' in attendance."

Ash's fist tightened around Modo's sticky note, crushing it in her palm. She could already feel it starting to catch fire, and small wisps of smoke drifted up between her fingers. Colt and the others had kidnapped a girl she assumed was Modo's girlfriend to lure him out into the open. Now he was potentially walking into a death trap, without Ash or the police to help him, in a futile attempt to save her. Why such a public place, though? If they were just going to off Modo, why not lure him to a secluded location instead of a bustling frat party in the middle of a residential college neighborhood?

And the lingering question: What did the death of some random blacksmith god have anything to do with Colt putting Pele back together?

Ash angrily flung the charred remains of the sticky note at the laptop screen and double-timed it back to the parking garage.

o o o

Ash arrived at the address just after dusk, parking Modo's car around the corner, out of sight. She didn't have to use her phone's GPS to find the house—even from the end of the street it was pretty obvious which of the old colonial homes housed the Delta Psi Omega fraternity. The music echoed out onto the road, and the porch was overflowing with so many people that it was a structural miracle that the railing hadn't snapped. As far as she could tell, there was just one underclassman guarding the front door, but he only smiled at her goofily as she climbed the front steps and crossed the threshold into the house.

The inside of the fraternity had been transformed into a forest, to match the *Midsummer Night's Dream* theme. Under any other circumstances Ash might have been impressed with how long it must have taken to cover the walls and ceiling with faux leaves and ivy. All the fraternity brothers were bare from the waist up, with fake horns on their heads and fur pants on their legs—satyrs, she guessed. The girls were swaddled in togas, some more revealing and risqué than others. Ash, in her jeans and T-shirt, earned looks that ranged from amused to disdainful as she cut through the crowd. Some of these party animals took the dress code more seriously than others apparently.

The good news: From the atmosphere of frivolity and fun, Ash was going to guess that Modo hadn't been publicly executed in front of everyone.

She found him in the kitchen, almost hidden by a

jumbled line of partygoers who were armed with plastic cups and waiting for the keg. Modo had his own cup gripped tightly in his hand and was staring forlornly into space, even as Tom—the guy Ash had met at the belfry yesterday—jabbered on animatedly.

Modo snapped back to reality the moment he realized Ash was standing there. With the same blank expression on his face, he just walked away from Tom while his friend was mid-sentence and crossed the kitchen to Ash.

"I had to," he said, hollowly repeating what he'd written on the sticky note.

"I know," Ash said, finding it hard to be infuriated with him for putting himself in danger. After all, how often had she thrown herself into perilous situations in the last few months to save someone she loved? She took his hand and pulled him back into the living room, so that they'd tactically have a better view of the entrance. She found them a dimly lit corner, where their only immediate company was a couple making out in the privacy of the green foliage dangling from the walls. "Modo," she said sharply, because he still looked dazed. She couldn't blame him, since his life had transformed overnight from that of a normal engineering student to a god whose life was in grave danger at the hands of a murderous pantheon. She waved her hands in front of his face until he snapped to attention. "I know you didn't think any of this was in the cards when you woke up yesterday morning, I know this has all blindsided you . . . but I need you to stay alert. I promised I would protect you."

"And Jenna?" he asked, and she figured he was referring to his girlfriend. His voice, which had sounded hollow before, grew inflamed with anger. "Those bastards took her while you were protecting me. I could have been there for her. Instead of her. We were safe and happy until you and your sister rolled into town."

She opened her mouth to protest, because in some ways what he'd just said was unfair . . . but in other ways he was just echoing her own dark thoughts. Colt was doing all this because of her. Because of who she used to be. There was a trail of bodies from California to Miami because of his crazed infatuation with Pele. And while some of them invited their deaths upon themselves, others—Rolfe, Raja, Aurora—might have lived full, rewarding lives if they hadn't crossed paths with Ash.

She was about to offer Modo some apology, some promise to him about getting his girlfriend back, when his eyes grew wide. "Jenna . . . ," he breathed.

Ash turned in time to see a shock of blond hair—the girl from the photograph earlier—as she rushed up the stairs. Next thing she knew, Modo was already plunging through the dance-floor crowd, even as she cried out for him to stop, her voice lost over the music. She tried to catch up with him, muscling the dancing satyrs and wood nymphs out of the way, but the crowd was far more yielding to Modo. Even despite his limp, his broad shoulders allowed him to cut a path through the dancers. And like that, he beat Ash to the stairwell and rocketed up to the second floor.

When Ash reached the steps herself, she took them two at a time. She hit the landing upstairs just as Modo disappeared into a bedroom at the end of the hallway. There was no doubt that the Jenna clone who'd climbed those stairs was probably the shape-shifter Proteus, luring him into some secluded trap where he could finish what Eve started. With a last sprint she barreled through the open door, expecting to find Modo with his neck broken, lying on the—

A hard fist, far too solid to be just flesh and bone, slammed into Ash's gut. When she looked up, Proteus was standing over her, his hair slicked back, and his greasy complexion glinting under the light of the room. Now that he'd shifted back into his own male form, he looked ludicrous in the one-size-too-small woman's shirt and jeans he was wearing as part of his Jenna disguise. Of course Ashline wasn't laughing—especially with the guy's fists transformed into cast iron, another one of his shape-shifting tricks.

He grinned savagely at her, clinking his iron knuckles together. Ash spotted the burn scars she'd left him on one wrist, the marks of her fingers clearly seared into his flesh. "Second time I've gotten the drop on you," Proteus said, reminiscing about the time he'd clipped her with a rock fist. "I'll let you pick what my fist will be made out of the next—"

Before he could finish his sentence, Ash transformed her own fist into igneous rock and landed an uppercut under his jaw. He dropped backward onto the oriental carpet, and Ash lunged at him, ready to take her second swing.

Someone else in the room applauded. "Now that's the Pele I remember."

Colt stood behind her. He softly closed the bedroom door and kept the gun in his hand trained down at Modo, who was curled up in a fetal ball on the carpet. Proteus must have given him an iron fist to the stomach as well.

Here he was, in the flesh again, the man whose life Ash was devoted to ending. Everything that had once seemed sexy and alluring about him—his sun-kissed complexion, his muscle-bound forearms, the mysterious music that always danced in his eyes—now disgusted her.

Then there was his smile, the same smile that he'd been giving her since the day he'd first introduced himself at a seedy bar in California. It was a soft smile, but disconcertingly sincere, as though the corners of it had been dulled or weighed down by history . . . a history that, until recently, she didn't know they shared.

"Turning your skin into volcanic rock," Colt said. "If I'm not mistaken, that's a new trick for you in this lifetime. Just you wait, though. There's so much power in you, Pele, waiting to be unlocked. I know . . . because I've seen it."

"I am not," Ash seethed, "Pele."

Colt clicked his tongue. "Soon, darling."

Ash crossed in front of Modo so that she was now between him and the bullets in Colt's gun. He wasn't about to shoot her. "Why this kid?" Ash asked the trickster, even though Modo was older than her and didn't really qualify as a "kid" anymore. "What will killing him accomplish?" Across the room Proteus was staggering hazily to his feet, using a window curtain to pick himself up. Ash wagged a burning finger warningly in his direction.

"Kill him?" Colt echoed, and even though Ash knew he was a practiced liar, the confusion on his face read sincere. He tucked the gun in his hand into his waistband. "I don't want to kill Modo. The gun was just to keep you from doing anything rash. No, I just wanted to offer Modo a job. Your friend has a unique skill set that will prove integral to my mission."

Modo tried to step out around Ash, but she held him back. "Some way to hire me," he shouted over Ash's arm. "Kidnapping my girlfriend."

"Ah yes," Colt said. "Ms. Paulson." He crossed the room to one of the windows and drew the curtains aside. Cautiously, Ash and Modo both joined him at the glass and peered out.

A van with tinted windows was parked on the side street behind the house. As soon as Colt waved his hand twice over his head, the side door rolled open. There were three people inside: Eve, who sat nearest the exit, had her hand clutched tightly in Jenna's blond hair, while Ash could see just the faintest shadow of a third girl—Rose—on the other side. Jenna was no longer gagged, but she looked too terrified to even try to scream out. All it would take was one hard electrical shock from Eve's hands . . .

It was hard to see very well in the low light of the streetlamps, but for just the briefest of glances Eve stared penetratingly at Ash, a look that Ash couldn't quite decipher. Then she slammed the door closed.

Ash was close enough to Colt to smell the cinnamon cologne wafting off his neck . . . which meant that she was also close enough to wrap her fingers around that neck and just let the fire pour out of her until she melted him alive—to test just how much bodily harm his regenerative abilities were capable of repairing.

But in her heart, even if there was the slightest chance she could end this now, she also knew that she'd be risking Jenna's life, and Modo's. And she couldn't take on Colt and Proteus simultaneously. Proteus could easily transform his arm into a shiv and put it right through her heart while she was trying to barbecue her ex-boyfriend.

Colt must have sensed her resignation, because he offered her another soft smile. Then he turned to Modo. "You are Hephaestus, god of the forge. I need you to use your powers of metallurgy to create me an ax."

Modo scowled. Ash could tell he was ready to claw out Colt's eyes himself. "If you wanted an ax, asshole, all you had to do was swing by the Renaissance fair yesterday and buy one for the low price of $79.95 plus tax."

"Not a toy, and not just any ax," Colt corrected him. "This needs to be stronger and more resilient than any blade ever created, with an edge so fine and sharp that it can cut through anything—an ax only a god like you could create." He tapped his skull. "Everything you need to forge it is stored up here."

"And you'll let my girlfriend go if I agree to do this for you?" Modo asked.

"Upon delivery," Colt said.

Modo nodded sullenly. When it had just been his own life in danger, he'd still retained a brightness, an aura of better days about him. Now it was like there was a vacancy sign dangling from his soul. "Sorry, Ash," he said. "It's hard to argue with an ultimatum like that. I . . . have to."

Proteus was beckoning Modo over, and the boy obliged. With metal fingers curled around Modo's shoulder, Proteus led him out of the room.

Colt shadowed the two of them to the door but lingered in the exit. "Why do you still resist, Ashline?" he asked her. "Rose is magnetically drawn to me. Eve has rediscovered the electricity, the charge between us. You're the only one, the only piece of Pele, who's fighting this now. Sooner or later, though, you're going to take a step back and appreciate all these elaborate measures I've taken, just to make you whole again. Sooner or later you're going to stop denying the old spark you've never stopped kindling for me."

"The only spark I'm going to rekindle," Ash said, enunciating each word sharply, "is the one I'm going to light beneath your funeral pyre."

Colt smirked one last time at her. "You always did say the most romantic things." Then he was gone, and Ash was left with only the fading traces of his cologne and a tightness in her chest.

She stayed in the frat bedroom for some time, staring out the window until Proteus and Colt had forced Modo into the back of the van, then driven off. Ash was struggling to put some of the pieces together. To start: What the hell would Colt need to cut with a special ax, and how could it possibly relate to melding Pele back together?

Remember Occam's razor, Ash thought, recalling a lesson from one of her teachers at Blackwood. Occam's razor, in short, was the philosophy that the simplest explanation was usually the best one . . . so Ash started simple.

Colt needed an ax.

Aside from medieval warfare—which wasn't exactly Colt's style—axes were most commonly used to cut down trees.

And if a real ax could be used to cut down a real tree, then a specially made ax could be used to chop down a specially grown tree.

Which left the question: Where on earth was there a special tree that Colt would want to get rid of?

When the answer dawned on Ash, her elbows slipped off the windowsill. "Oh my god . . . ," she whispered.

She'd asked herself the wrong question when she wondered where on "earth" this special tree was . . . because it wasn't on earth at all.

The Cloak Netherworld revolved around a towering "life tree," a mystical organism that the oily creatures apparently drew their power from. The tree was also a sort of jail for gods who the Cloak had taken off-line, ones who they'd deemed too sadistic and dangerous to exist in circulation anymore. Each of those gods was plugged into the tree to rehabilitate them, like acorns on an oak, to teach them selflessness and peace by forcing them to exist as part of a communal organism, for the common good.

Both Eve and Colt had at one point been imprisoned within that tree . . . only Colt was so wretched a soul that his very presence had proven toxic to it.

Now he intended to chop it down. It could prove the end of the Cloak . . .

. . . and it could jailbreak a whole lot of twisted, deranged gods.

That still left one last question though. Colt needed Modo, alive, to build him the tree-killing ax . . . yet Eve, who supposedly now sided with Colt, had attempted to murder Modo the day before.

What's your angle, Eve? Ash wondered. *Why destroy the very tool your would-be lover needs to complete his vile mission? Unless . . .*

Ash pressed her hand to the glass pane, which was cool beneath her palm. Pictured the look that her sister had given her before she drove away. Listened again to the words Eve had heralded yesterday before Ash subdued her: *You don't know what you're doing, Ashline. If you knew who he is—what he is—you wouldn't be protecting him.*

Ash let her forehead slump against the window. *You have got to be kidding me,* she thought. Her next words she actually uttered out loud, because they were so ludicrous, so unfathomable that she needed to hear them to believe them.

"Eve . . . ," she whispered, "is on my side?"

It was a restless and haunted eight hours
of sleep back in the hotel room. Ash woke up at least once
an hour to gaze at the empty bed where Modo should have
been. In between she suffered through nightmares, from
which she would wake up sweaty and with only a loose
grasp of what had happened in the dream. Only vivid
but fleeting images remained, burned into her memory
upon waking—of giant falling trees, of her body wreathed
in fire as she held hands with Colt . . . of flames spreading throughout a city as Pele allowed it to be consumed
in lava. People screaming up and down the streets. Fire
devouring everything. Everything.

She prayed that these were truly just nightmares, and
not visions of the future.

By morning Ash was short on options. She couldn't
in good conscience stop Modo from making the ax unless

she rescued Jenna before he created it, and she couldn't rescue Jenna without knowing where they'd taken her. Colt was smart enough to keep Modo's girlfriend in some secluded location, away from Modo, so the metallurgy god wouldn't try anything stupid.

What Ash needed was to talk to someone higher up than her.

Someone omniscient.

She needed to have a conversation with the Cloak.

After devouring a quick breakfast in the lobby restaurant, Ash hopped in Modo's car and drove out of the city. The Cloak were a strange race. As powerful and all-knowing as they were, they had a weakness: They were allergic to hate and violence, though not exactly in the way a human might be allergic to peanuts or dairy. When they were exposed to it, they transformed from a wise, sentient super-race into uncaged, animal-like monsters. For that reason they could only tolerate quick visits to Earth before retreating to their home world, where only their magnificent tree could detoxify them.

Ash wasn't sure precisely how the "hate allergy" functioned, but she had noticed that the Cloak more frequently appeared to her in natural settings—the woods, the ocean. That much at least made sense, since cities and populated areas were more likely to be tainted with hate and violence . . . whether it was residual or fresh.

So with that in mind, she kept driving down Route 117 until she hit the town of Lincoln, fifteen miles outside Boston city limits. There she parked in a dirt lot just off the road and headed out into the woods. A few joggers and locals walking their dogs populated the trail here and there, but by the time Ash crossed a train trestle and veered off the path, she found herself alone.

She'd never actually summoned the Cloak before, so she cupped her hands around her mouth and called the name "Jack" over and over again. It was the human name with which the Cloak identified themselves, as if it somehow made them more mortal and less terrifying.

Ash was about to give up and wander, defeated, back to the car, when she heard the softest rustle of leaves, just behind her. "Calling our name?" an inhuman, gender-neutral voice said into her ear. "That's a new trick."

Ash spun and found herself gazing upward, face-to-face with one of the Cloak. The single fiery blue flame that it had for an eye drifted just slightly with the breeze that was blowing through the woods. Its oily black flesh moved fluidly around it, more like an ink than a skin. Its teeth were bared, a massive gray bear trap of a mouth that looked like it could chew through a tree in one bite. Ash couldn't be sure whether it was smiling or about to devour her . . . or possibly both.

She tried to swallow the lump of fear in her throat. "I didn't know how else to reach you," she said, trying to take a casual step away from Jack. "It's not like you guys carry cell phones or check your e-mail."

Jack didn't laugh. "I don't have long here," he said.

"Even in the wilderness the hate from other areas of your world blows like a foul wind. In time it won't be safe here for us . . . or for you." Beneath those words Ash heard what he was actually saying: *In time, you won't be safe from us.* Even though Jack had only materialized for less than a minute, Ash could already see how his inky body was starting to bloat outward, growing less humanoid and more animal in shape.

"I summoned you because of Colt," Ash said, skipping to the chase. "In order to fuse me and my sisters back together, he's decided to get rid of you . . . and to do that he's commissioned Modo—Hephaestus—to forge an ax to chop down your life tree."

"We know," Jack replied calmly.

After a few seconds, when Jack offered nothing else, Ash shrieked, "Then stop him, damn it!"

Jack shook his head, which was starting to elongate into more of a snout than a face. "You know that's not how we operate."

Ash did, and it was infuriating. The Cloak had been charged with overseeing the gods, the way the gods were originally supposed to oversee the humans . . . but according to their bizarre, inhuman code of ethics, they refused to directly meddle in the affairs of the gods unless they decided it was absolutely necessary.

Of course Ash guessed that from their perspective, the few times they'd meddled had only given birth to more problems. When they'd split Pele into three goddesses, they'd created sisters who warred among themselves. And when they'd stripped the gods of their old memories to give them a better life, they'd opened the door for Colt's manipulations to flourish, lifetime after lifetime.

Ash couldn't think of a time more urgent than this for them to at least try again. "Forget your stupid hands-off policy, Jack. Colt is coming for you. With a big-ass ax, too, which he's going to use to go Paul Bunyan on your stupid tree if you don't step in and stop him now. Don't you get it? He is going to kill you."

Jack snarled a little, his back bucking with uncontrollable spasms. It wouldn't be long now before the hate really started to leach its way into his consciousness and transform him. "Even with the ax he can only get to the tree by traveling through our Netherworld, at our mercy." His voice sounded strained and phlegmy now, his words echoing up from the back of his throat. "And should he somehow succeed, we don't fear death the way that you do. All of you, humans and gods alike, base all your rash decisions on your fleeting mortality. You've convinced yourselves that behaving like you will die tomorrow is the admirable and adventurous way to live. That," he said, spitting out the word as though it left a bad taste in his mouth, "is what we call a stupid policy."

Ash pounded her fist on the trunk of the birch tree next to them. With the heat rising in her, she left a faint char mark on the flaking bark. "You could probably end all this in a second," she protested. "Instead you're going to stand by and watch me struggle, on my own, to bring down Colt Halliday? While more humans and gods die at his hands?"

Jack dropped to all fours as a pair of clawed arms emerged from his body where there had only been a dark amorphousness before. Ash had never seen the transformation progress this far. "You are missing the bigger picture, Ashline Wilde. Back in California, when you were first discovering your abilities, we sent you a scroll with instructions. Do you remember what it said?"

Ash nodded impatiently. "'Kill the trickster.' I could have gotten a head start if you'd told me my target was also my fucking boyfriend."

Jack ran a talon down the birch tree's trunk, scoring a line through the char Ash had left. "When we gave you that task, we were looking for someone to show us that this world is worthy of being saved. We were looking for . . . a champion. And if the best this world has to offer can't vanquish the worst it has to offer—if good cannot ultimately triumph over evil—then give me one reason why you deserve our intervention."

Ash could see that it was a lost cause trying to convince Jack and that she was quickly running out of time. There was a hunger in his eyes, as though he were absorbing the violence of the world like a sponge . . . and that hunger had fixed Ash as its prey.

She was backing away now, as Jack sauntered forward. His mouth parted, and each of his gray teeth glistened with the same oil that writhed over his body. "If you won't help me directly," Ash implored him, "then at least give me a push in the right direction." She thought back to the cryptic directions the Cloak had once delivered to her and her friends and how they'd provided her with visions of Rose to set her on the correct path. "You were never against dropping a hint from time to time to help me stay the course. So tell me this: Where are they keeping Hephaestus's girlfriend?"

Jack paused and cocked his snout to the side, as if deciding whether to answer her question. "Greymoor Hotel . . . top floor," he growled out finally, each word a struggle. "You'll find . . . her there."

"Alive?" Ash asked, but just then Jack bellowed and lunged for her. Ash held up her hands to shield herself, as his gray jaws snapped open. . . .

And then, like that, his body burst into a million particles of darkness that evaporated as he returned to the Netherworld. Only the spectral image of his blue flame eye lingered in the air in front of her, shimmering until it faded, but it left her with a very clear message that Jack had left before:

We'll have our eye on you, Ashline Wilde.

As Ash returned to Boston, Jack's final hint wasn't sitting well with her. In the last few months Ash had found herself in several kidnapping situations. First there were the mercenaries who tried to toss Serena—the tiny, blind siren that Ash went to school with—into the back of a windowless van. Then she'd had to rescue Wes from being tortured in the humidor of a cigar shop, and just a couple of days later she nearly died rescuing Ade, her thunder god friend, from a mafia safe house.

Those environments all seemed fitting under the category of "places to kidnap someone or hold them hostage." Shady, secluded, populated with men for hire.

The Greymoor, however, was one of the finest four-star hotels in downtown Boston. With its sweeping views of Boston Common, right in the heart of the city, it was about as conspicuous a place you could choose to bring a captive. Ash's parents stayed there on business trips, for crying out loud. At four hundred dollars a night it wasn't exactly the kind of hotel where you dragged a college-aged girl, bound and gagged, through the marble lobby and expected a bellhop to help you haul her over to the elevator on a golden cart.

Ash earned a few looks of disdain from the concierges on her walk through the Greymoor's regal lobby but she couldn't look *that* out of place—surely they must be used to spoiled teenagers staying with their loaded parents. So she walked with an air of self-entitlement through the elevator's silver doors and rode it all the way up.

Ash's uneasiness only grew when the doors parted and she stepped out onto the twenty-seventh floor. The luxurious top level was adorned with all sorts of abstract modern sculptures, and Ash was having a real hard time imagining some girl gagged and tied to a chair behind one of these doors.

So, Ash thought, looking at the four top-floor rooms. *I have a one-in-four shot of choosing the right one on the first try.* She glanced up to the ceiling at the fire alarm that was silently blinking red every few seconds, and she felt her lips forming a smile that they reserved only for when she was about to do something particularly devious. *Time to improve my odds.*

With the same flicking motion that one might use on a lighter, Ash ignited her thumb and held the flame up to one of the ceiling's steel sprinklers.

It only took a few seconds. As one, the sprinklers on the top floor all whirred on, sending curtains of water raining down over Ash and everything else in sight. Red lights pulsed down the hall, and the fire alarm picked up to an almost deafening level. Ash reached up and melted the nearest one so she could hear better.

The occupants of two of the rooms exited almost immediately. First a mother and her grade-school-aged son from one, then a couple—both in bathrobes and looking more than a little flushed—from the other. All of them rushed past Ash and headed for the stairwell to begin the long trek down.

That left only two rooms, neither of which had produced any guests. Ash headed for the nearest of the two and wheeled back, ready to kick the door down . . .

But then she heard just the faintest peal of laughter from the other room. When she listened more closely with her ear against the door, she could hear two people inside giggling over the alarm—a man and a woman. There was a hard wrenching sound, then the alarm on the other side of the door cut out altogether.

Until now Ash had sensed there was something shady about this kidnapping, but that hunch was quickly transforming into understanding. And with that Ash felt her anger heading for its boiling point.

Ash took a step back and unleashed a devastating kick on the door in question, her foot connecting hard, right next to the lock. The door imploded, slamming against the wall inside with its mangled dead bolt protruding like a broken bone. The scene inside the hotel room brought Ash's rampage to a momentary but very abrupt stop.

On the bed, as she predicted, Modo's girlfriend lay only half-dressed, tangled up in a bedsheet with the water from the sprinklers cascading down on her. Her matted blond hair was so long that it practically flowed off the mattress, and she pulled the covers more tightly over herself when she saw Ash. Although she was no longer laughing or smiling upon Ash's entrance, the expression on her face wasn't a "thank God someone's come to save me" look that would make sense for someone who'd been kidnapped.

It was the guilty expression of someone who had just been caught in a lie.

That much Ash had expected. But the other man in the room was the true surprise. His name was Brett Hardeson, and Ash knew this because he was a musician— a pop star. His infectious breakout hit "Star-studded" had been ravaging the Top 40 radio stations for the last two months. Now here he stood in front of Ash, wearing only a pair of boxer shorts and the fire alarm that he'd ripped out of the wall, while the sprinklers continued to wet his boyish haircut and his bare chest.

Before Ash's brain could properly compute "Modo's supposedly kidnapped girlfriend is sleeping with a pop star," Brett lunged for her. Water droplets flew off his wet body, and one of his fists transformed into wood midair, on a collision course for Ash's face.

Ash dodged the punch, letting the wooden fist clip her shoulder, then seized her attacker under his bare armpits. With her strength still fully engaged, she lifted him off the carpet and hurled him into the wall behind her.

His body struck the ornate sculpture that had been nailed to the wall, which looked like a pair of twisted antlers. Both the man and sculpture fell, but the pop star's face smashed into the cherry dresser on his way down.

His eyes rolled back into his head, and his body transformed. Hair sprouted out of his smooth, toned pale chest, which lost all its muscle definition. An angry red burn mark appeared on his wrist, and when the metamorphosis was complete, Proteus lay on the carpet, unmoving.

Someone squeaked behind Ash. She turned to find

Jenna, still wearing only lacy lingerie, darting off the bed and toward the exit.

Ash was too fast for her. In one jump she blocked Jenna's escape, slammed the broken door shut, and then grabbed Jenna by the throat. While Jenna flailed futilely, Ash threw her out the sliding doors onto the balcony.

Jenna curled up in a ball, quivering against the railing. Tears were streaking down her classically beautiful face—it was the kind of face that could probably make a man do anything. Ash towered over her. She was so angry that the water from the sprinklers evaporated right off her red-hot skin and into a fine mist. "Right now," Ash said, "you're probably wondering what you should be more afraid of: the twenty-seven-story drop behind you"—Ash pointed to Tremont Street, so far below them—"or the angry Polynesian volcano goddess in front of you. If you don't tell me who you are and what's going on, you're going to get a taste of both."

"Okay, okay," Jenna shrieked. "My name really is Jenna Paulson. But my goddess name is Aphrodite."

Ash choked on absolutely nothing at all. No wonder the girl was obnoxiously beautiful—she wasn't even human. Then Ash had a funny thought and glanced back through the window to where the unconscious Proteus had his face pressed into the soggy carpet . . . and she began to laugh. "Now I get it," Ash said. "History's most famous lover . . . is hooking up with the god who can be any lover that he wants. Tell me . . . ." She stooped down so that she was closer to Jenna. "When you make Proteus shift into a new celebrity every night—because let's be honest, who wants to shack up with his real face?—does he feel empowered, or does he feel . . . inadequate? And who did you have him transform into last night, to celebrate your fake kidnapping? Matt Damon? Ben Affleck? Angelina Jolie?"

Aphrodite just whimpered and said nothing, pressing her face into the bars of the balcony railing. Maybe the drop was starting to seem like a more pleasant fate than being interrogated by Ash.

"So you're a goddess masquerading as human, who seduced a god who actually believed that he was human," Ash went on. "I'm not even going to ask if you've been working for Colt, since the answer to that is pretty obvious. But what I don't get is: What the hell do you get out of this? You worm your way into Modo's life, make him love you, all so he'll unquestioningly build the ax that Colt needs, in order to 'save your life,' . . . But what's in it for you? Money? Fancy rooms at the Greymoor? Or do you just get your jollies hurting good men you think are beneath you?"

"You wouldn't understand!" This time Aphrodite actually snarled, the first time that she'd shown any sort of anger since Ash kicked down the door. She quickly softened her tone, though, when she remembered it was Ash she was talking to. "You said it yourself: I'm history's most prolific lover. . . . And those oily, hell-dwelling Cloak bastards took all my memories from me! Thousands of years of lovers and affairs in cities across the globe, and I don't get to remember any of it? It's bullshit. Colt promised me that if we cut down the Cloak's tree, he'd get those memories back for me."

Ash laughed, but she was so disgusted that it sounded more like the bleating of a sheep. "Fake relationships, fake kidnappings, emotionally torturing some innocent kid—all this bullshit—because you can't remember who you shagged a hundred years ago?" Ash pressed a heel into Aphrodite's sternum, forcing her up against the railing. "Where is Colt holding Modo?"

Aphrodite let out a wheeze. "Modo interns for a technology company, RazorWire. Their HQ is a tall glass building down in Fenway, and they were so impressed with Modo's work that they gave him his own lab on the top floor. Please . . . ," Aphrodite pleaded. "You have to understand. I just wanted to remember. I just . . ." Then she started sobbing, her tears flowing off her face and onto Ash's foot.

Ash shook her head as she removed her shoe from Aphrodite's breast. "If I ever cross paths with you again . . . Let's just say that I'll give you some memories you won't be so keen on remembering in your next life."

Then she turned fast, stepped back into the flooded hotel room, and slammed the glass door. With a quick flame from her hand she heated up the lock enough from the inside so it would jam shut, then drew the curtains across to hide the balcony. Aphrodite would have to break her way through the dense glass door or wait until a housekeeper came to clean up the room.

Either way, no one on the street below was going to hear her cries from the top floor.

Either way, Aphrodite was going to have to spend a long time out on the balcony thinking about what she'd done.

Unfortunately, Ash discovered when she turned back to the room, the spot on the floor where Proteus had supposedly been unconscious was no longer occupied by the shape-shifter. The coward had fled, leaving his supernatural lover to fend for herself.

He was probably also making his way back to Colt to warn him that the ruse was up. Ash just prayed that Modo hadn't finished the ax yet.

The front door to the room flapped open, revealing two men in Boston Fire Department gear. "What the hell are you doin'?" the firefighter in front yelled at Ash. "Head to the staircase and get outta here."

"Yessir," Ash said with a salute.

"Anyone else in the room with you?" the second firefighter asked as she started to pass him.

Ash smiled darkly. "Just me and my lonesome."

Then she headed for the stairwell, taking the steps two at a time all the way down to the lobby. There was no time to waste.

After all, she had a laboratory to infiltrate.

RazorWire Laboratories was an intimidating tower of glass and steel that looked more like a massive modern sculpture than the headquarters for a technology company. It sat squarely in the middle of a series of liberal-arts college campuses, not too far from Fenway Park. The reflective glass windows blazed a blinding orange under the setting sun.

With the regular work day over there was only one security guard manning the check-in station, his legs up on his desk and a magazine open in his lap. Ash tried to exude an "I work here" confidence as she strode past the desk, but the guard was shrewder than she thought. "Miss," he called out, and was already starting across the lobby for her.

Ash was prepared. She telegraphed a point of heat to the magazine the guard had left on his desk. "Fire!" she cried, pointing behind him before he could get to her.

Sure enough, when he turned, his issue of *Maxim* had gone up in flames. He sprinted back to his station. Ash tried not to giggle as the fan behind the desk blew some of the burning pages from the magazine, scattering them across the lobby floor.

While the guard was busy trying to stamp out all the burning debris before a fire alarm went off, Ash darted for the elevators and slipped into one just as an employee was exiting.

It only took the high-speed lift a few seconds to rocket her to the top floor of the laboratory, and another couple of minutes before Ash found a door marked R & D - NANO-TECHNOLOGY that she could hear voices behind.

She threw open the unlocked door.

Everyone in the laboratory froze as soon as they saw her. For a second, with the harsh setting sun backlighting the occupants of the room and gleaming off the high-tech machinery, it was hard to sort out who was who. Gradually, however, Ash saw that Modo was presenting a six-foot-tall ax to Colt. Proteus and Eve stood to either side like sentries, their eyes fixed on Ash to see what she planned to do next.

"Don't give it to him, Modo," Ash yelled. "This whole thing was a setup."

Modo paused. Even though the silvery ax was as tall as Modo, he held its leather grips in his massive, callused palms as though it weighed nothing at all. The blade, Ash noted, looked sharp and refined enough to slice through stone like it was jelly. "But Jenna—" Modo started to say finally.

"Is a double-crossing, goddess bitch who's been working for these guys all along," Ash said. "She conned you, Modo."

It was like someone had attached weights to the bottom of Modo's face, his sagging jowls nearly falling to the floor. His head started trembling as he turned to regard Colt. Then he cranked on the machine behind him. The fans inside began to whir rapidly, and a red beam—a laser—materialized between the two diodes.

Modo spun around, pushing the blade of the ax toward the open laser.

But Colt was too fast for him. In a blur the trickster god ripped the cumbersome ax out of Modo's fingers. With his other hand he grabbed Modo by his hair and forced his head down toward the machine.

Ash took a few steps forward to save him, but Colt shook his head at her, stopping her in her tracks. He held Modo's face so that his cheek was just inches from the laser. If it was powerful enough to cut through steel, Ash guessed, then it would certainly cut through flesh as well.

"You're making my job awfully difficult, Ashline," Colt said. "Although it's really adorable that you show up wherever I go. Like a puppy dog. That sort of persistence reminds me of the old Pele. . . ."

"You're not leaving with that ax," Ash told him. She sized up the fifteen feet that separated them, figuring out if it was possible to dodge both Proteus and Eve, get to Colt, and wrap her fingers around the blade long enough to melt it. Even if she had the agility to pull that off, however, there was a good chance Modo's head would get sheared in half by the laser in the process. It seemed they were at a stalemate.

That is until Proteus surprised all of them by pulling a pistol out of his pocket and pointing it at Ash's forehead.

"What are you doing, Proteus?" Colt asked, and the look of sincere terror that overcame him told Ash that this was definitely not part of his game plan. "I need all three of the sisters alive to put Pele back together again."

Proteus kept the gun trained on Ash. "This chick keeps popping back up like a cold sore, and sooner or later she's going to get the drop on us. I think it's about time that I put her down like the dog she is."

"Proteus, lower your weapon," Colt said sternly.

"Shut up," Proteus barked. "I am so sick of taking orders from you. You completely lose all perspective when this bitch is around. You think I give a damn about your love life, Halliday? You've got these delusions of grandeur that you're this master puppeteer pulling everyone's marionette strings, and that you've got every single god and goddess in your pocket, doing your bidding. I just want my damn memories back, you asshole. So maybe I should just take that ax, have Rose cut me a portal into the Netherworld, and cut down that tree myself."

Ash considered reaching out and trying to burn Proteus's hand with her mind, but his aim was steady, and she might just cause him to pull the trigger instead. Eve must have sensed this too, because she gave Ash the most fractional shake of her head.

Colt laughed dryly at the mutinous shifter. "If you go to the Cloak Netherworld, they will eat you alive and cast you into oblivion before you take three steps on their home turf. I, however, hold the secret to passing safely through their realm."

"What is it then?" Proteus demanded, then shrieked, "Tell me!" Colt still said nothing, so he moved the gun just a hair to the left and fired a bullet past Ash's face. Her eardrum sang as it whistled past and smashed through one of the big windows. Glass rained down, littering the floor and falling twenty stories to the parking lot below.

Colt, Ash could see, was losing his cool. He still had Modo held against the laser machine, but his attention was completely on Proteus's pistol. In his own deranged, twisted way, he really did want to make sure Ash stayed safe. Still, he remained silent. *He doesn't want the Cloak to hear his secret plan,* Ash realized. The oily creatures had ears and eyes everywhere—but they couldn't read minds, so Colt had the upper hand as long as he kept his mouth closed.

"Fine," Proteus said. He aimed the gun back at Ash. "Let's find out if her fire's quick and hot enough to stop a bullet to the face."

Just as his finger went to squeeze the trigger, Eve sent a lightning bolt sizzling from her outstretched hand across the room and into his chest. The machinery all around them exploded with sparks, and Proteus writhed with convulsions. Ash dove for the floor right as two bullets discharged from his gun, nearly hitting her.

In just a few furious strides, Eve crossed the room to where the shifter was still shuddering on his knees. Her fingers wrapped around his neck, and she lifted him up in one hand. "Bullets are for cowards," she scolded him, and sent another electric current through him until his pistol clattered to the floor. With his toes just barely brushing the tile, she dragged him over to the window he'd shattered. Eve smiled sweetly up at him. "For your next trick, let's see you transform into a pancake."

Then she threw him out the window.

There was a very short-lived scream, which ended suddenly with the crunch of a body landing on the top of a car.

With Proteus dead, Ash straightened back up. Eve turned around slowly. They locked eyes briefly to acknowledge that, for the first time in over a year, the two of them were now on the same team.

Then they started to converge on Colt.

The lightning bolt had short-circuited the laser, so Colt finally released Modo, who crab-walked behind the shelter of another machine. It was like he was a bystander in a ghost town who sensed the duel that was about to happen.

Meanwhile, Colt backed away toward the corner of the lab, with the ax gripped in both hands. "So," he said to Eve. "You were just playing along the whole time, thinking that I might share my plan with you?"

"You got it," Eve said. She spread her hands and let electricity pass between her palms, like an accordion made of lightning. "When you tried to recruit me again in Miami, it was tempting for me to send one hundred thousand volts through you to find out how much pain and punishment that regenerating body of yours could endure . . . but you're a slithery one and good at escaping.

So I decided to out-trick the trickster and earned your trust instead."

It was Ash's turn to smile as she sauntered toward Colt. Smoke rose threateningly from her palms. "Eve and I barely coexisted in the same household growing up without killing each other. How could you possibly think either one of us would want to coexist in the same brain for eternity?"

Colt bumped into the window behind him and seemed to realize that he'd run out of room. Ash and Eve fanned out a little to either side to make sure he didn't try to escape around them.

His expression should have looked helpless as he watched the volcano and storm goddesses closing in on him . . . but instead he just nodded resolutely at both of them. "It's good to see you two working together," he said softly. "Actually, it's . . . kind of a turn-on. With every fiber of your being that you resist becoming Pele, you actually become more like her. The ruthlessness. The brutality. The carnal appetite for destruction."

"Sometimes it takes a bastard to corner a bastard," Ash said.

Colt raised the ax and at first Ash thought he might be so desperate that he intended to swing it at one of them. Instead he drove the butt of the ax backward, hard, into the window, shattering the glass. "What corner?" he asked innocently.

And with the ax still in hand, he jumped out the window.

Ash and Eve both rushed to the window's edge, careful not to throw themselves out as well.

For a moment Ash thought that maybe this really was the end of the road for Colt Halliday. His body lay in a messy splatter on the grassy hillside below, a puddle of blood spreading through the earth and down toward the parking lot curb. Not too far from him, Proteus was sprawled dead on the roof of the car that had "broken" his fall.

Unlike Proteus, however, Colt eventually stirred. With a groan audible to Ash even on the top floor, Colt rose onto one arm, then the other. The regenerative magic in his body shifted the bones around, setting and mending all the ones that had snapped during the fall. When his spine healed, he was at last able to stagger to his feet. The indentation in his skull popped outward, and his healing flesh repopulated with his close-cropped hair.

When the process had finished, he limped over to the ax, the entire blade of which had sunk into the ground during the fall. He ripped it free of the earth, like he was drawing Excalibur from the stone. With the ax hoisted in one hand and a congenial wave up at the two Wilde sisters, he loped off into the trees.

A speechless minute passed while Ash and Eve just stared out the broken window at the place where Colt had disappeared. He would be in his car and gone by the time they took the elevator down anyway.

"How bad do you think that hurt?" Ash asked Eve finally, breaking the silence.

Eve grunted. "Not bad enough."

Outside, sirens of the police and the paramedics were just arriving in the parking lot—someone must have heard Proteus hit the car. But even though Ash knew they should get going before the police traced the body to the broken windows in their laboratory, she couldn't help but study Eve in the glow of the sunset. The girl had double-crossed her before. She may have saved her life from Proteus tonight, but trust still wasn't going to come easy.

"So is this real?" Ash asked at last. "The two Wilde sisters, teaming up to hunt down the trickster?"

"On one condition," Eve said, and she flashed a grin that would scare off a grizzly bear. "That when we track the bastard down, we play rock-paper-scissors to decide who gets the pleasure of ripping out his heart."

Of all people, you never thought you'd develop a deep friendship with a mortal.

In fact your friendship with Colt Halliday is in a lot of ways your only true friendship, even among the Council. Papa and Rangi are far too stern and inwardly focused to properly bond with anyone else. Tu is more the silent, brooding type, and Tane spends the majority of his time either haunting the influx of foreigners who've started to visit Hawai'i or seducing girls from the village. You wonder how many fathers will never know that their children are not their own.

Then there's Tangaroa. The more time you spend with Colt, the more distanced and callous the sea god grows. He barely looks at you at Council meetings, let alone flirts or paws at you the way that he once did. It had always been assumed that you would both pair up, but jealousy has deadened any romantic momentum the two of you had before.

Somehow you don't really care. You'd fully expected Colt, marooned as he was, to be desperately seeking a way back to the mainland . . . but as far as you can see, he's adopted the islands as his true home. He shows a persistent and insatiable inquisitiveness for the ways and customs of the different peoples, for mastering the language, for getting to know the personality and geography of each of the main islands.

It's been six months since you found his body in the surf, and he's given no indication that he ever plans to leave. You like that. You like it so much that you haven't even bothered to hide your godliness from him. Who would he possibly tell anyway? And it's not like the others have made strict efforts to conceal their own identities. Tane's girls know full well that they're not being seduced by an ordinary man. Tu, in his former life, supposedly counseled King Kamehameha in the ways of conquest, while Papa regularly moved through the fields, bringing fertility to the soil wherever she tread.

So you use your portals to speed up your travel as the two of you jump from island to island, and light fires for Colt in his cave before you leave him each night, so that he'll remain warm until morning, when you both do it all over again.

One morning you arrive beneath the sea arch to find Colt's cave empty. This isn't unusual—it's not as though he's always by your side. You still travel to the summits of Haleakalā and Kīlauea for contemplation, and bring rain to the forests when they desire it. But this morning is special. Until now you've never taken Colt to the summit of any of the volcanoes. They are a sacred place, your place, and only this morning did you decide he'd earned this special privilege. The volcanoes are the last key to Colt understanding your importance here, how the islands would never have come into being without the raw, molten power source that lurks beneath the earth's crust.

When you get to the cave and find Colt missing and the bonfire extinguished, you don't panic. By now you've figured out which bays and forests and reflection pools are his favorites, and unless he's constructed some sort of raft, there are only a limited number of them he could have traveled to on foot without your portal-making abilities.

You find him on the second try, when you step out into a glade on the southeastern side of Maui. You hear the dramatic whoosh of Waimoku Falls before you even see it, the four-hundred-foot waterfall that cascades down the rocky cliff carved into the side of Haleakalā. But the more breathtaking sight is the young man standing knee-deep in the water, at the base of the moss-covered cliff.

It's Colt, of course. He's standing beneath the rushing falls with an untamed strength, as though it were just a trickle and not the weight of four hundred feet of water crashing down on him.

He's also completely nude.

Before you can escape, hide, or even just look away, Colt turns and spies you standing there between the trees. You expect him to show some embarrassment or shyness—you've seen most of his body every day in the malo that you fashioned for him, but never this much.

Instead his expression remains placid, and he steps just out of the waterfall, so that his naked body is no longer obscured by the rushing water. He wipes the last droplets of water from his scalp, but then leaves his hands at his sides, letting you take in all of him. You sense the invitation lingering there.

The blood pulses in your temples, and a new heat burns in your chest. Your heart feels like it's pumping out magma in double time. Your relationship with this outsider has already crossed so many forbidden lines, but the threshold that hangs between you now is the one you never thought you'd cross.

The one you've always secretly wanted to.

Even though the faces of the Council—of Tangaroa, especially—materialize in your mind, logic slips away under the burning tides of temptation. *You are Pele*, a voice whispers inside of you. *You made these islands, so you should walk among them wherever you please.*

And lie down with whomever you please.

You step out from between the tree trunks. Colt hasn't moved. As you walk toward the edge of the pool, you untie the kapa wrapped around you and let it fall to the stones, leaving your body completely bare. Colt's eyes never leave yours as you stride slowly but purposefully out into the pool. With each step the fiery soles of your feet cause plumes of steam to rise up.

Then your bodies come together, your flesh hot to the touch, his flesh a stirring cool from the Waimoku waters.

When it's over, you both lie beneath the falls. His arms have never unwrapped from their position around you since your bodies first came together. There's nothing desperate in the way he holds you, like he thinks you might run off through another portal, to leave him for good. There's no fear in it either.

There's only a powerful certainty.

You press your face into the crook of his neck and you whisper, "So that's how it feels. . . ."

"That's how what feels?" Colt asks, running his hand through the wet strands of your hair.

"The stillness," you say, picturing the rocky volcanic bay where you first found Colt. "That's how the lava feels when it joins with the tide."

You lose yourself over the next few weeks. You stop showing up for Council meetings. After all, what function do they serve anyway? So Tane can brag cheekily about his latest exploits? So Tangaroa can scathingly ignore you? If anything, it's just a formality to maintain a bond between six people with nothing in common except for their mutual godhood and shared heritage.

For true passion and friendship, it took an outsider.

You've even started sleeping in the sea cave with Colt, instead of the crater atop Haleakalā where you used to curl up most nights before you met him. You wake up in his arms every morning, greeted by the cool breath of the tide and the warm breath of your lover. You spend your days hunting and fishing, showing Colt every tiny islet he's never seen before in the archipelago, gleefully sprinting through the bamboo forests. He may be mortal, but he always keeps pace with you.

He never seems to get hurt either, which is something you can't even say for your godly self. Even when he lost his footing on a climb up Kīlauea and tumbled a hundred feet down the hillside, he just brushed himself off and stood up. Not one bloody scrape or scratch visible on his body.

Somewhere in his home lands, the gods are still smiling upon him.

One morning you wake up to a sound that your sleepy brain can't make sense of at first. It's a deep and distant musical note, and the echo of the cave tunnel distorts it. . . . But after you've gathered your senses, you realize what you're hearing.

Somebody's blowing into a pu conch shell in the distance. And not just any conch—this shell is among the largest ever found, with a deep sonorous note that you were forced to memorize.

It is the Council's horn, blown by Rangi's deep sky-wielding lungs so that its sound will carry to any of the islands. The conch is only to be blown in the event of an emergency meeting when the immediate gathering of the gods is imperative.

Colt stirs next to you. "What . . . ?" he mutters.

You're already on your feet, but you kneel back down and press your lips to the short, bristly hair on the top of his head, the hair that he never cuts but it still never grows. "I must obey the shell's call and gather with the others," you say, as the conch lets loose another deep blast. "I'll be back in time to fish with you on the banks of Lāna'i, as I promised." You carve a portal into the air and you're gone.

In the bamboo grove Rangi and Papa have already assembled as usual. The other three are nowhere to be seen. Rangi holds the conch shell to his mouth, ready to blow a third time, but he lowers it when you appear in front of them.

"What is it?" you bark. "Why have you blown the horn?"

"Patience, Pele," Papa says in her soothing alto. "We shall explain when the others arrive."

You squint at the two of them. They've summoned you here at dawn with the utmost urgency, and even their normally stoic façades betray the faintest signs of nerves. Now they want to linger around and await the arrivals of the other, slower gods when you could already be taking action?

Minutes pass. Something is off. While the others may not be able to move instantaneously through portals like you, traveling between two places miles apart as though they were side by side, they can also travel lightning-quick when necessary by calling up their various elements. So where is Tangaroa? Or Tane? Or Tu?

Then you notice an even more chilling detail: Rangi is no longer sounding the horn. The rules say that he must continue to blow into the conch until the others have come to the Council in case, for instance, Tangaroa should miss the initial call while swimming deep around the reefs, as he often likes to do.

Instead Rangi holds the horn half-cocked at his side, while his other hand keeps tightening then relaxing, as though he's prepared to use it. Papa, too, maintains a defensive stance, subtle but tight in her legs.

"What have you done?" you say finally; then in a harsher voice that sends tremors up the slopes of Haleakalā: "What have you done?"

"What needed to be done," Papa says, circling around to the other side of you. "Let them do what they must with the Driftwood Stranger and then come back to us. Peace will be restored."

"The time for peace is over," you growl.

You feel the sky breathing in as Rangi circles his hands, preparing to flatten you with a harsh gale. Unfortunately for him, lightning moves faster than wind—you thrust out a hand in his direction, and a bolt forks down from the heavens and spears him through the chest. He crumples to his knees, and his face slumps into the dirt.

You spin and grab Papa by the neck before she can run. She wheezes as you lift her off the ground and hold her up over the short cliff. The water in the pool below looks too blue and serene for a place where they've forced you to spill blood.

"Please," Papa gasps out. "I always thought highly of you, Pele."

Your fingers tighten around her neck. "I always thought you were boring." With your free hand you fire an explosive burst into her chest, and she sails into the pool below. When her body resurfaces, it's facedown and unmoving.

With no time to lose you gouge another portal in the air and lurch through it. You pop out beneath the sea arch, where the waters had been calm when you left.

Now they're frothy and angry with a raging, stormy tide. The waves pound against the cliff wall, and the tide has risen so high that the entrance to the sea cave has completely disappeared below the surface.

"No . . . ," you breathe out. Then you inhale deeply and dive into the maelstrom.

Tangaroa's deadly tide batters your body as though you were a minnow as you try to flounder your way into the underwater cave opening. Each current that pulses through the water slams you against the jagged walls of the cave, tearing into your skin. You still press on, guided by dread that you may be too late to save Colt.

Finally, just as your lungs are burning and the rush of

the water around your ears is starting to fade, you breach the surface into an air pocket. Ahead you discover why both Tangaroa and Tane are missing. Colt lies where you left him, only he's very much awake. The waterline has crept nearly up to his head. In any other situation he might have been able to lift his mouth clear of the water and retreat to an air bubble, but Tane has summoned vines out of the rock to tether Colt firmly in place. The two gods aren't in the cavern, but they can't be too far off.

You swim to Colt, but not before a sharp stalactite bites into your shoulder. With your burning hands you easily shear through the vine bonds holding Colt down. The plant matter withers and retreats into the stone, singed and blackened with fire.

Up the slope, at the dead end of the cavern, you cast a new portal into the air. You push the half-drowned Colt toward it, and he catches himself before he goes all the way through. He spits up more water onto the ground, then holds out a hand for you to join him.

"No." You shake your head. "I'm sending you to Ni'ihau," you say, pointing to the vision of the arid cliffside floating in the air. "It has no forests for Tane to track you in, and Tangaroa won't be able to sense you unless you go into the sea."

He tries to protest for you to come with him, but you have one more Council "meeting" to attend. You push him through, and the portal snaps shut before he can scramble back to you.

Eventually, Tangaroa and Tane must sense that they've lost their prey. The storm tide recedes and the waves flatten out, until you can see back through the cave entrance ahead.

It isn't long before Tangaroa and Tane arrive. They wade through the now-placid waters but stop when they see that you're alone. "Where is the mortal?" Tangaroa barks at you.

Tane tilts his head back and sniffs. "I can still smell him. He hasn't been gone long."

You hold out your hand, letting an explosive orb hover over your palm. Fire laps around it as it grows bigger until it's twice the size of your head. It needs to be big for what's going to happen next. Tane and Tangaroa shrink back toward the exit, but ultimately hold their ground.

Once you're certain it will do the job, you spin and wing it down the cave tunnel. Tane and Tangaroa both dodge to the side, clinging to the cave walls as it zips past them.

"You would try to maim me?" Tangaroa cries out, beating his chest.

You smile. "It wasn't meant for you."

The orb completes its trajectory through the cave opening and slams into the base of the sea arch outside. The cave trembles, and the tremendous sound of cracking stone echoes down the cave walls. Tane and Tangaroa turn to flee, sensing all too late what you've intended.

They don't make it to the entrance in time. The sea arch collapses over the mouth of the cave, and as the enormous mound of stone blocks the last of the exit, the cave falls into pitch blackness.

But not for long. Your eyes flicker red, glowing through the dark just enough to see the terrified expressions of the two men in front of you. Even gods and forest spirits know fear.

The ground trembles again, this time behind you. The stony surface where you've slept for the last month splits open as magma bubbles up through the surface. The molten lava flows around you, lapping at your legs, but of course you're impervious to it—you could swim in an erupting volcano unscathed if you wanted to.

You are Pele.

Tane and Tangaroa stagger back toward the blocked cave entrance. "Stop this madness," Tangaroa orders you. The lava rolls down into the water, which slows it down at first. But as the shallow pool turns to steam, new lava starts rolling right over it. With gruesome certainty it boxes in Tangaroa and Tane.

They're still close enough for you to see the sweat dripping from their brows, and it's not just from the intense geothermal heat rising off the lava.

"Please," Tangaroa pleads in the missionaries' language, his courage evaporated just like the water. He huddles next to Tane as the lava starts to eat up the last of the cave floor. "We were like a family before the stranger came here."

"Yes!" Tane agrees vigorously. "You were our cherished sister!"

With a tiny detonation behind you, you carve a new portal in the air, to Ni'ihau, where Colt awaits. "Cherished sister?" you echo. "I'm afraid you're mistaken. I'm an only child." You hop through the rift in the air onto a barren cliff on Ni'ihau. For a few seconds two tortured screams sear through the opening before the portal closes behind you.

It won't be long before the cave fills in completely.

Colt waits nearby like you expected . . . and so does Tu.

You immediately take a defensive stance between the war god and your lover, but Tu holds out a hand for you to stand down.

"I mean the Driftwood Stranger no harm," Tu offers. "I was not part of the plot to destroy him."

"Yet you knew about it, didn't you?" You try to be fierce with him, but after destroying four members of the Council you're exhausted, and your anger sounds weak. "You could have warned me before it turned to this."

He indicates one of the many tattoos that cover his body. It's made of many triangular strokes and waves, but you recognize it as a spear wrapped in kapa leaves. "Sometimes," he says ruefully, "being a good god of war means knowing which battles are not your own."

Colt steps up behind you and rests his hands soothingly on your shoulders. You press your back into his chest but keep your eyes on Tu. "So you're not here to avenge the Council?" You want to believe him, but it's hard to trust anyone after the four people you knew best in these islands just conspired against you.

Tu shakes his head. "What the Council sought was murder. What you just accomplished was justice. And I believe in justice." After a pause Tu adds, "I also believe in prophecy. The Driftwood Stranger may not have intended to bring destruction to Hawai'i, but just as the prophecy foretold, he has. So for the good of our people, I ask you to leave these islands."

From his tone it's clear that there's no "asking" about it.

"Where will we go?" you ask.

"Somewhere you'll find peace, I hope," Tu says. The irony that he's a war god offering this advice must not be lost on him, because his lips form a stiff smile—it may be the only time he's ever smiled. Then he wanders off down the beach.

You'll never know how he predicted where he could find the two of you after the Council's mutiny . . . or that you'd emerge alive at all.

Colt spins you around and holds you tenderly by the elbows, drawing you to him. He rests his head on yours. "I would never ask you to leave your home for me, Pele. Say the word, and I shall swim away from these islands, the way that I came."

"My home is with you now." You look meaningfully

to the east, where the sun lingers over the blue horizon. "Wherever we may go."

"You're willing to put your faith in a man you barely know, who washed up into your life without invitation," Colt says, somewhere between gratitude and confusion. "Why?"

"Because . . ." You swallow. "Because . . . I love you."

It's the truth, but not the words you didn't have the courage to tell him. Not the words that have died on your lips every time you've tried to say them this last week.

Because, you had wanted so badly to tell him, *I'm carrying your child.*

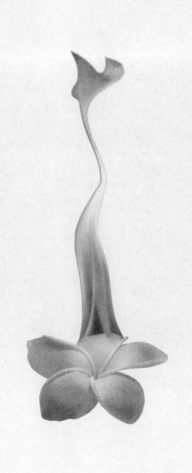

PART II:
NEW YORK CITY

As far as car rides went, this had to be one of the more awkward ones in Ash's life.

The two Wilde sisters had agreed to a ceasefire, yes, and yes, they'd also agreed to hunt a common enemy . . . but that didn't mean that everything was going to be instantly warm and sisterly again.

Eve had insisted on driving the rental SUV, even though she looked horribly uncomfortable behind the wheel. Ash was sure Eve would rather be back in the saddle of her Honda Nighthawk, the bike that Colt and Ash had sort of blown up in a car accident on a joyride to Canada.

Ash rolled down the window and dangled her arm out of the car, letting the seventy-mile-an-hour roar of the passing wind on the MassPike fill the silence that neither sister could. After the incident at RazorWire labs the previous night, they'd raced back to Colt's hideout, only to find that he'd taken Rose and left town fast. Ash had expected to find Raja's orphaned baby, Saga, there as well, but Eve explained that Colt had dumped her at an orphanage days ago. After he'd used the baby to manipulate Raja back in Miami, the child was no longer of use to him. The thought of Saga alone, with both her parents murdered, broke Ash's heart like a porcelain figurine, but for now Saga would be safer in the care of an orphanage.

After dropping Modo off at MIT so he could try to put his life back together—without his treacherous girlfriend—the Wilde sisters were New York City–bound. According to Eve, before she'd blown her cover, Colt had revealed the Big Apple to be the destination for some sort of heist he'd conceived. Whatever object he planned to steal was somewhere in Manhattan . . . but beyond that detail Colt had kept the cards close to his chest. Maybe he didn't trust Eve completely. Maybe he was afraid the Cloak would overhear him and intervene. Regardless, Colt seemed sure that with the object in his possession he'd be able to walk safely through the Cloak Netherworld without getting devoured alive.

Which would mean that he could walk right up to their big Tree of Life and chop it down with a few powerful strokes of the ax.

Which also meant that the Cloak might die, and the evil, twisted gods imprisoned in the tree would be liberated, placing an army of supernatural gods at Colt's disposal.

"Worst of all," Eve had said, looking genuinely unnerved, "Colt has all of the gods on his payroll convinced that killing the Cloak will bring all the memories from our old lifetimes back. But I think he's been lying all along and it's just the opposite. If the Cloak die, I think it may mean we *never* get those memories back."

It was a terrifying concept. As much as Ash found herself overwhelmed and confused when an old memory resurfaced in her sleep, she saw the big picture now. Even if Ash and Eve stopped Colt tomorrow, they'd forget all about his manipulations when they woke up in the next lifetime, while he would remember everything. With the Cloak gone, what was to stop him from coming back time and time again until, one lifetime, he finally succeeded?

After Eve brought Ash up to speed on Colt's scheming, the two sisters fell into an icy silence. In the quiet Ash felt a year's worth of frustration with Eve coming to a boil. She wanted so badly to be happy to have Eve back by her side, but instead she felt more distanced from her sister than ever.

Finally, Ash rolled up her window, unable to keep her annoyance contained any longer. "Why didn't you just tell me?" she demanded. "Why didn't you let me in on this whole double cross, instead of letting me believe that you really were in league with Colt?" She thought back to their skirmish at the Renaissance fair. "I could have killed you."

Eve didn't take her eyes off the road, but her arms stiffened. "Kill me? As if." She chuckled softly under her breath. "Look, Ash. We both know that I'm the conniving one here, while you, on the other hand . . . well, you've always been a terrible liar. You know how I always used to call you the human mood ring? It's because your emotions, your push-buttons, your insecurities . . . You wear them with the subtlety of a goddamned fireworks display. As much as I wanted to let you in on it, it was much more convincing when your seething hatred for me looked all the more real to Colt. But the other part of it . . ." She trailed off, then finally took her eyes off the road long enough to appraise Ash. "I worry that when the time comes, you won't have it in you to do what's necessary . . . especially if it's dirty."

Ash crossed her arms. "Dirty? Eve, you haven't seen the depths of hell I've had to descend into—the people I've had to hurt, the people I've had to kill, even—to get our baby sister back, and now to track down Colt. I'm not proud of some of the things I've done . . . but don't sit there and question my motivation because you think I'm too dainty to get the job done."

"So what?" Eve snapped. "You've killed a couple of people who attacked you first? They were bad fucking people, rotten apples to the core, and you killed them in self-defense. But what about Colt? The guy has done some deplorable shit to mold us back into his freakin' volcano goddess Barbie that he can play dollhouse with.

Deranged as he may be, though, he really does love us—or at least what we could become. So can you live with the fact that you might have to kill a man who refuses to physically hurt you even as you're ending his miserable life?" Ash said nothing, because she had no answer. She'd been so focused on ending Colt's reign of death and misery that she'd never stopped to consider the actual act of killing him. Self-defense was one thing, but the cold-blooded murder of a man who might not fight back . . .

"Then there's the collateral damage," Eve rattled on. "Hephaestus—Modo, Limpy McLimperson, whatever he goes by—that kid might have been the only god in the world with the supernatural acumen to make a weapon to cut down the Cloak's Tree of Life. One stroke of lightning through his body and Colt's plan would have gone to shit, and our fight would be over for good. You wouldn't let that happen. Sure, you didn't know why I was playing assassin with him at the time, but even if you did—you're too precious to acknowledge that in the big picture a few innocents might have to die to keep a hell of a lot more people alive."

Ash's hand fastened around Eve's wrist. "No more innocents die. At our hands or anyone else's."

Eve glanced knowingly down at Ash's hand, then at the scars on her own wrists—the permanent burn scars Ash had seared into Eve's flesh only months earlier. "That's exactly my point. You see everything as black and white, that one lonesome engineering student shouldn't have to die. The way I see it? This Pele chick that we used to be was one crazy, hot-tempered biatch. She wasn't just like you and me and Rose added together; she was us *multiplied* together . . . and let's face it, the three of us are no charm school graduates. Now let's say Pele does come back to life, and marches into Times Square in rush hour, and thinks, 'I'm having a real shitty day,' and next thing you know, she's summoning a volcano in the middle of Forty-second and Broadway, enveloping a few thousand tourists in lava and bringing buildings crashing down . . . all because a waitress served her morning cup of coffee cold." Eve let that image sink in. "Tell me preventing that isn't worth the life of an innocent bystander or two now."

Ash groaned and looked out the window at the approaching golden arches that advertised the upcoming rest stop. Maybe Eve had a point about killing a few to save thousands . . . but it was Eve's complete disregard for the value of human life that had always bothered her. "Some days," she said, "I really wonder how we're related."

With a hard jerk of the wheel Eve swerved across traffic into the rest-stop plaza, as the cars she'd cut off blared their horns. As soon as they rolled into a parking space by the gas pumps, she engaged the emergency brake and the car screeched to a halt.

"What, do you need to pee that badly?" Ash asked, her hand still with a death grip on the door handle.

Surprisingly, Eve was regarding her with a soft, almost

affectionate expression—a look that Ash couldn't remember seeing once in the last decade since they had drifted apart.

"Look, no matter what the Cloak and Colt say about us being shards of the same person," Eve said, "to me, you'll always be my baby sister. Growing up, you were always the good apple. Sure, you had some brushes with trouble here and there. And I'm not going to turn this into some after-school special by saying that I looked up to you or anything . . . but you were the daughter Mom and Dad wished I could be more like." She shook her head and stared out at the cars rushing by on the highway. "I'm not here to make you change into some immoral monster like your older sister. All I'm saying is that, when the shit hits the jet turbine, you're going to have to decide whether you've got it in you to do the kind of dirty, soul-staining things that might keep you up at night for life. If you can't commit to doing what's necessary, then all that I ask is that you get the hell out of my way when it's time for me to take care of it."

"I mean this in the most positive way possible," Ash said slowly. "But sometimes, you're one scary chick."

Eve snorted, fished a twenty-dollar bill out of her jeans, and flung it at Ash. "Now go inside and get your maniacal older sister a double cheeseburger with extra pickles."

After Ash had used the bathroom and picked up fast food for the two of them, she made one last stop to grab a copy of the *New York Times* before she returned to the car. With a big bite of cheeseburger still in her mouth, Eve wrinkled her nose and waved the sandwich at the newspaper, letting a drop of mayo land on the front page. "Since when do you care about current events, Ash?"

Ash fanned through the pages. "All we know is that Colt is after something in Manhattan, and twenty-three square miles and one-point-six million people is kind of a lot of area to cover when we have no leads."

"And you figured," Eve said through another mouthful of burger, "that Colt might have placed a classified ad with the headline 'Hopi Trickster God Seeks Mythical Object to Help Him Journey through Hell'?"

Ash shot her a dirty look, but went back to scouring the paper. While she didn't find anything that screamed "item that Colt would be after," she felt her internal furnace freeze when she came across one human interest story on the back page: THE FIVE-BOROUGH VIGILANTE.

According to the story, for the last several nights a modern-day "superhero" of sorts had been incapacitating muggers, drunken rabble-rousers, and gang members from sundown to sunup, all across the city. On Tuesday he'd left seven suspects on Staten Island beaten, hog-tied, or in need of hospitalization. Early Wednesday morning, just after midnight, it had been eleven in Spanish Harlem, and fourteen in the Bronx on Thursday night. The mugging and assault victims saved in each of these incidents reported the Five-Borough Vigilante to be massive in stature, standing at least six and a half feet tall, with broad shoulders and a threateningly muscular build. In a few situations, where he'd battled multiple gang members at once, bystanders reported that his body took a number of hard, punishing hits—in one case from the blunt end of a lug wrench—yet in all the cases, he seemed unfazed by the attack.

The few people who'd gotten a look at his face beneath his hood had identified him as a Hispanic male in his late teens or early twenties.

Holy shit, Ash thought.

The Five-Borough Vigilante had to be Wesley Towers.

The timing made perfect sense. She'd last seen Wes on Tuesday night, in Miami. Distraught by the gruesome murder of their mutual friend Aurora, the Aztec god of night had told Ash that he couldn't bear to stay in Florida another day. Everything there—including Ash—reminded him of the horrible events that had led up to the fateful night when Aurora was sacrificed. It had just been too painful, so Wes left Ash alone with the key to his Miami penthouse and the awful, stomach-tearing feeling that she'd never see him again.

Ash had only known the Aztec god a week, but there had been something there, something more than a high school infatuation—this awe and admiration for the boy that made even her grave circumstances feel lighter. Wes had inherited a fortune, yet instead of retiring early to a carefree, self-indulgent poolside life, frivolously enjoying fine dining and piña coladas until he became a part of the tropical landscape, he'd devoted his life to protecting the people of Miami—the city he'd adopted as his home after a tragic childhood.

Now it seemed that he'd relocated to a new city, where he'd wasted no time in using his supernatural abilities to lay down the law. Thanks to his godly powers his body was uncannily strong, agile, and resilient under the cover of night.

He would make the perfect superhero, so long as the sun was down.

But as Ash read through the article, there was something dark and savage about the events described. He was saving innocent people, there was no argument about that . . . but she almost got this premonition that he was reveling in the brutality of it. Like hurting bad people was the only thing that could distract him from the agony of losing his best friend, Aurora. After all, Lily and Thorne—the two people responsible—were dead now. If he couldn't punish them . . .

Ash was hypnotized by the newspaper article until Eve cleared her throat. When Ash lifted her head, Eve was squinting at her out of the corner of her eye, her attention only half on the road. "Either you found a lead in the paper, or you were getting really into a crossword puzzle."

"No, it's . . ." Ash folded the paper closed and took a deep breath. "It's somebody I know."

"Damn." Eve snapped her fingers. "I was hoping you'd found Colt Halliday's obituary."

Ash knew that her older sister had expensive tastes when it came to just about everything—food, clothes, motorcycles—but she was taken aback when they finally got into Manhattan, and Eve pulled the car up in front of the Plaza, one of New York's most luxurious hotels.

Before Ash could stop her, Eve was already out of the car, popping the trunk for the bellhops to take their luggage, and tossing her keys to the red-jacketed valet.

"Eve!" Ash whispered harshly, finally catching her as she ducked past the doormen and into the extravagant lobby. "Don't you think we should stay someplace a little more discreet? And where the hell did you get the money for this anyway?"

Eve stopped finally and blinked twice at Ash. "Stock market," she said, deadpan. "I have a really good investment portfolio." Then she walked up to the concierge to check in, presumably under one of the false names she'd conjured for herself.

Ash decided to let it go for now; after all, it was hypocritical to judge Eve for whatever (probably) illegal means she used to pad her bank account when they had been a bank-robbing duo in a previous lifetime. . . .

After they'd checked in and settled into their ludicrously sized suite, they sat down to brainstorm how they were going to canvas the city for Colt and Rose. "So Colt never said exactly what kind of object he was looking to steal here in New York?" Ash asked. She was curled up on one of the king-size beds with her laptop, scouring the Internet for any special events or exhibits that were happening this weekend . . . but there was a hell of a lot going on in the city.

Eve stood at the window, peering out through the curtains at Central Park below. "He referred to everything in code names. All I really know is that he said he was in search of three things to defeat the Cloak: the door, the blade, and the armor. The door clearly refers to Rose, and her ability to open portals into the Netherworld. The blade is obviously the ax. But the armor . . ."

Ash tried all sorts of searches for armor-related items that might be in the city. Everything from medieval exhibits at museums to an antiquities collector on the Upper East Side who had a private collection of battle gear from the ancient world. Nothing Ash came across, however, screamed "this could be the one!"

Ultimately, her search turned back to the Five-Borough Vigilante. According to the latest news report Wes (if it was him after all) had struck Queens last night, and the police were still calculating the number of victims he'd sent to the hospital. From the news article Ash also learned that the majority of the ruffians Wes had beaten senseless potentially belonged to a new, but rapidly expanding criminal organization that called itself Bedlam. The gang prided itself on disseminating crime and fear into all the boroughs of New York City, rather than sticking to a single home base or neighborhood. And what made them truly terrifying was how they would flood one particular, very contained region of the city— sometimes within a few city blocks—with a large number of criminals all at once. They were believed to have a membership of at least five hundred thugs, although that number had started to dwindle since the Five-Borough Vigilante crashed the party.

This article also contained a picture of the alleged Bedlam leader, Cesar del Frisco, who, until his recent disappearance, had been openly taking credit for the syndicate's crime spree. *What an idiot,* Ash thought. Forgoing anonymity just for the sake of infamy. Still, the guy had to be pretty smart to unite so many gang members and convicts under a single umbrella.

On a whim Ash pulled up a map of the five boroughs of the city, each one identified with a single color. Ash traced the vigilante's path from neighborhood to neighborhood. On Tuesday, he'd hit Staten Island. Then Manhattan. Then the Bronx. And finally Queens. Four nights, four boroughs . . . one left.

Wes was cycling through the major areas of the city to show them that no neighborhood was safe for Bedlam. That wherever they went, so too would he.

Which meant that if his pattern continued, Wes would be standing guard over Brooklyn tonight.

If I were a gang set on instilling fear in the defenseless, Ash hypothesized, *where the hell would I go to find easy prey? Or to find a big herd of prey?*

This time her search finally yielded some positive results. The Brooklyn Cyclones, a minor league baseball team, were having a grudge match tonight against their rivals, the Staten Island Yankees. The slugfest was going down at the Cyclones' stadium, in the southern part of Brooklyn, not far from the amusement parks of Coney Island.

"Hey, Eve?" Ash said. "The whole armor thing isn't turning up any leads, but I think I might have located a friend who can help."

Eve was pouring herself a tumbler full of scotch from the minibar. "Let me guess—you want me to help you scour the city for your Aztec lover-turned-crime-fighter? Oh come on," she added, and flung the open copy of the *New York Times* onto the bed. "It wasn't rocket science after I found the page where your fingertips lustfully smudged the ink. And I've got more productive things to accomplish around here without helping you chase your rebound romance around the city." She took a long sip from the scotch, and Ash wondered if "getting drunk" was Eve's idea of productive.

"What if I told you," Ash said, "that there's a slight chance you might get to electrocute some people who really deserve it?" She twisted the laptop screen around to show Eve the Cyclones' page.

Eve stopped mid-sip and lowered her glass. "I'd say," she said after a pause, "that the forecast for tonight's game just got dark and stormy."

The crack of a bat echoed over the field, and cheers rose up from the bleachers. Ash watched from by the concession stand as a tiny white comet streaked toward the right-field fence. It clattered off the green wall, bounced back into the outfield, and the cheers redoubled as the runner who'd been on first base beat the throw home.

Ash's phone rang right as she took the soda from the concessions cashier. When she flipped it open, Eve didn't even wait for her to say hello. "You promised," Eve muttered grudgingly on the other end, "that I'd get to electrocute some people." As she said it, the clouds that had slowly been gathering over the field since they'd arrived grumbled with impatient thunder.

Ash chuckled. And people said Ash's moods were transparent—her sister's changed the damn weather. "Patience, oh stormy one," Ash said. "It's not even the seventh-inning stretch yet. And I offered to be the one who patrolled the streets outside, but you said you'd rather gnaw off your left foot than watch a ball game."

"The actual sport, yes. But I'd go for a cold beer and a few of those concession hot dogs just about now," Eve whined. "I'll give it another hour, and after that, you can take the subway home by yourself." Then she hung up.

Ash headed back to her seat, and instead of watching the game she stared out over the home-run fence. The fence provided a picturesque frame of what lay beyond: the Atlantic Ocean to the south and the amusement rides of Moon Park to the east. The magnificent roller coaster, the Tempest, had been one of Ash's favorites during summers in grade school, and its wooden tracks blazed with lights as the sun set. But the only sounds that Ash could hear from the ballpark and the amusement parks in the distance were sounds of happiness and cheer.

Maybe this was a stupid idea. What if Bedlam opted for someplace less public? And what if they'd also deciphered the pattern of Wesley's crackdowns and were avoiding Brooklyn because of it?

Ash shook her head. If this Cesar del Frisco asshole thought he was untouchable and infamous enough to publicly acknowledge that he'd masterminded Bedlam, then he was also governed by pride. Which meant that Cesar wasn't the type to back down from a fight. No, he'd just up the ante to show the vigilante that this entire city belonged to him.

Innings passed, numbers filled the scoreboard as the game headed into the eighth, and Ash's doubt was beginning to grow.

That is until just after sundown, when a blackout hit Brooklyn.

As one, the massive tower lights around the ballpark flickered off. The pitcher had been just releasing his pitch, but as the players on the field were swallowed by the darkness, there was only a loud "ow" as the batter got drilled with the ball.

With Eve's storm clouds still blotting out the stars and moonlight, Ash stood in near blackness. The people around her were only silhouettes, shades of gray that were slowly rising to their feet and taking out their cell phones for light. In fact the screens of phones around the stadium all flickered on in rapid succession, like a nest of fireflies coming to life. Ash could feel her own phone vibrating in the pocket of her jeans—probably Eve calling about the blackout—but she didn't take it out. Instead Ash telepathically willed the spectators around her: *Don't panic. Remain still and don't panic.* All it would take was one sudden move for a stampede to happen.

Was this a product of Bedlam? Ash wondered. Was this just a coincidental blackout, or was this some platform for the crime syndicate to instill fear and anxiety in the people of Brooklyn?

Ash got her answer just moments later when a small but loud explosion popped in the air overhead.

It was a firecracker, Ash realized, lobbed up into the air by someone in the next section over. The noise and burst of light caused the chatter around her to erupt into a frenzy.

All around the stadium Bedlam members planted in the crowd started to toss burning firecrackers over the heads of the people in the arena. They were just miniature fireworks, but the effect was as if MCU Park were suddenly being shelled by enemy forces. The bystanders across the stadium cascaded into full-blown hysteria and started pushing and shoving for the doors.

Ash was knocked backward and dropped painfully to

her own metal chair, as terrified spectators climbed over the rows of seats, bypassing the stairs, which were already clogged with people trying to escape. The weaker folk— children, the elderly—were barreled over and trampled in the chaos. A fight between two fans erupted a few rows forward as one jostled the other one in his attempt to flee.

Meanwhile, firecrackers continued to shell-shock the stadium. Ash held her ground and even had to throw a few overly aggressive passersby off her. With each hit she took she grew more enraged. All the time, however, she kept her gaze fixed on the nearest Bedlam hooligan. His red Mohawk looked razor sharp, like the blade of a table saw, and he was strong enough to manhandle the one guy who tried to stop him from lighting another firecracker. The do-gooder tumbled over two rows of seats before getting trampled by the crowd.

Once the damage had been mostly done, and the hordes had started to make headway in funneling out of the park, the firecrackers stopped. Ash bent down to help an older man up, where he'd been wedged between two seats. As soon as he assured her that he was just a little shaken, she turned her attention back to Mohawk . . . only to find his stupid hair retreating with the rest of the crowd.

Ash zeroed in on his spikes and trailed him at a distance through the chaos. The masses were pouring out through the front gates and fanning out onto Surf Avenue. Several squad cars were already on the scene, with the police officers approaching the stadium, but they had to fight their way against the current. Of course, by the time they muscled their way into MCU Park, all the perps would blend into the crowds just like Mohawk had, so they were running a fool's errand.

Which left Ash with two questions: What the hell was Bedlam's endgame tonight? And more importantly, when the hell was Wes going to show up?

Interestingly, as the panic-stricken spectators turned up Stillwell Avenue toward the train station, Mohawk continued east toward the amusement parks. It was hard to keep tabs on him with all the streetlamps still lightless . . . which was why it was all the more impressive when Eve came up alongside Ash. "Following a lead?" she asked Ash, as they brushed past a couple of Staten Island bodybuilders.

"Literally," Ash confirmed, nodding to Mohawk ahead in the thinning crowd.

They followed him to the entrance to Moon Park, where he jumped the gate without ever looking back. Not that he had much to worry about, since the amusement park had been closed for an hour and all the available police officers seemed to be responding to the baseball stadium.

And that's when something clicked with Ash. What if the blackout and the firecrackers had all been just smoke and mirrors? Like they were drawing all the cops to one bug zapper, so they could get away with something even bigger, undisturbed?

Ash and Eve both clambered over the gates to the park. It was near pitch-dark with all the rides and lights zapped by the blackout, so if Mohawk noticed them, then at least they could pretend to be with Bedlam. With five hundred members no one could know everybody in the gang, right?

Up ahead they spotted the silhouettes of four more gang members moving beneath the massive Tempest coaster. Even in darkness it wasn't hard to see exactly what they were doing.

The Bedlam members were pouring tanks of gasoline around the wooden supports.

They were going to torch the roller coaster.

Sure enough, after they'd sufficiently doused the support beams, the guy in the center took the lit cigarette from his mouth and tossed it into a puddle of gas. A shimmering fire trickled up where the butt landed, then spread outward rapidly. In just a few seconds the flames engulfed the wooden beams they'd targeted, then started to climb into the rafters. In no time at all, it seemed, the coaster tracks were going to go up like they were made out of matchsticks.

The inferno provided light where there had been none before. Of the five men who'd been admiring the blaze, one turned around before Ash and Eve could retreat into the shadows. His face flickered a demonic red in the firelight, but with the shaved sides of his head, his long braid in the back, and the scar that puckered one of his cheeks, Ash recognized him.

It was Cesar del Frisco, the Bedlam mastermind whose picture had been in the papers.

Apparently Ash had been wrong about Bedlam being too big for Cesar to know everyone, because he stuck out his lower jaw then said, "Carnival's closed, ladies."

"Then why are you five carnies still working?" Eve asked. "I hope the freak show labor union is paying you good overtime."

The five men laughed darkly, but even as they did, they fanned out around the two sisters, quickly surrounding them. It might have felt threatening if either of the Wildes had planned to flee or back down.

They weren't planning on doing either.

"You girls are very pretty," Cesar purred. In his blood-shot eyes, Ash could practically see a slide show playing of all the terrible things he wanted to do to them. "Won't you stay and"—he glanced up at the burning coaster—"enjoy a good ride."

One by one the Bedlams were drawing weapons from their waistbands. Box cutters, a machete, a hatchet. "Seriously?" Ash asked, unfazed. "Five guys versus two girls . . . and you think you'll need weapons?"

"Bedlam's not about what's fair," Cesar informed her, twirling his butterfly knife in one hand like he was carving the air with a jack-o-lantern face. "Bedlam's about what's fear."

"I'm not even going to try to tackle the grammar in that sentence," Ash said, and Cesar squinted at her.

Either he didn't understand what grammar was, or he was trying to understand how two defenseless girls could dare to be so cheeky to five armed goons.

It probably only unnerved them more when Eve seemed to be fighting back a smile. She turned to the thug nearest her and pointed to his machete. "Could you raise that just a teensy bit higher, cupcake?"

The thug laughed a little, then looked confusedly to Cesar before he shrugged and raised the blade higher.

What he didn't notice was the tiny point of electricity gathering on the tip of the machete.

Or the fact that his long, dirty hair was starting to float around his face with static electricity.

He did, however, notice when the lightning bolt sizzled down from the clouds and zipped through the machete before it pumped his body with enough electricity to power Brooklyn for a few days.

When it was over, and the blinding light of the bolt faded, the thug collapsed to the dirt in a violent seizure before his body went still. Only a low moan escaped his mouth, and even that soon faded to a whine as he succumbed to unconsciousness.

When Eve turned back to the four remaining Bedlams, who were all standing too stunned to move, her eyes fluoresced with an electrical sheen. She tossed a ball of lightning back and forth between her hands. "Take me out to the ballgame . . . ," she started to sing creepily as they all watched her. "Take me out with the crowd. . . ." She windmilled the orb of lightning around, then whipped it at the thug to the left of Cesar. He flew back into one of the wooden supports of the burning roller coaster, and Ash couldn't be sure whether the *crack* sound she heard on impact was the wooden beam, or the vertebrae in his back.

Ash couldn't help but join Eve's creepy sing-along as she continued. "Buy me some peanuts and Cracker Jack . . . ," they both sang together.

Ash spun on her heel and slammed a fireball into Mohawk's chest. The explosion of fire rocketed him back over a concession stand counter, where he smashed into a wall of popcorn and cotton candy.

Cesar and his remaining man backed away toward the flaming roller coaster, apparently more terrified of the two Wilde sisters than of being burned by the inferno. Still, Ash and Eve sang in unison as they slowly edged forward: "I don't care if I never get back! Let me root, root, root for the home team, if they don't win it's a shame. . . ."

Eve pointed at the guy next to Cesar with her thumb and forefinger, forming a fake gun. When she clicked the imaginary trigger, another bolt of lightning forked down from the clouds and incapacitated him.

Ash shook her head at Cesar. "Come on, Cesar, sing along for the finale." Then she and Eve turned to each other, and in their most boisterous voices they shouted, "For it's one, two, three strikes you're out . . ."

Behind Cesar, in his blind spot, an enormous

silhouette emerged from the flaming underbelly of the roller coaster—a man over six and a half feet tall wearing all black. Wes drew back his hood, so that the firelight illuminated his handsome Latino face. He reached up and snapped one of the burning crossbeams off the coaster like he was breaking a twig off a tree and cocked it back like a bat. Then he enthusiastically finished the song for the Wilde sisters in his deepest, manliest, opera voice. "At the ooooold baaaaall gaaaame!"

Cesar turned just in time to catch the swing of Wes's "bat" full-tilt in the chest. The gang leader somersaulted backward three times until he hit a trash can. He used one arm to try to pick himself up, before he wheezed heavily, then dropped unmoving to the dirt.

"Babe Ruth called," Eve started to say. "He says he wants his swing ba—"

But by then Ash had already squealed, taken a few running steps, and pounced up onto Wes Towers, wrapping her arms and legs around his enormous upper body. She reveled in it as the muscles in his arms tightened around her back. Then they kissed, long and hard, while the chassis of the Tempest still burned around them like a flaming picture frame.

"God," Eve said, disgusted. "Let a girl at least finish her joke before you start sucking face." Still, Ash and Wes didn't pull away from each other, so Eve muttered, "Fine—I'll just, you know, extinguish the burning roller coaster while you two go at it."

Soon the rain from Eve's storm clouds spattered down on them. Ash and Wes finally pulled away from the kiss, leaving just an inch between their faces. Water cascaded down their cheeks, which Ash was grateful for because her tears blended right in. "You sure know how to make an entrance," she told him finally, and then half-laughed, half-sobbed with relief and joy, and so many other emotions that were vibrating in her. It had only been four days since they had last seen each other, but with the intensity of all that had happened these last few weeks, it felt like it had been years.

As he peered at her, she saw that the bags beneath his eyes had darkened with sleeplessness. Other than that, though, it was the same old Wes. He planted a feverish kiss on her forehead, then let his words whisper through her hair: "I should have never let you go, Ashline Wilde."

"Duh!" Eve called from somewhere in the rafters, where the heavy rains were finally extinguishing the flames. The upper parts of the roller coaster remained intact, but some of the charred lower supports looked like burned up matchsticks.

"Sisters," Ash mused. "Their number one job description is apparently to ruin moments like these."

"Speaking of ruining moments . . ." Wes glanced up at the Tempest through the steam billowing around them. "I'm trying really, really hard not to make a horrible pun about love being a roller coaster. It's just so tempting."

Ash pressed a finger to his lips to silence him. "You

are the worst." But they kissed again, and this time they didn't let up until the sirens of the approaching fire engines wailed. Eve insisted they get the hell away from the crime scene before they were charged with trespassing and arson along with the unconscious Bedlams.

On the walk back through Brooklyn, with Eve ten paces in front of them as though she were allergic to romance, the streetlamps flickered back on.

With her hand tucked into Wesley's, Ash felt as though power had been restored inside of her, as well.

Ash woke up with Wes's massive arm draped over her body. It was sort of like being trapped beneath a heavy tree branch, but in a good way. Wes was on his side, with his cheek pressed into the pillow. His chin-length hair was matted to his face with sweat, but a strand billowed in and out with each of his light breaths. Eventually, he opened one big, brown eye and regarded Ash soporifically. "Were you . . . were you just watching me sleep?"

Ash offered him the craziest joker grin that she could. "I am one hopelessly creepy romantic. And you . . ." She ran her hands from his cannonball-size shoulder down his ribs and to his waist. "You give a whole new meaning to 'big spoon.'"

He glanced down toward where his toes—and his calves, and his knees—were protruding off the end of the mattress. "I miss my custom-made bed in Miami. It's always nice to, you know, fit on a bed without turning your body diagonally."

Ash climbed on top of him. "I'll turn your body diagonally, if you know what I mean." She winked at him saucily.

Wes bit his lip. "The horny eighteen-year-old boy in me is turned on by the way you said that, yet my internal Hemingway is really struggling to decipher that metaphor." Still, his hands closed around her waist.

Ash had a funny thought and abruptly started to laugh. Wes peered up at her inquisitively, so she said, "I just had an epiphany. I met you for the first time beating the living pulp out of a cigar shop full of gang members. . . . Fitting that beating up some more people should bring us back together."

"Let no one say we haven't had a classic fairy-tale romance," Wes joked, then turned serious. "I really thought that leaving you was the right thing to do in Miami. I selfishly thought that was the only way to ease this pain inside with Aurora gone." He turned to the window, as though he might see the winged goddess flutter past their hotel room, her wings filled with Manhattan wind as she sailed back to the Hudson River. But there was only an unwavering morning light. "But she's gone, either way. And when I saw you last night, the firelight from that roller coaster washing over you, I realized that you're all I've got left in this world right now. You're the reason for me to not give over to hate and rage."

Ash pressed her face into his stubble. "God, put it in a song, Towers," she whispered, then kissed his neck.

Just then Eve kicked open the door to the room without knocking and walked in, fully dressed and very awake-looking. Since when was she a morning person? Ash wondered. And Ash certainly didn't remember giving her a key to the room she and Wes were sharing.

Eve was either oblivious to the romantic moment she'd just interrupted, or she didn't care. She tossed a bag of fresh bagels onto the bed next to them, the smell of still-warm dough washing around them. "Chop chop," Eve snapped, cracking an imaginary whip. "Less snuggling, more hunting the evil trickster god bent on world domination. And eat your bagels before they get cold."

After bagels, with only one computer between the three of them at the hotel room, the three gods went mobile, commandeering three computer stations at the New York Public Library. For hours they plugged away, cross-referencing "armor" with "Manhattan" in search of anything helpful. But by the afternoon the text on the screen was beginning to swim in front of Ash's eyes, which felt like they were about to bleed. What if Colt had already stolen what he needed and was on his way to the Cloak Netherworld? What if he wasn't even in Manhattan, and he'd given Eve a false lead when he sensed her deception?

But something began to tickle her mind when she was going through the thousandth search result. She lifted her head from the screen and said aloud to the two others, "What if we're taking 'armor' too literally?"

Wes and Eve squinted at her, partly out of confusion, but partly because they too were half-blind from all the Web surfing.

"Think about it," Ash said, getting more excited as the idea planted seeds in her brain and started to grow. "Armor is meant to protect your body on its way through battle. But the Cloak aren't going to give a rat's ass about some metal or leather suit. They're too powerful for that sort of mortal concern. So ask yourself: What *does* concern them?"

"They're allergic to hate," Wes said cautiously. "But . . . armor implies something you wear. And you can't wear hate."

Eve snorted. "Have you seen Ashline's closet lately?"

Ash rolled her eyes but continued. "People—both gods and mortals alike—create hate. But we leave trails of it wherever violence or cruelty happens. That's why the Cloak can't even go to a secluded forest without it transforming them. Hate is like some deadly particle that we're slowly filling this world with. If that's the case though, what if it's not just places where we leave hate trails . . . what if we can taint objects, too?"

Both Eve and Wes were starting to catch on. "So you get an object that's imbued with hatred," Eve said, "and you wear it almost like a protective amulet to walk through the Cloak Netherworld."

"But," Wes interrupted, "and I hate to play devil's advocate here . . . shitty, hateful things happen every day, in every city, around the world. There would be millions of objects that are hate infused, if that were the case. So if what Colt led Eve to believe wasn't more smoke and mirrors, then why is he so fixated on a single object here in New York?"

Ash considered this. "Yes, violence happens every day, and yes, violence seems to be an inherently hateful thing. But so many other factors go into most acts of violence. Just think of all the terrible stories you hear about from friends or see in the news. A mugger corners and attacks his victim in a dark alley . . . but the victim is probably anonymous, and the attacker is just looking for quick cash. A man comes home to find his wife cheating on him and turns a gun on both her and her lover. A terminated employee walks into the workplace that fired him and starts shooting at random. There's some semblance of hate in all of these situations, but it's not pure, or focused, or calculated. They're crimes of passion, because they're governed by things like envy, greed, self-loathing, fear of poverty, fear of the future . . . a whole bouquet of motivations that Freud couldn't sort out in a flowchart if he wanted to."

"We get it," Eve said, cricking her stiff neck. "Violence is complicated. What's your point?"

What is my point? Ash wondered, but then she felt her mind zeroing in on the idea that had been just barely eluding her. "So if you want something so poisonous to the Cloak that they can't come near you, even when they have home-court advantage, you don't walk into the Netherworld with a mugger's knife, when it probably belonged to some scared, stupid kid who only used it because he was looking to get his next drug fix. Colt wouldn't take a gamble like that. No, he wants an object that is pure with evil, overflowing with hatred so intense that those other factors barely play into it."

"So in summary," Wes said, "you mean that we should be looking for an object that is one hundred percent hatred not-from-concentrate?"

"Bingo," Ash said, then flagged down the librarian who'd been helping them. He practically pranced over, just as ecstatic as he'd been in the first place. He looked more like a bashful, blond-haired Baywatch cast member than any librarian stereotype that Ash could think of. Even though it was Ash who'd summoned him, his gaze kept flitting to Eve, who'd shown him no interest or eye contact since they'd arrived. Apparently he was into the dark, brooding, slightly sociopathic, hard-to-get type.

"We were wondering," Ash asked him, "if there are any current events happening in the city right now that might center around . . . hate. Evil. That sort of thing."

He idly twisted the lanyard around his neck, which had his name—Ephram—printed on it in big block letters. "Well, there's an opera about vengeance going up at the opera house next week, and there are several memorials and monuments around the city, but those are more about the memory of the victims than the violence that took them." From the murky database of his information-loaded brain his eyes widened with clarity. "'The Seven Deadly Sins, Realized,'" he said with a snap of his fingers.

"What the hell is that?" Eve snapped, finally acknowledging him. "Some sort of amateur Broadway musical?"

His bashful eyes met Eve's and quickly glanced away. "It's a new exhibit at the Metropolitan Museum of Art. Not your typical art gallery kind of thing—there are seven artifacts, each with major historical significance, that speak to one of the Seven Deadly Sins. Sloth. Lust. Pride . . ."

"Wrath?" Ash finished for him.

He nodded. "Exhibit opens to the public tomorrow. I actually might make a trip there if"—he glanced at Eve again—"any of you wanted to check out the exhibit with me."

Eve yawned. Wes pretended to cough to cover his snickering. Ash had already turned back to her computer to research the exhibit, so Ephram awkwardly shuffled away to straighten out some books that didn't need straightening.

According to the Met website Ephram was right—the exhibit didn't open to the public until tomorrow morning.

However, the museum was hosting a private, rooftop gala with the artifacts tonight, just for donors and historians.

Where Colt's scheming was involved, even twelve hours could make a big difference.

Ash took Wes by the hand and fluttered her eyelashes coquettishly at him. "My dearest trust-fund baby," she cooed at him. "How do you feel about making a last-minute museum donation? Philanthropists really, really turn me on."

Wes rolled his eyes. "I am way too young to be someone's sugar daddy. . . . Fine, how much do you think it's going to take?" He already had his phone out, looking for the Met's fund-raising number.

"However much it costs to get three tickets to tonight's cocktail party," she said absently, but her mind was already spinning, fantasizing about finally getting the upper hand on Colt.

You want an object that will allow you to safely walk through hell, Colt? she thought. *I'll show you a girl that won't let you safely walk through Earth.*

As Ash, Eve, and Wes followed the flow of guests through the grand halls of the Met, they earned their fair share of admiring or envious looks from the normal museum goers. At first Ash figured it was just because they looked real sharp in their black-tie formal wear—Ash and Eve in cocktail dresses of, respectively, red and gold, and Wes in the three-piece tuxedo from the men's big-and-tall section. But after a girl shyly approached them to ask Wes for his autograph, Ash burst out laughing when she realized what was going on.

"What?" Wes snapped, then lowered his voice. "Do you . . . do you think they recognized me as the Five-Borough Vigilante?"

"No," Ash said when she finally stopped cracking up. She shifted the satchel slung across her dress from one shoulder to the other. "You bear a striking resemblance to a certain player on the Knicks. They probably think we're your arm candy for the night."

"Ugh," Eve groaned in disgust. "I'm no concubine, especially for a professional basketball player."

Ash figured that most of the museum donors would be on the older side, but when they emerged onto the moonlit rooftop gardens, the three of them really didn't look that out of place. In addition to the more mature patrons she'd expected, there was a smattering of young donors too—probably real estate brokers, Wall Street types, or dot com entrepreneurs, she guessed.

Fortunately, Ash didn't immediately have any Colt sightings on the crowded rooftop, although it was tough for anyone to stand out among all the men wearing tuxedoes. Instead she wandered carefully through the crowd, with Eve and Wes in tow, while she went from glass case to glass case to investigate the new exhibit. The items the curator had chosen to represent each one of the sins weren't much on first look—mostly timeworn relics that looked like throwaways from *Antiques Roadshow*.

But when she stopped at each of their glass encasements to read the plaque below, she felt a growing sense of awe. For instance, at the installment for the sin of pride, there was a gold-trimmed mirror. According to its caption, the mirror had purportedly belonged to the Countess Elizabeth Bathory of Hungary—or the Blood Countess, as she was known later in history. Bathory had been infamous for a sense of vanity so intense that in order to preserve her youthful looks she'd allegedly stooped to black magic by torturing and murdering young virgins.

According to some accounts she actually bathed in their blood.

"Jesus," Eve muttered after she read the caption. "Maybe she should have just tried Botox."

When Ash skimmed through the captions of the exhibit's other antiquities—gluttony, envy, lust, sloth, greed—they were just as unsavory. But it was when she finally came to the wrath artifact near the far end of the exhibit that she felt truly sickened.

For all appearances, the wrath object looked like a tobacco pipe, although oddly it was made out of a scuffed bronze metal. Only when Ash peered closer did she recognize the pieces that had been sculpted and welded together to form the pipe.

They were shell casings from a rifle.

The caption explained that the pipe had belonged to an officer in the Nazi Gestapo during the Holocaust.

Apparently his favorite sport had been to corral groups of concentration camp prisoners that he no longer needed for his labor efforts.

Then he would line them up.

And he would see how many human beings his bullet could pass through in the lineup before it would come to a stop.

The bullet casings that he'd saved and fashioned into a pipe—which he apparently smoked out of every day— were from the bullets that had gone the farthest.

This truly is hate, Ash thought. No ulterior motives. No desperation because of poverty, no jealousy over an unfaithful wife. Just one man who so unconditionally loathed another group of people that he killed them without provocation, and without mercy, and with so much pride that he made this pipe to remind him of his own hatred on a daily basis.

Ash was very relieved to see that the man had been executed as a war criminal in the wake of the Holocaust, but she still felt a desire for retribution and vengeance for victims that she would never know. Who knows how many had been slain to make this pipe—fifty, sixty, maybe even more? All she knew was that the mere sight of it made her vision swim.

"So this is it," Eve said, and she seemed equally mesmerized as she peered at the pipe. "A couple of old bullet casings, and our boy Colt buys himself a get-out-of-jail-free pass to walk untouched through the Cloak Netherworld."

Ash nodded absently, but before she could speak, another party guest caught her eye through the glass case. The young girl was breathtaking in her floor-length black gown, and there was a willowy elegance to her with her one-size-too-long arms and legs. Her dark hair was so straight and well cut that it seemed to fall in one seamless curtain.

But her expressive brown eyes and her face, which looked like Ash's own, only harsher and more angular, needed no introduction.

"Oh my god," Eve said, apparently noticing the girl at the same time. "How did Colt manage to get her hair done and have her dress fitted without her blowing anyone up?"

It was Rose, after all, and even though she'd only been in a teenage body for less than a week since Raja aged her, she'd already shed the initial awkwardness of her newfound, taller body to reveal a powerful grace.

Still, despite the façade of beauty and elegance, Ash only saw the deadly darkness that lurked beneath it.

For the first time, as Ash gawked at her younger sister, she realized it wasn't Eve she was most terrified of sharing a head space with again for eternity if they failed to stop Colt. It was Rose, who was volatile and alien and oblivious to just about anything human, like an incurable psychopath.

"Breathtaking, isn't she?" Colt said. He had snuck up beside them and was leaning against a patch of railing with a martini in hand. Ash could tell he was trying to look composed, as always, but he had to be surprised that they'd worked out what "armor" he was after. His eyes kept flitting to the glass case beside them, then down at the satchel slung over Ash's shoulder.

"That girl," Ash said, pointing across the way to Rose, who was looking curiously at their group but not approaching, "has the mind of a six-year-old . . . and you're playing dress-up and house with her as though she's Evening Wear Barbie?"

Colt swilled his drink around. "You know one of the things I loved most about Pele? She—you—would never impose such rigid human morality on the gods. We make our own rules."

"Cool it, James Dean," Ash said.

Meanwhile Wes positioned himself between Colt and Ash, ever the protective boyfriend, even though Ash and Eve were both arguably more dangerous than he was. Colt, who was six feet tall himself, had to gaze up at Wes, but there was no fear in Colt's face. Fear doesn't function the same way when your body can repair itself from even the most horrific injuries.

Wes leaned his head down just slightly, to remind Colt who the big dog was. "The last time we crossed paths, I seem to remember telling Ash that I didn't trust you as far as I could throw you . . . and that I'd be happy to find out exactly how far that was."

Colt gestured to the other museum patrons around

them, who were completely oblivious to the tense confrontation happening near the wrath artifact. "Really, Towers? Let's save the primitive fisticuffs until we're no longer in civilized company."

Wes glanced up at the gibbous moon, the moon from which he drew his night powers. "Okay," he said.

Then he grabbed Colt by the front of his tuxedo shirt, spun him around a few times like he was a discus, and then launched the trickster with every ounce of his super strength off the roof.

Colt's body sailed over the museum and across Fifth Avenue, until he smashed into the fifth floor of the building across the street. He left a visible dent in the brownstone exterior before he dropped out of sight to the Fifth Avenue sidewalk below, where the screams of pedestrians echoed up even into the rooftop gardens.

They were followed by a second wave of screams, probably as the man who had just plummeted five stories magically began to peel his broken body off the sidewalk.

There were plenty of shrieks on the roof, as well, from the patrons who'd seen Wes toss Colt like he was made of balsa wood. People slowly drifted away from them, while two security guards edged closer, walkie-talkies in hand.

"How about another blackout, Eve?" Ash murmured out of the corner of her mouth.

Eve knelt down to the nearest electrical socket and put two of her fingers where a plug would go. She sent a hard burst of electricity into the circuitry.

The lights all around them burst, immersing the rooftop in darkness. Ash felt panic rise within her. Colt might have been subdued for now, but he was nearly impossible to kill and relentless as hell. Plus it was only a matter of time before security came to confront and detain the three of them. She needed to get the wrath artifact as far from Colt as she possibly could before he had a shred of a chance to steal it himself.

Ash plated her fist with volcanic rock. Then, under the cover of darkness, she wheeled back and slammed her knuckles into the glass encasement.

Her punch passed right through, shattering the glass around it. She groped around until her hand found the pipe. She put a hand on Wes's shoulder and said, "Keep the trickster and the explosive one off my tail for as long as you can."

Then she took off running across the rooftop . . .

girded her legs with the same volcanic plates she'd used on her fist . . .

and vaulted off the back of the roof into Central Park.

The impact with the grass below sent through her a tremor so violent, she almost forgot her own name for a second. But the volcanic reinforcement on her legs prevented them from breaking. By the time she emerged from her awkward roll through the grass, she was already back on her feet and running, the pipe still tightly clutched in her hand, and her satchel slung over her back.

As Ash sprinted through the dark park, with no real

destination in mind, she briefly contemplated just throwing the pipe away. Central Park was almost eight hundred fifty acres, and maybe it was safer just to melt the object and leave it in a gooey metal puddle somewhere.

But if anything, Colt was supernaturally resourceful. He'd managed to find Ash lifetime after lifetime, in a world with over six billion people. The gods and goddesses made up only an infinitesimal fraction of that population, yet he'd sought each of them out and wrangled them together in no time at all. Knowing Colt, the guy would just bankroll some god of magnetism to play metal detector in the park until they found it.

Ash's legs (which she had returned to flesh so she could run more freely) began to burn. Ahead she saw the banks of Turtle Pond, a little wildlife preserve in the middle of the park. She started to change her trajectory to circumnavigate the pond . . . when a hard object cracked her on the side of the head.

Pain sang through her skull, and suddenly she couldn't tell which direction was up. She distantly felt her body tumble to the grass, but her limp limbs no longer felt like her own. Darkness convulsed in and out of her vision as she struggled to retain consciousness. Somehow she regained enough feeling to touch the side of her skull, and felt a hot stickiness where blood was flowing out of a wound near her temple.

A foot caught her by the shoulder and flipped her over so that she rolled onto her back like a beached turtle. A demonically gleeful face stared down at her from behind a head of long red curls. Epona held a cricket bat, tinged red with Ash's blood. The Celtic nightmare goddess pressed her riding boot down hard on Ash's wrist, driving her sharp heel into the flesh until Ash painfully relinquished her hold on the pipe.

As soon as Epona had the wrath artifact in her possession, she tilted her head back to the sky and let out an animalistic shriek that sounded like a hawk's cry. At first Ash thought that Epona was just going berserk with pleasure at having thwarted her. But thirty seconds later, even through the church bells that were tolling in her ears, Ash heard the pad of footsteps coming toward them.

It was Colt. His tuxedo coat was gone, as was his tie, and his tuxedo shirt was shredded and stained with his own blood from the long fall. Unfortunately, thanks to his regeneration, he looked healthy as ever.

He caught Epona by the back of the neck and kissed her hard. Ash wasn't sure whether the need to throw up in the grass was because of the concussion Epona had given her, or from watching the two of them go at it.

Colt pulled away first, even as Epona lunged in hungrily for more. He stayed her with a hand. "Do you have it?" he asked.

She coyly held up the pipe, twisting it between her fingers while she gave Colt a naughty smile.

"Good," Colt said. "Let's get this over with then."

Ash tried to pull herself into a kneeling position, but

her legs were still refusing to cooperate, so she curled back up in the mud. What happened next, while she watched, was a scene of horror far more grotesque than watching the two of them kiss.

Colt stripped off his tuxedo shirt and turned so that his bare back was exposed to Epona. The nightmare goddess reached into her belt and plucked out a long dagger.

"It's going to heal quick, so you'll have to work fast," Colt reminded her.

She nodded. With a pained expression, Epona held the dagger up so that the blade pointed down . . . and then she plunged it into Colt's back.

Colt let out an agonizing cry as the blade sank into the flesh beneath his shoulder, buried in his body all the way up to the hilt. The cry turned into choking sounds as Epona dragged the dagger down, creating a long, deep incision in Colt's body.

Then, before the muscle and tendons and skin could repair themselves, a process that would happen almost immediately, Epona took the metal pipe and forced it into the open wound. She pushed it hard, gritting her teeth, until it was firmly embedded in his body.

She removed her fingers just in time. Like Ash had witnessed many times before, the flesh over the blade's incision zippered back together on its own. Within ten seconds the skin sealed the pipe inside Colt's body and left his back as smooth as it had been two minutes ago, without even the faintest trace of a scar.

Colt raised his arms over his body in a stretch, letting his musculature get used to the collection of bullet casings that was now lodged inside his body. It was buried so deep that Ash couldn't even make out a bump on his back.

There was more padding in the grass, and Ash prayed it was Eve or Wes, coming to stop this for good. It was Rose, however, who appeared through the trees. She'd abandoned her heels and walked barefoot around the banks of the pond. She looked curiously at Ash, who was still curled up in the grass, but there was no sisterly warmth behind her gaze. Ash could only guess that Colt had given Rose some sort of Stockholm syndrome through his manipulations, convincing her that he was the only person who could make her feel whole again, to stop the loneliness inside her.

Rose wanted to be part of Pele again.

Colt gave Rose a big smile and an even bigger hug. Epona looked disgusted to see Rose there, and Ash was sure the nightmare goddess would try to slit Rose's throat the moment Colt left the two of them alone—if he was stupid enough to do that.

Ash hadn't regained her strength enough to even half-ass chase after them, but she did have one last idea left in her arsenal. She reached a trembling hand into the satchel lying in the mud beside her and pulled out the secret weapon she'd brought with her.

It was the music box from Rose's demolished home in

western Massachusetts. After a few quick cranks of the key by Ash, it began to twinkle its soft melody across the park.

Rose stopped dead in her tracks, leaving Colt and Epona to walk ahead of her. Soon they noticed she was no longer following, but by then she was already under the trance of the music box's song.

Rose took a shaky step in Ash's direction, drawn toward the music. Then she stopped again and gazed back at Colt. Soon her head was twisting frantically back and forth between the trickster god and Ash, who held the music box out for her little sister, beckoning her over. She looked like she was being physically torn apart, like a human tug-of-war rope.

Tears streamed down Rose's cheeks. Then she let out a wail so deafening that it probably could be heard all the way across the Hudson River in Hoboken.

That's when Rose detonated.

The blast of intense energy burst out of Rose in a magnificent orb. The blinding explosion threw the bodies of Colt and Epona into the woods and reached far enough to send Ash tumbling into Turtle Pond.

When Ash spluttered to the surface, she saw just the tail end of Rose's black dress as the girl disappeared through a portal she had carved into the air. Then the air fused closed behind her, and the rift was gone.

Ash only managed to crawl out of the shallows onto an algae-covered rock before her concussed brain gave way to unconsciousness.

SHATTERED LANTERN

North America, 1831–1832

Your journey across the eastern continent begins on its Pacific shores.

When you first make land in the boat you stole from the Hawaiian missionaries, you've drifted farther north than Colt anticipated. It's colder here, and the misty shore air has the same crisp morning bite that the sea does. Your first thought, as your bare feet touch down on the rocky sand, is that you've made a big mistake. Maybe you and your beloved should have remained on the islands, despite Tu's warning. It was your home after all.

How could this place ever be your home?

But some of that trepidation disappears the moment Colt's hand finds yours. Together you wander up the steep hill into a forest that leaves you breathless. The forest here is unlike anything you ever saw back home, even on the most fertile slope of Kīlauea. The trees are so thick that

180

even ten of you couldn't make it all the way around one trunk if you were holding hands. The bark is a funny red color, not crimson like volcanic fire, but instead a deep earthy clay. The giant trees journey so far up into the sky that they might even penetrate Rangi's clouds.

If only Rangi and Papa were still alive to see these sights.

The going isn't easy—the two of you have to survive off what you find, sleeping under whatever natural protection the landscape can provide for you. It will be a long time before you encounter another human being. But Colt is truly a child of these lands. He knows what berries and leaves you can eat, and which are poisonous. He can catch fish from mountain streams and lakes, fell birds with a single stone, and catch game from rabbits to deer just by using the natural elements around him. Of course, when you're lucky enough to gather meat for dinner, you're more than happy to light a fire for him to cook it.

At night, under the stars, he tells you stories from his own ancestors, who were the first to inhabit this strange and ever-changing landscape. His favorites are tales of the trickster, Kokopelli, a god among men who would travel from village to village, bringing spring and fertility wherever he traveled with his magic flute. Whenever you ask exactly how Kokopelli brought fertility to the women of his people, Colt just smiles mischievously and says, "Let me show you."

Even after you've made love, you still can't bring yourself to share with him the news of your own fertility. Do you think he'll be angry? Do you think it will change the way he looks at you? It's hard to say, but something makes the word "pregnant" wither as soon as you've gathered it on your tongue.

Eventually, however, once the forests and mountains give way to sweeping prairies, you start to notice the swelling bump of your belly . . . which means that soon so will he. And because you still don't have the courage to say the words, you wait until one night, nestled in the prairie grass, as Colt leans in to kiss you. Before his lips can meet yours, you sweep open the fur coat he made for you, and you place his hands on your bare stomach.

He stares into your eyes for the longest time, only breaking away to glance down at your belly. "Really?" he whispers finally, just to be sure, and you nod.

The way he smiles at you is the biggest relief of all. When you wake up later that night, you find his head tucked under your chin, the ghostliest touch of his fingers still resting protectively over your belly.

You reach the cities to the east just in time, because the chill of winter is settling into the landscape, and you're growing large enough that travel on foot is becoming difficult. You stop in the major cities—Washington, DC, first, then up to Philadelphia, New York, and finally Boston. But the closer you move to civilization, the more Colt changes. It's not that he doesn't love you. In fact, if anything, he's grown more protective as his child grows within you. The cities bring with them a different species of danger from the wilderness of the frontier, but Colt seems especially distrustful of the city folk and their fast-paced lifestyle. You can tell he's more at ease out in the wild.

Then there's the secrecy. In each city you visit, mostly at night, Colt meets with strange men, offering only the vaguest explanations as to how he knows them. "Business associates" he calls them frequently, but you never see what sort of business transactions occur between them. From what little you can tell, as you eavesdrop, they bring Colt news about his various interests and tasks he entrusted them with before his disappearance. But how did a man with so much invested here end up washing ashore on your distant islands in the middle of the great ocean? How does he know so much about wilderness survival, in isolated patches of the frontier that few men have ever seen . . . but also have such deep social and business involvements with the Americans?

And where did he accumulate the money that magically waits for you in banks in every city?

Neither you nor Colt blend in with the city people. Maybe it's Colt's wealth that encourages the people here to be more tolerant of your presence. Colt maintains a compelling level of respect from and control over the men who visit him that leads you to believe he's more their boss than their equal.

In Boston your journey finally seems to have come

to a complete stop, at least until the baby is born. Colt sets the two of you up in a cozy but lavishly furnished home in Boston's North End, in the shadow of the North Church's steeple. It's warm, it's luxurious . . . and you resent it. You've spent your entire life sleeping under the stars. This is . . . safe. With or without child, you're the most powerful goddess in all the islands.

Now you find yourself cooped up in a musty armchair, with a roaring fire in the fireplace and an absentee lover who comes and goes with increasing frequency.

That's why, one night, you decide to tail him.

The baby bump doesn't exactly make for a very agile Pele, but fortunately, what you lack in stealth, your supernatural abilities compensate for. It takes a little bit of concentration, but you summon a thick fog, which rolls off Boston Harbor and into the narrow streets.

Shrouded in the mist, you follow Colt at a distance, far enough away that he won't hear the pad of your bare feet on the wet stone, or catch any shadows you cast in the lantern light. He follows the curve of the road until he reaches the Charles River Bridge. The toll collector nods curtly at Colt as he strides past with purpose, headed for Charlestown on the opposite side of the river.

The same tollman eyes you as you slip past him. You can't be sure what's raised his hackles more—your skin color, or the nine-month swell of your belly. Either way, he lets you pass with an "Evenin', ma'am" that sounds more like a question than a pleasantry.

The fog you've created is so effective that you momentarily lose sight of Colt. You briefly entertain the idea that maybe he sensed you on his heel and broke out into a run, disappearing off into the streets and alleys of Charlestown on the opposite riverbank.

When you let the fog dissipate just enough to see a little farther, you discover that he's actually stopped partway across the bridge.

He's not alone either.

The redhead's hair is pulled so tight to her skull that you mistake her for a man at first. It's not until you see the subtle swell of her breasts under her green cloak that you gather that she's a woman. Colt rarely collaborates with female business associates, from what you saw before he became more secretive about his work, so this is unusual to begin with.

Unless she's not an associate of his at all. Even as you go to strike that unthinkable image from your mind, the girl flashes a smile at Colt that's very unbusinesslike.

And then they kiss.

You freeze, your hands unconsciously straying to your swollen stomach. You watch in horror, with a rising, uncontrollable heat building in you. For months now you've resisted any sort of volcanic transformation for fear that the child growing in you might lack your resistance to fire. Now, however, it's a struggle to stop the slow boil of your blood. How could he? All this time, holing you up in that insufferable apartment under the guise of coddling you and keeping you safe, and he was off gallivanting with ginger-headed waifs, making a fool of you—of you! The goddess, brought low by this thieving Irish whore?

Colt has his back to you, but the redhead's eyes flutter open from the kiss. At first she blinks dreamily, but then she squints at your outline, at your hands almost clawing into your own stomach.

Control is slipping away from you. You don't *want* control. The old Pele is taking over, casting aside this weak, domesticated shadow you've felt yourself becoming.

"Colt," you hear the redhead say. "Do you know this girl standing behind—"

She doesn't finish the sentence because a heavy current of water slams into the bridge, an angry torrent that washes over the road and plows into the couple. Colt reflexively latches on to the edge of the bridge, but the tsunami carries the spritely girl over the side and into the Charles. She lets loose a last yelp before the current drags her beneath the surface, a final freckled hand disappearing into the murk as the river carries her out to the harbor and the sea beyond.

Colt has noticed you at last. He scuttles backward as your hands ignite. His mouth opens, probably to offer some weak protest about how it's not what it looks like, but you don't want to hear it. You jet forward and unleash the burning, untrimmed nails on your hands across his cheek and forehead.

When you pull back to admire the four-lined claw of blood and burns you've left on his face, something unusual happens. The wound shimmers ethereally. The skin moves just in the slightest, replacing the fresh burns with even, healthy flesh. The lacerations cinch closed, two weeks' worth of healing accomplished in just a matter of seconds. Colt wipes the final lingering drops of blood off his face, erasing any last evidence that you'd hurt him.

If it's at all possible, you're even more shocked and furious to discover that he's got abilities of his own. "All this time," you hiss, "and you're not even a mortal?"

He doesn't seem to hear you though. Instead he's trembling and gazing down at the harbor waters. "You don't know what you've done, Pele . . . ," he moans. "You really don't know."

You pause. Colt is—apparently—a god whose body heals in an instant. Now he lies before you, overcome with terror . . . but that terror doesn't seem to be directed at you.

The waters under the bridge bubble, like a fire was lit beneath them, a fire that you didn't ignite. As the frothing intensifies, a dark mass rises through the surface.

The substance isn't water. The gelatinous oil continues to pile on top of itself until new color emerges within it: a blue flame. Then another. Miniature fires populate the surface of the black ooze like candles from hell. All the while two projections grow from the side of the thing, elongating, thickening, until you recognize them for what they are: arms.

And when the blue flames angle down to take in Colt, still cowering on the ground, then swivel around to take in you, standing frozen over him, you know that they're actually eyes.

Your initial gut instinct is that this abomination is here for you, some hellish demon that's come to punish you for casting the redheaded outlander into the sea.

But then Colt speaks. "I didn't do anything!" he shrieks, pleading at first. "I'm innocent!"

At first the oil creature doesn't move. Your concentration is so broken that the flames on your hands extinguish themselves, as though the fire might ignite the oily substance of the beast.

Then, in the center of the obsidian creature, a tear opens laterally across its flesh, beneath the fiery eyes . . . a mouth. With gray, fist-size teeth, it rasps, "Innocent? Your treachery knows no boundaries. When your lies cut so deep that even a woman who loves you—the mother of your child—desires you harm, then it is time for your reign to end."

Colt's face twists unattractively with anger. "You're the guilty ones," he rages. "You tamper with us like we're broken dolls, meddling in our affairs. Why can't you just stay in your godforsaken nether realm, and rule yourselves?"

But his wrath has no effect on the creature. "We've been waiting far too long for this, trickster."

Colt hops to his feet and succeeds in running a few

steps. The creature's oily arms shoot out, brushing past you, stretching until the emerging claws fasten onto Colt's shoulders.

With one hard jerk Colt flies backward over the railing of the bridge and is swallowed into the creature's voluminous belly.

Before you can process any of this, or realize that you may have seen your spurned lover, the father of your unborn child, for the last time, the oil creature plunges back into the Charles River.

You stand there, staring at the river's surface until the water goes still. Until the bubbles stop rising. Until the fog fades and you can see the moon's reflection bouncing off the water.

It's only when you feel a dampness on your legs, a trickle of liquid running down your thigh, that you snap out of your stupor.

Because your water has broken.

When Ash emerged from her latest vision,

she was in the backseat of the rental Escalade, which was in motion. Her head throbbed something fierce as she picked it up off the armrest. Wes sat in one of the middle seats, his seatbelt off as he turned around to tend to her. He held out a Pepsi in one hand and a bottle of Advil in the other.

"You sure know the way to a girl's heart," Ash said, her words a little slurred as she swiped both of them from him. Dehydration had set in for sure, so she popped the tab on the soda first and took a few long, greedy gulps before it had even stopped hissing. "Hello carbonation, my old friend," she whispered to the soda can.

"I hate to ask an obvious question," Wes said, "but how you feeling, champ?"

Ash popped three pills into her mouth and took

another swig of soda. "I'd say my headache is somewhat slightly worse than a hangover, but a step up from permanent brain damage." She touched the hair that was matted to her forehead. "And I'm feeling feverish enough that I must have somehow contracted malaria in Central Park."

"You've been fading in and out since we found you on the banks of that pond—almost ten hours ago," Wes said. "You mumbled an only slightly coherent explanation of what had happened to you. The rest has been gibberish, but from the way you've been mumbling and sweating through the night, I'd say you were having some pretty vivid dreams. . . ."

"And you accused me of creepily watching you in your sleep," Ash joked. But inside she shuddered, just thinking about this latest vision of her life as Pele.

She finally took notice of her surroundings. Eve was up front, with a lead foot down on the gas as they coasted along the highway—the Saw Mill River Parkway, she recognized. "We're heading north?" Ash asked.

Wes nodded and slipped next to her in the backseat. "Colt and Rose were gone by the time we found you, although Rose left a healthy crater in her wake. Actually, if it hadn't been for the sound of that explosion, we might not have found you as quickly as we did." He tried to tuck a sheet he'd stolen from the hotel around her, but she waved it off because she was still feeling feverish. "Anyway," he went on, "while I was staying up watching you at the hotel, I was half-paying attention to the morning news when they started reporting unexplained explosions throughout Westchester County."

Westchester County—Ash's home of sixteen years before her life at Scarsdale High degenerated into a nightmare.

Before Eve murdered Lizzie Jacobs in cold blood, just for being a "mean girl," and Ash was forced to start over three thousand miles away in California.

Now Rose was clearly tearing her way through Ash's old stomping grounds.

"Nobody's been hurt so far," Wes continued, "just a few buildings damaged here and there—but those explosions were around dawn, when the streets were empty. Even now, people are waking up to go to work. If we don't catch your sister soon . . ."

"Where exactly in Westchester were these explosions?" Ash asked.

Wes scrunched his eyes shut as he tried to remember from the news broadcasts. "So far, Silver Lake, Tarrytown Music Hall, Saxon Woods Golf Course, and . . . Sarah Lawrence College."

Ash's grip tightened around the headrest in front of her. *Shit,* she thought as the pieces started to come together. What if Rose wasn't just heading through Westchester County? What if it was actually her destination?

Ash unbuckled her seatbelt and squeezed between the seats so that she was closer to her sister. "Eve," she said, "please tell me you see the pattern in the places Rose has been choosing to visit?"

Eve turned down the Led Zeppelin song that was spilling out of the front speakers. "What's the big deal, Ash? We were in New York City, and now she's moving north. She could be headed for her hometown, or the Canadian border. . . . Who the hell knows?"

Ash shook her head. "Where did you always sneak off to to see rock concerts when you were dating that metalhead?"

Eve shrugged. "The Tarrytown Music Hall."

"And that summer when Dad insisted we take golf lessons and kept dragging us to the driving range, he took us to Saxon Woods. I used to sneak off to Silver Lake in Rich Lesley's pickup truck while we were still together. And Sarah Lawrence was—"

"Where Mom took me for a college visit right before I ran away. I get it, I get it. So the crazy little tyke is . . . what, visiting places from our childhood?"

"You and I started having visions of Rose last year, while we slept," Ash said excitedly. "Because we all came from the same person, there's clearly still some psychic link between the three of us. Which means that if we could see her life through her eyes, then there's a very good chance she's been reliving moments from our lives as well. The girl can barely make sense of what she's experienced in her own body; maybe now she's looking for answers by revisiting the other places she's seen, popping in and out of portals at key milestones from our lives."

Eve drummed her fingers on the steering wheel. "A college, a concert hall, a driving range, the lake where you'd straddle your dumb-ass ex-boyfriend . . . so where does that leave?"

The two sisters looked at each other.

And then Ash's phone started buzzing.

She clawed her way into the satchel and found it buried beneath the muddy music box. The screen was newly cracked, probably from when Rose detonated on the banks of Turtle Pond, but Ash could still read the name on the screen:

Home.

Thomas and Gloria Wilde had called several times in the past few days just to protectively check in on Ash and make sure she was on her way home with the newly found Eve. Ash had lied, even when it looked like Eve was in cahoots with Colt, saying that the two sisters were just taking their time on the road trip back to Scarsdale.

Before Ash even picked up, she knew they weren't just calling to say hello this time.

"Mom?" Ash asked once she'd clicked the call button.

There was a short, static-filled silence on the other end, and she could hear her parents whispering to each other before her father put the phone back to his ear. He cleared his throat. "Sweetheart, we're having a . . . bit of an unusual morning here at the Wilde residence."

There was the sound of a slight tremor in the

background—not like a bomb had gone off, but as though a train had passed near the house.

The Wilde house was nowhere near a train.

Ash buried her face in her free hand. "I'm going to take a wild guess," she said. "There's a girl in the house who looks like she could be related to Eve and me. She probably hasn't said much of anything. And the house is mysteriously rumbling."

There was another long pause on the other end while her father probably tried, unsuccessfully, to figure out how she knew all that. "Yes, how did you . . . ?" He trailed off and lowered his voice. "She just wandered in while we were having breakfast in the kitchen, and immediately started up the stairs without even saying hello. I just caught a quick glimpse of her face and thought at first it was one of you two . . . but when we raced upstairs and found her in your bedroom, we realized the girl wasn't either of you at all. But the resemblance . . ." He trailed off again as the house rumbled a second time. "Ash, what the hell is going on?"

Ash snapped her fingers at Eve and pointed frantically at the phone. Eve got the message and rammed her foot down on the gas as they sped up the parkway toward Scarsdale. "Look, I'll explain when we get there," Ash promised her father, "but for now, I need you to do me a big favor: Get out of the house. I don't care where you go—grab some patio chairs and sit in the far corner of the backyard if you can." In truth, she'd feel much safer if her parents got in a car and booked it out of town, but she knew she'd never convince them to leave the house with a strange girl wandering around inside it. "When we hang up, don't call the police; just wait for Eve and me to get there in about fifteen minutes."

"Wait," her father said, "you two are in New York? Why didn't you—"

"Do not," Ash interrupted him, "go up and interact with that girl anymore." She pictured Rose's home in Massachusetts, and what the girl had done to the bedroom.

The blood patches on the wall.

Her father was asking more questions, but Ash just said, "See you soon," and hung up.

Thanks to Eve's maniac driving, they made record time getting to Scarsdale. After cutting over to the Bronx River Parkway, Eve nauseatingly veered off onto the Fenimore Road exit, and the pain in Ash's skull ignited all over again as she was tossed up against the car window.

When they swerved into the Wilde's driveway, Ash and Wes were out the passenger doors before Eve hit the brakes. Thomas and Gloria Wilde had honored Ash's cryptic instructions and set up two lawn chairs by the bird-feeder mailbox. They looked dazed, and a million questions danced in their eyes as they stood up—most notably, *Who the hell is this giant man-boy that's next to you?* when they spotted Wes.

But all those questions disappeared into a galaxy of emotion when Eve stepped out of the driver-side door. Eve visibly grimaced, flinching like she was about to be lashed, the moment she locked eyes with her adoptive parents.

Thomas and Gloria didn't miss a beat. They both rushed forward and wrapped their arms around Eve at the same time. There was a lot of crying involved, from both of Ash's parents. Eve just stood there stiffly, trying not to let the cracks in her hardened exterior show. In another life, or another road in this one, maybe she would have hugged them back.

Impenetrable though her armor may have seemed, and even though Eve was the type who'd rather die than let any vulnerability show, Ash caught just the lightning-quick glimpse of an embarrassed, remorseful, but ultimately happy smile flicker across her face.

Ash stepped up behind them. "Don't worry about me," Ash said, "I just, you know, brought your rogue daughter home safely." *And rescued her from hell,* she added silently. *And, uh, sort of banished her there in the first place.*

Her parents laugh-cried and took her in their arms too, while Wes tried to stand unobtrusively in the background—a tough feat for someone the size of a Kodiak bear.

Before the Wildes could fully squeeze the life out of Ash, the yard rumbled just slightly beneath their feet. In the window to her own second-floor bedroom there were brand new spiderwebbed cracks in the windowpane. Ash knew that there was very little time before Rose threw a tantrum and took a large fiery chunk off the side of the house.

"There will be time for happy reunions and explanations later," Ash said, though she had no idea how to really explain any of the last few months to her parents, who were still oblivious to the fact that their daughters were reincarnated goddesses. She pointed to the house. "The three of us are going to go have a little chat with the Polynesian orphan that's running amok in there."

Eve and Ash took the lead on the walk up the stone pathway, while Wes offered a sheepish wave and an awkward "Uh, nice to finally meet you both" to Ash's parents.

Once they were inside, the house rumbled again. Ash wondered what sort of fiery "redecorating" the little Rose was doing to Ash's bedroom, and whether she should consider grabbing the fire extinguisher from under the staircase.

At the top of the landing, where the door to her bedroom was ajar, Ash held out a hand to stay the other two. "Maybe I should go in alone at first. She's not exactly a . . . social butterfly, so bombarding her with three of us at once might prove overwhelming. Since the sound of a music box was enough to make her self-destruct and run off last night, I'm really hesitant to push her."

Eve nodded. "I guess between the two of us, you're the more 'personable' sister."

This made Wes snicker, but he shut up as soon as Eve

held up a warning finger glowing with electricity. "We'll wait out here in case you need backup," he promised Ash.

"Okay, but if I yell something like 'She's gonna blow!' then get the hell out before this house turns into a fucking meteorite crater." Then she took a deep breath and slipped through the space between the door and the frame.

Rose sat on Ash's twin bed, staring down at a picture frame cradled in her hands. She was still wearing her black dress, although by now it was singed and hung in tatters from all the self-detonation she'd been doing. Her legs were coated with mud, and her hair hung in matted strands, which had a few twigs and leaves clinging to them. When Ash had seen Rose in a dream for the first time, Rose had been a girl lost in a jungle, but who looked like she belonged in the wild, as though civilization would never truly hold a place for her.

Even though Rose's body had aged ten years since that vision, the girl sitting on her bed still looked like the same lost six-year-old.

Rose didn't even look up to acknowledge her visitor, so Ash decided to take a big risk: She sat down on the bed beside Rose, gently though, as though there were a land mine hidden somewhere beneath the covers. Still, Rose didn't lift her head, so Ash peered down at the photo she was admiring so intently. It was a five-by-seven black-and-white shot of Ash and Rich Lesley, her tennis-playing jerk of an ex-boyfriend. The candid shot had captured the once-happy couple in front of a bonfire, while Ash hand-fed a gooey marshmallow into Rich's mouth. It was from last summer—almost exactly a year ago—and had been snapped by one of the fair-weather friends who'd abandoned Ash in the wake of the breakup.

"Have you seen the boy in this picture before?" Ash asked.

Rose nodded, almost imperceptibly, and traced her fingers over the face in the photograph. Her fingertips left soot trails over the glass when she pulled them away. "I want to live like this," she said cryptically.

"You're only six," Ash said, then grimaced when she took notice of Rose's prematurely aged teenage body. "Kind of. In time you'll get your own memories, ones you get to create and weave yourself. Some of them will be beautiful. Some of them . . ." She glanced at the picture in Rose's hands. "Well, some of them you'll at least be able to laugh at later. But if you don't learn to control that rage and loneliness inside of you, people are going to get hurt. And then all you'll be left with are a collection of bad memories and no one to form new, better ones with. You just have to be patient . . . Penny." Ash knew it was risky using Rose's given name, but she didn't know how else to get through to her. Maybe if she appealed to a happier time in her life . . .

Apparently it was the wrong move. "Don't call me that . . . ," Rose said in a low voice, and as her hands tightened around the frame, a long diagonal crack ripped across the glass from corner to corner. "Colt said to forget that name. He said I'd feel better if I helped him. He said I'd find home again."

Ash sighed. Colt was the emperor of false promises. Here he was, promising her a home, when all that was left of her real one was a shell of a house with no occupants . . . and no family. "You're my sister, Rose," Ash said, and pointed to the door, where Eve was cautiously peeking in. "Eve is your sister too. We might not be the home you're used to, but I promise that we can be your family."

Rose's forlorn expression hardened, her eyebrows folding down in an unmistakable scowl. "Colt showed me what you did to me," she snapped. "That bad man tried to kill us, and you and Eve ran away and left me in the barn, under the wood and hay with that man's dead body."

Ash's stomach lunged. She was referring to their previous life, almost a hundred years ago, when the three of them had been adopted by a farmer in Maine. When a violent neighbor came to fulfill a vendetta—to kill the sisters—Ash had tried to lead him away from Rose's hiding place in the old barn.

But then the barn had exploded. Ash and Eve had presumed Rose dead in the rubble and left the state altogether to start over in the South.

Only Rose hadn't been dead after all. She'd returned years later to exact her own vindictive revenge on her older sisters for leaving her behind.

"You left me so you could be a family without me," Rose snarled. The house around them rumbled. Dust rained from the ceiling. "I was all alone!"

Ash's vocal chords were paralyzed. She'd barely heard Rose utter more than three words in a row in the brief time she'd known her . . . and now she'd snapped out of her mute stupor to go on a tirade against Ash and Eve. All because Colt had manipulatively shown Rose a memory that would make the two of them look like the bad guys. No wonder Rose was willing to follow Colt to the ends of the earth.

Ash knelt down in front of Rose. She took the picture out of her hands, set it aside, and then grasped the girl's hands suppliantly in her own. "We never meant to leave you behind . . . but there's no excuse. No words I can offer you to make it better. But Eve and I, we can make up for it as best we can now. What do you say?"

Rose stared silently at her, which she supposed was as much of a tacit agreement as she had earned for now. At least they'd had a relatively human conversation without anything blowing up in the process.

"Now," Ash said, nodding toward the window. "There are some nice people who are very dear to me that I'd like you to meet. Do you . . . do you think you could try to not explode this time?"

As Rose followed Ash out of the room, the girl moved so soundlessly that she could have been levitating behind Ash. Wes and Eve gave them a wide berth as they came out, as though Rose were an overflowing barrel of nitroglycerin—which in a lot of ways she really was. The four of them descended the stairs and then exited the house to finally begin introductions with Ash's parents.

Only when they stepped out onto the stoop, Thomas and Gloria Wilde were no longer alone.

Ash's parents were writhing in the grass. Her mother was moaning something about snakes and compulsively brushing off her body when nothing was actually there. Her father was on his butt, scuttling backward away from some invisible creature that seemed to be attacking him.

Epona loomed over them, her sadistic smirk trembling with excitement as she telepathically filled the minds of the Wildes with nightmarish visions. Colt lingered patiently by the mailbox with the enormous ax strapped to his back.

A third boy, whom Ash didn't recognize, was leaning up against the driver-side door of the Escalade in the driveway. He was probably only five-foot-six, but his black muscle T could barely contain his barrel chest, which had the sort of thick, stocky, almost steroidal build that might belong to a wrestler. He had a goatee that tapered down to form a dagger point beneath his chin, and he appeared to be Latino in origin.

Ash, Eve, Wes, and Rose had all frozen in front of the house. Ash wanted to run to her parents' aid, but Epona wagged a finger in her direction as if to say, *One more step, and I'll really make your parents suffer.*

Eve jutted her chin out in the mysterious boy's direction. "That's Itzli," she whispered to Ash. "Aztec god of stone and sacrifice. I met him once, when I ran away to Vancouver. He's Colt's favorite enforcer . . . and contract killer."

So a hit man, a deranged nightmare goddess who wanted nothing more than to murder Ash in a jealous rage, and Colt . . . and her parents were rolling around in the grass, right in the cross fire.

Colt clapped his hands together. "Everybody ready for our happy little field trip to hell?" he chirped. "Did everyone get their permission slips signed and remember to pack a brown-bag lunch for the big yellow bus?"

"No one's going to the Cloak Netherworld, Colt," Ash said. Her blood was literally boiling the more she watched her parents suffer. "Rose is with us now. Let my parents go, and maybe I won't rip the heart out of your chest right away."

"Fine," he said. "Then I guess I'll just have my colleague put them out of their misery. Itzli?"

The Aztec hit man started across the lawn toward her parents. He reached toward the ground just as a stone sword emerged from the soil, and he plucked it free. It must have weighed a hundred pounds, but he brandished it like it was made of tinfoil.

Ash recognized this all for the bluff that it was—Colt

had no bargaining chips if he killed the Wildes now—but both Wes and Eve lunged across the lawn to intercept Itzli.

Itzli turned and thrust out a hand.

A thick slab of stone burst out of the yard, and Wes and Eve collided with it at a full sprint. The two of them dropped, dazed, to the ground. Before Ash could get to them, three more stone walls sprang up around Wes and Eve. The tops of the stone slabs angled in until they formed a point over the box.

When the massive stones finally stopped moving, Wes and Eve had disappeared behind a gray prison of seamless stone. She could hear the muffled slaps of them pounding on the inside of the foot-thick slabs, but Wes's super strength had vanished with the sunrise. And what were Eve's weather abilities going to do to the heavy rock? Erode it away over a thousand years?

"Did you at least leave them an airhole?" Colt asked Itzli. "I don't care if your Aztec brother asphyxiates, but I need the stormy one."

Itzli grumbled, held up a finger, and twisted it in the air. Rock dust rained down on the lawn as an unseen drill punched the tiniest of holes in the prison roof.

To Ash's further surprise, Rose walked casually past her, heading for the other gods ahead. Ash caught Rose by the wrist. "What about what we talked about up there?" She pointed back to the bedroom window. "You don't understand what's at stake here, Rose."

Rose jerked her arm free. "You want me to wait to feel better. He promised I'll be happy tomorrow."

"His promises are full of—" Ash started.

"He keeps his promises," Rose said. "You just leave me alone." Her voice softened. "When he puts us back together, you won't be able to leave me . . . and I'll never be lonely again." With that, she turned and joined the other gods near the mailbox.

Ash glanced next door, where their neighbors had come out to watch the spectacle. Mr. Glassman had his cell phone out, and Ash could hear the approaching wail of police sirens. A cruiser whipped around the corner at the end of the street, gunning for the house, even though the police officers inside of it had no idea what they were getting themselves into.

Itzli looked bored as he turned to the road. Another flick of his hand and a stone wall exploded out of the asphalt.

The Crown Victoria collided with it at a full forty miles an hour before the police officer driving it even had a chance to apply the brakes. Ash couldn't see behind the wall, but the cruiser's horn blared . . . and no one seemed to be getting out of the car.

"You know what to do?" Colt asked Rose, and she nodded. "Good girl," he said, and patted her head. Patted her like she was a dog.

Still, she smiled.

Then she hurled an explosive blast across the yard.

It detonated near the stone jail cell containing Wes and Eve, sending a massive crack through one slab, though unfortunately not enough to liberate its prisoners.

When the explosion cleared away, a jagged rift had ripped through the fabric of space and time, a window to a dark realm on a different plane of existence.

Epona arched her fingers over Ash's parents, and both of them rose to their feet. They'd stopped moaning and were no longer fending off imaginary creatures, but they weren't conscious, either. Instead they sleepwalked toward the open portal. Epona and Itzli followed close behind them, with the latter twirling his stone sword at Ash. Any funny business, she was certain, and he'd be delighted to shish-kebab her sleeping parents.

Colt and Rose were close behind, and Colt motioned for Ash to join him. "Come, Ashline Wilde. You need to see what happens next."

Ash didn't have much of a choice. Her parents' lives were at stake. Wes and Eve were trapped in a prison that they wouldn't likely be able to break out of until nightfall, when Wes's strength was reinstated.

So she did the last thing she thought she'd ever do:

She willingly followed Colt and his evil partners through the portal and into the Cloak Netherworld.

When the portal snapped shut behind Ash, she found herself sprawled on a familiar beach. The sand was black as a starless night, and stormy waves crashed against the shore, as though the ocean could sense the intruders. Out at sea, where the thunderclouds churned and grumbled, a large ship protruded from the waters like a gravestone, and if Ash looked carefully, she could still see the bloated corpses of sailors bobbing over the ocean swells.

This was it—the Cloak Netherworld.

The place that Ash had prayed she'd never have to return to again.

Colt flexed his back and touched the ax strapped across it to make sure it was still in place after they'd passed through the rift. Then he gestured for the others to come closer to him. "Stay near me as we make our way to the tree," he instructed all of them. "The pipe buried in my body will give me freedom to pass safely through the landscape here, but I can't guarantee how far the sphere of protection will extend."

They formed a tight caravan as they headed toward the tree line ahead. Colt made Ash walk out in front, with Ash's parents marching hypnotically behind him. Every time she even tried to look back at them, to strategize some way to break them free, Itzli leaned menacingly between Thomas and Gloria and pressed the edge of his stone sword to one of their necks.

On Ash's last visit the forest had been made up of enormous black calla lilies, but now it had transformed into a thick, impenetrable rainforest. Lines of brambles as sharp as razor wire and as thick anchor chains hung between the trees in tight lines.

Clearly, the Cloak had tried to prepare for Colt's arrival. They must have underestimated the poison-ousness of both Colt and the wrath artifact entombed within him though . . . because when Colt stepped up to the tree line, all of the vegetation began to wither. The thorny vines liquefied onto the soil, and the trees groaned as they dried up, until they cracked and toppled aside. With each step Colt took, a path formed through the previously impassable forest. Even the grass browned and dried up under his feet as he walked slowly but confidently forward.

Halfway through the forest, they were attacked by their first Cloak.

The creature appeared in their path, where Colt's aura was gradually gnawing through the trees. It materialized in humanoid form first, only eight feet tall, with a black oily coat and that wavering blue flame of an eye.

The closer they approached, however, the more its body degenerated into something wild and animal, a supernatural beast that had crawled out of a tar pit. It dropped to all fours. Its legs articulated back, and its body grew bloated. Its gray fangs lengthened and sprouted an extra row.

And when the animal instincts became too much for it, it reared back onto its haunches and pounced for Colt.

Ash experienced a brief moment of hope while it lingered midair that Colt hadn't thought this through, that the Cloak were finally going to put a stop to his deadly antics once and for all. She pictured the Cloak's inky talon plunging into Colt's chest, cracking open his ribs, and tearing out his heart with a snap of its claw.

Instead, when the Cloak was only a few yards away, it struck some invisible wall in the air formed by the extreme concentration of hate and evil . . . and it simply evaporated. Its body exploded into a million particles of darkness and rained down around them like confetti.

These attacks happened several more times throughout their journey—from the dying tree canopy overhead, from the sides—but always to the same result with deadly efficacy. Even though Ash would never have called the Cloak friends, exactly, there was something truly chilling to see a being so otherworldly, so omniscient, dying in the blink of an eye.

By the time they reached the great stone dais—the hub of the Netherworld—the Cloak had given up altogether. It was snowing on the dais, which ended abruptly in a cliff that overlooked a vast and chilling nothingness—just a gaping void. Ash could theorize that if you fell off the edge, you might simply fall for eternity.

The real attraction here, however, was the towering life tree, which was every bit as breathtaking as it had been when Ash first gazed upon it. The tree was a skyscraper of spiny wood and gnarled branches and thick, vibrant leaves . . . and if you looked closely enough you could see the faces of imprisoned gods just visible through the foliage. They had been plugged into the tree the way Eve had been while she was imprisoned here. These were the most sordid gods that history had to offer, preternatural beings so vile and destructive to the people around them that the Cloak had crossed the threshold between worlds and taken them "off-line." So long as they were imprisoned here, they couldn't be reincarnated like the other gods; instead they were supposedly rehabilitated by the tree's cleansing powers—the same cleansing that gave the Cloak their life energy and restored them after they came in contact with evil.

Across the stone amphitheater, at a safe distance for now, the remaining Cloak had gathered and coalesced into a single entity. Ash had seen them do this before. Their oily, viscous bodies just melted into one super-Cloak, thirty feet tall. Twenty collective blue eyes flickered out of its amorphous head, but the flames were dimmer, less vibrant than usual. With each Cloak that had just perished trying to protect the Netherworld, Colt seemed to have chipped away at their overall life force.

However, even recognizing that they were about to die, the Cloak maintained an eerie calmness. They had solemnly accepted that their time had come.

Colt didn't even give the Cloak a casual look. He just strode across the dais and drew the enormous ax from its sheath on his back. Then he wheeled back, spun a hundred and eighty degrees, and drove the head of the ax into the tree trunk.

The Cloak's life tree had stood tall for centuries and imprisoned some of the most powerful, vengeful beings to ever roam the earth . . . yet with just the first swing, the ax cut a third of the way through its intimidating trunk before it stuck. Ash decided that even if the wood had been reinforced with titanium or carbon steel fibers, the blade that Modo had fashioned would have cut through it as though it were a warm stick of butter.

As Colt pried the ax from the trunk and prepared for another swing, the branches of the tree rustled with discontent overhead. Colt took another massive swing from a different angle, sheering through another third of the tree trunk. The rustling grew louder, and at first Ash hoped that maybe the tree was coming to life and preparing to fight back.

Instead it was something far, far worse.

The gods imprisoned in the enormous tree were being liberated.

One by one they dropped out of their stations where they had been attached to the tree like acorns. Their bodies plummeted toward the stone dais below, but the vinelike plant fibers that had wired them into the tree slowed and stopped their fall before their bodies could splatter on the stone.

And as they dropped, their eyes flickered open. They were gods of every race, men and women alike, some of them dressed in ancient, foreign garb. One of them was a nightmarish creature, with dark sinewy wings and red, glowing eyes. As they reawakened from what had been centuries' worth of slumber for some of them, they dazedly reached back and snapped the vines suspending them from the tree, like marionettes casting off their puppet strings. Among them Ash even recognized two from her visions—Tane and Tangaroa, the forest spirit and the sea god she'd condemned to death in that sea cave on Maui. They showed no signs of knowing Ash, so they must have been imprisoned by the Cloak during their last lives.

Ash looked over at the Cloak super-creature—Jack, as it called itself. It hadn't moved from its perch, but with the power draining from the tree, Jack's massive dark body was hunched over, one hand bracing itself against the earth. Its blue flame eyes looked dimmer than ever before.

Colt must have noted the fallen Cloak too, because a triumphant smile—the grin of a true trickster—was smeared across his face. He gazed up into the branches one last time, probably to make sure that all the gods had been successfully relieved of their botanical prison.

He drew back the ax, and, with all his accumulated vengeful hatred for the Cloak, he drove the blade home.

This swing didn't even catch on anything. It sheared straight through the remaining portion of the trunk and kept right on going through the other side.

For an agonizing moment, the tree precariously tottered upright in one last act of defiance. But then gravity caught up with it, and it fell in the direction of the cliff. The awakened gods had emerged from their stupor enough to stumble out of the way before it crushed them, except for one blond god who didn't even see it coming. One of the enormous branches of the tree struck him in the chest as he was climbing almost drunkenly to his feet. The force of the impact knocked him off the edge of the stone dais, and with a quick yelp he tumbled into oblivion.

None of the gods—Colt, Itzli, and Epona included—looked like they cared enough to mourn his loss.

With the tree destroyed and Jack collapsed in an oily, melting heap, Colt climbed up onto the stump that remained of the life tree. The awakened gods gathered around him, and Ash noted that none of them looked particularly confused by Colt's appearance. In fact there was a recognition, a respect, in all of their expressions.

Because they'd all met the trickster in their previous lives.

Because they'd maybe even looked up to him like a boss, or as their king.

For all appearances, Colt was a made man among the gods, the crime overlord who had directed the morally dubious deities for hundreds of years.

Epona flashed Ash a sarcastic thumbs-up. The nightmare goddess had directed Ash's parents to sit cross-legged on the stone dais, while they stared catatonically off into nothingness.

"Brothers and sisters," Colt boomed over the dais. "Today is a great day. We have finally brought about the extinction of the vile shadow creatures that have meddled in our affairs since the dawn of our race. We have freed you from your eternal, dormant purgatory here in the Netherworld. And now, as one, we can return to Earth as the triumphant superior race."

The crowd of gods offered a positive reaction to this: nods and cheers of agreement. Ash had never heard Colt give a damn about making the gods some "superior race," but she had encountered quite a few evil gods who felt that way—gods who were sick of living silently among the mortals, gods who longed for a new era when they would be worshipped, even feared once again.

Gods who were willing to kill to see that happen.

And now, trickster that he was, Colt was telling these power-hungry deities exactly what they wanted to hear. He'd be perfectly content to rile them up and unleash them upon the world if it meant he could manipulate them to do his bidding later on.

"The world has changed a vast deal since many of you last saw it," Colt went on. "As the gods retreated to the shadows, choosing lives of anonymity and banality over the dominance we once held, the humans have almost completely forgotten about us, made us footnotes in the history books as they worship their new idols—wealth, technology, sex. Well the time has come for us to reclaim our rightful throne." He hoisted the ax over his head. "The time has come for us to step out of the shadows, as one. The time has come to remind the human race that to us, they are ants."

Colt stepped down off the stump. He motioned someone to join him, and Ash couldn't initially see who it was through the crowd of gods . . . until Rose stepped into view. He took her hand and looked lovingly at her. She returned his gaze with a bashful affection, the kind of crush that a child might have on an adult.

Ash had witnessed many horrors these past few months, but the bond Colt was fostering with Rose . . . Just watching the two of them together knotted Ash's insides like a wet dish towel.

Colt let go of Rose's hand and turned back to the

assembly. "We need to rescue one more member of our family first before we're ready to strike—one of our finest, fieriest warriors," he continued, and Ash had no doubt he was referring to Pele. "So we will gather in the solitude of an ancient forest on Earth for just two nights . . . and on the third day we will sweep across the world as an unstoppable flood and re-establish our authority, no longer as mortals . . . but as gods once more."

A cheer rose up from the freed prisoners, a riotous frenzy as they all became swept up in Colt's powerful presence. On cue, Rose doled out a series of explosive blasts that ripped portals into the air all around the dais. The floating windows back to Earth all showed the same backdrop of a familiar forest that was near and dear to Ash's heart.

Towering trees with trunks of burnt umber.

A daffodil afternoon light filtering through the green canopy.

And in the distance, just visible through the thicket of trunks, the faux-wooden buildings of a boarding-school campus.

Colt was convening his council of murderous, evil gods back at Blackwood Academy.

Where Ash had first come into contact with her fellow gods.

Where the bloodshed began.

The gods all poured through the inter-dimensional rifts, and Ash could hear joyous, crazed laughter from the other side as they gratefully left the Cloak Netherworld for their home planet . . . the very planet that they were about to immerse in a plague of violence and fear.

Epona jerked on some imaginary reins, and Ash's parents hopped to their feet like they'd been shocked by a cattle prod. The current of gods carried them out into the redwood forest as well.

Ash started to follow the flow toward the forest, but Colt, who had lingered behind with Rose, shook his head at her. "I'm afraid we must part ways for one night, Ashline . . . though I know you're anxious to remain in my presence."

Ash spat on the stone in response.

Colt whispered something to Rose, and she nodded and cast a new fiery orb toward the back of the dais, where the Cloak lay unmoving. It ripped open the air next to Jack, and through it Ash saw the backyard of the Wilde residence.

"Return to New York and collect your older sister," Colt instructed Ash. "That will give me time to make preparations without the two of you meddling again. You and Eve will have until midnight tomorrow to meet me at the banks of the redwood forest. Come to the stone lighthouse just offshore, where you will begin your rebirth as Pele. If you fail to arrive on time, or refuse to follow my exact directions upon your arrival, or resist in any way . . . then I will be forced to crush the two mortals who took you under their wing for the last sixteen years. If you cooperate, then

218

I will allow them to live, although in a few nights' time, 'life' for any mortals will never be the same."

With that he drove his ax into the stump of the life tree, and left it planted there, a flag claiming the Netherworld for his own. Then he and Rose both jumped through the last of the closing portals to Blackwood, before the seam in the air closed altogether.

Ash knew that she only had a limited time before her own portal back to Earth vanished, but she couldn't help it—she jogged over to where the Cloak lay and knelt down beside it.

Jack's enormous mouth hung open, and only shallow, wheezy breaths whistled through his teeth—although Ash had never even been sure if the creature breathed, or ate, or did anything remotely mortal, for that matter. The blue flames that made up his collective eyes were winking out one at a time as his collective consciousness died.

Still, his voice was strong as he spoke to Ash for the last time. "Colt has gained the allegiance of many of his followers by promising that in killing us, it would restore all your memories in the next lifetime." He drew in one long, ragged breath, before he continued. "But the reality is just the opposite—with us gone, the damage to your memories from previous lives will prove permanent."

And now Ash had glimpsed the true genius behind Colt's scheming. With his regenerative abilities, his brain repaired itself lifetime after lifetime, so that he had a monopoly on remembering his extensive past. Meanwhile all the other gods were cut off from their own.

Colt had just secured that monopoly from now until eternity. Even if Ash somehow succeeded in destroying him in this life, she'd forget all about him in the next, and the cycle would begin anew. He would continue to use the other gods, and they'd never be the wiser.

Ash was overcome with a heavy exhaustion and a sense of futility. Tears welled in her eyes. There was almost nothing human to Jack, to the Cloak, yet she still felt a mixture of anger, sorrow, and fear at his imminent death.

The anger is what came out first. She pounded the stone dais nearest Jack's face. At this point all but one of the blue flames had been extinguished. "It didn't have to go this way," she shouted at Jack through her tears. "I warned you this would happen. You could have ended all this and saved so many lives. Instead you're going to die because you couldn't be more like us."

"No," Jack whispered, as the final blue flame gradually dimmed. "We are dead because *you* could not be more like *us*." The last flame flickered out and Jack was gone. His body simply dissolved into tiny black particles, which a low wind blew toward the abyss.

The Cloak were no more.

Ash wiped her eyes with the back of her hand. There was nothing left for her in the Netherworld, so she jumped through the open portal and landed on her grassy backyard in Scarsdale just as the rift snapped shut behind her.

Back on Earth, Ash moved quickly to the edge of the house and chanced a look toward the street. Her boring suburban neighborhood had transformed into a crime scene since she had left. It looked as though the entire Scarsdale police force—and maybe some units from nearby towns as well—had responded to the crashed squad car. The paramedics tended to the two officers who must have been in the car; one was being loaded onto a stretcher, and the other was pressing an ice pack to his head. Either way, Ash was relieved to see both of them alive.

The stone prison containing Eve and Wes hadn't changed in her absence. At some point she'd have to go at it with the sledgehammer her father kept in the garage, but not now, with twenty police officers and half the neighborhood watching. As long as Wes and Eve weren't asphyxiating in there, they would have to wait.

She had another order of business to take care of first, anyway. Ash returned to the Wildes' patio and took out her cell phone. She scrolled through her contacts until she came to the *S* section and found the number she'd never once called since she had programmed it in before summer break.

Serena Andreotes was a petite blond girl who'd been a classmate of Ash's at Blackwood Academy. Despite her incredibly expressive gray eyes, which flickered with vitality and near constant amusement, Serena was entirely blind.

She was also the reincarnation of a Greek siren.

While other gods like Eve and Ash had powers that manifested themselves physically in the elements, Serena's abilities were far more subtle. Her telepathic voice could reach anyone in the world, anywhere in the world. While it didn't involve actual words per se, and it wasn't as forceful as mind control, her siren's call could project emotions into the minds of those she called. It was Serena who had drawn several gods, including Ash, to the Blackwood campus, by appealing to those gods who felt a need to belong. They had never even realized until later that it hadn't been their own idea to matriculate at a boarding school in the redwoods.

Serena picked up on the second ring, and before they could even go into pleasantries or small talk, Ash unloaded an abbreviated version of everything that had happened in the last few weeks onto her. The blind girl listened in near silence, although when Ash reached the part about Raja's death, Ash heard a crackling sound over the receiver—Serena tightly clutching the phone in her hand.

When Ash concluded her story, there was only a brief silence before Serena said calmly, "Just tell me what you need me to do."

Ash took one last minute to contemplate whether the plan forming in her head was really the right thing to do. Lately, allowing others to help her in her quest had proven a death sentence for just about anyone involved— Rolfe, Aurora, Raja. Ash hadn't exactly pushed any of them in front of a bullet, but they'd all died because in hanging around Ash they'd wandered into Colt's web of trickery as well. To that end, she never wanted to ask for anyone's help ever again.

But the game had changed. This wasn't just about preventing Colt from tampering with her soul anymore; it wasn't just personal. He'd freed a cellblock's worth of crazy, malevolent gods, riled them up with his trickster rhetoric, and now intended to submerge the world in pure chaos until the gods ruled the human race as its merciless enslavers. From the events that had recently happened while Ash was in Miami, she'd seen how much trouble and destruction four power-hungry gods could rouse.

With an armada of them under Colt's direction, it would be genocide.

Ash had no choice but to ask for help this time. "Reach out to any god with a good heart left in them. Summon them to drop what they're doing and find a way to our meeting place in Crescent City, California, by tomorrow afternoon. Ultimately, it will be their choice whether or not they want to fight, but for those brave enough to join me, we'll storm the Blackwood campus . . . and we'll strike those bastards down."

"That much I can do," Serena offered, "but the siren's call is no exact science. I can hone the frequency all I want, but there's always a chance that one of Colt's people could pick up my broadcast too. That may have been how Colt found you on the Blackwood campus in the first place, you know. If anyone overhears, Colt may know we're bringing a wildfire to his forest."

"Maybe so," Ash said. Despite everything, she couldn't help the killer smile that tested the waters of her lips. "But you know the thing about wildfires and forests? Even when you see one coming, you can't put it out." She turned to the sliding door to observe her own reflection in the glass, and when she put her hand to the pane, she left a softened, molten imprint. "Even when you see it coming . . . it'll still burn everything in its path to the ground."

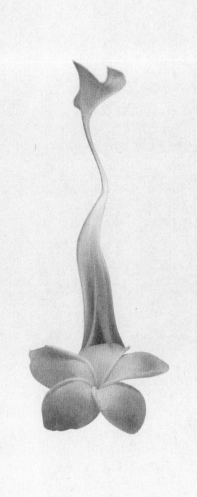

PART III:
CALIFORNIA

A FIERY DYNASTY

There's no way you're going to give birth to your child on the middle of a dark bridge in a dank, cold city like Boston. So even as you feel yourself go into labor, you carve a rift in the air and crawl through it.

Back to Hawai'i.

On the banks of Haleakalā, alone on a bed of hastily gathered palm fronds, you bunch up your knees and push. You push until you feel the splitting agony, unlike any pain you've experienced before. You push until your screams echo down the volcano, until you feel a sudden give and a soft thud in the bed of leaves—

—until you hear a high-pitched cry that's not your own.

It takes all the strength (not to mention the courage) you have left to draw yourself up onto your elbows, use your knees to pull yourself into a sitting position, and get your first look at the creature you've just birthed.

It's a girl. She lies on her back in the leaves, just between your legs, and she stops squalling as soon as your face comes into view. In fact she stops squirming at all and studies you intently. There is a moment when, despite everything that's happened, you feel the first jolt of love for this life you've created. During the course of your pregnancy, you'd often wondered whether you were capable of motherly affection, since you never really had a mother of your own.

Perhaps you would have been a great mother, had it not been for the events of the last few hours.

But all it takes is one turn of the child's head for you to see her in profile and recognize just how deeply she resembles her father.

That instant of recognition washes away the foundations of love you were just starting to experience.

You know that you must get rid of her before that affection resurfaces.

There can be nothing left to remind you of him.

So, even as the baby coos at you, maybe confusing your tight hold on her as affectionate and warm, you stride determinedly down Haleakalā.

You do your best to quiet the child on your descent into the forests, toward the shoreline. You pass Waimoku Falls, where your "intimate journey" with Colt began. The child, who you've refused to name lest you get more attached, could have been conceived under the falls for all you know.

You have every intention of making it as far as Kīpahulu, but when you reach Oheʻo Gulch, you hear someone singing.

The woman is bathing in one of the larger pools, where the stream makes a short drop off a basalt cliff and into the basin below. These pools were one of Tangaroa's sacred spots, another place where water and volcanic rock have come together. He thought of it as an allegory for the union the two of you might have had one day.

What's more, you recognize the bathing woman, who's dipped up to her neck in the water. You haven't always been as friendly with the locals as Tane once was, but there were certain favorites you'd met on the islands—people you might even call friends. She is one of them—a mother of two who lives with her husband down in Kīpahulu.

Well, she's about to inherit a third child.

You get as close to the pool as you can without making your presence known. The baby, who has fallen into a fitful sleep, twitches in your hands as you lay her down at the grassy edge of the water.

Then you dart back into trees.

The baby senses that your touch is gone, because she wakes with a resounding shriek that stops the bathing woman in the middle of her song. The sound is so heartbreaking that you can't help but stagger through the brush a few steps back toward the child, to rectify the impetuous, anger-driven mistake you're probably making. This child didn't ask to be brought into the world. Didn't ask to be born of such a conniving father, who was so vile that even the dark, unworldly creature had desired him dead or gone.

But the woman in the gulch is already swimming for the water's edge, toward the newborn child.

You vanish into the trees and through the bamboo forest before she sees you.

That night, alone in the enormous, arid crater of Haleakalā, the madness infects you.

Dusk comes and goes. Clouds swirl around the summit, and you try to lose yourself in them, but instead they just provide a blank canvas to paint the awful, too recent memories of Colt, and his mistress, and the dark executioner who'd taken him.

Every time you revisit that memory, your rage grows.

Every time you revisit that memory, the earth shifts beneath you.

The rumbling intensifies. You lose yourself in it, willing the magma up out of the earth. This crater—a red, dry bed of porous rocks—reminds you of your existence now, lifeless and barren. You killed Tangaroa, Tane, Papa, and Rangi before you left. Colt swims in the belly of an unfathomable beast. And your love child will live her life without ever knowing you.

You pluck an *ahinahina* from the rock bed and hold it up—the spiky, resilient plant is the only living thing capable of growing here, where the porous stone soaks up the rain. You've always admired the plant for its ability to thrive where other things could not.

Now you let it smolder in your palm.

As it burns, a rift tears through the crater bed. The trembling jaws of stone open up to the sky, and the first flickering glow of molten rock throws shadows against the crater wall. Part of you desperately wants to stop the fires from coming, knowing full well that an eruption now might destroy the villages below. You picture with horror the lava cascading down the shallow slope, toward the helpless child you just abandoned, whose tiny little heartbeat you swear that you can still hear all the way up in your castle in the sky.

But then another darker, primordial part of you bubbles up, with a single word.

Good.

You couldn't stop the fires now, even if you wanted to. So you stand at the edge of the once-dormant crater and watch the molten earth rise up. Soon it will fill this crater and spill over the edges. Soon the pressure beneath the earth will grow so intense that it will burst outward and rain rock and fire down into the Maui jungle.

Amid the dancing firelight you notice an odd shadow slowly growing over the basalt.

But when the dark blue fires begin to spring up on its body, you see that it's not a shadow at all.

The oily creature glides along the rim of the crater,

faster and more agile than you would have ever imagined. Its dark arms firmly wrap around your biceps in an unbreakable hold. Where it touches you, your body goes eternally cold, never to feel warm again. Even the lava pooling in the crater starts to cool as your concentration wanes, embers dying in the night air.

Thirty blue eyes flicker in the wind, and the gray mouth of the creature finally opens to speak. "Your own kin sleeps in the village below," it rasps, "yet you would still bring destruction to the island?"

You should probably struggle to break free, to flee down the volcano and take refuge in the jungle. Instead you let go. You let the creature absorb you into the lightless womb of its gelatinous belly.

Before the world goes dark, the creature offers you its final words:

"You will get a second chance, Pele. You will walk the earth again, to hopefully bring life where you have brought destruction and catastrophe before." There comes a long silence.

"But first," the creature continues without apology, "we're going to have to break you."

It wasn't the first time Ash had gathered with other gods on a California beach, but it was the first time she'd gathered with this many.

When she, along with Wes and Eve, had arrived at the Crescent City airport in the morning, she felt this strange mixture of fear and relief at the thought of no one responding to Serena's call for help. Her fear stemmed from the fact that they might have to face Colt's new pantheon of evil gods on their own, a few versus twenty, and that Colt might grow one step closer to his reign of terror over the human race. It would be a relief, however, that she wouldn't have to put any innocent strangers in harm's way.

For better or worse, as she stood with Wes, Serena, and Eve in the warm Pacific breeze on a beach just outside Crescent City, gods began to filter in. They were coming from all over, so their flights were staggered, and they all wore the same perplexed expression once they discovered the "welcoming committee" waiting for them at the beach. Serena's siren call had only broadcast a desperate sense of urgency for the courageous at heart to assemble at this location. One by one, Ash had to fill them in on details when they arrived. Some seemed angry to have been lured away from their everyday lives; some continued to look dazed, feeling like they'd somehow sleepwalked through the last twenty-four hours as they traveled halfway around the world to convene with a series of strangers on an unfamiliar beach. Most of them had trouble swallowing Ash's story as she explained it; she couldn't blame them for wondering if she was a complete whack-job.

When the shock wore off, all the gathered gods shared one thing in common, however: They all seemed relieved to come in contact with others of their own kind. Remaining camouflaged as a mortal was a taxing job for people who had to conceal such extraordinary, supernatural gifts.

Serena had come up with the idea of turning the assembly into a barbecue. The idea of loafing around the beach like they were on spring break, chowing down on burgers and hotdogs, felt a little off-kilter to Ash, especially given that they were possibly going to war later that same day. But they did need to fuel up, and the food helped to diffuse whatever tension the newly arrived gods were feeling as they tried to soak in the story Ash was spinning for them.

It was also worth it to watch as Serena, blind though

she might have been, manned the charcoal grill like a culinary master.

The best surprises were two arrivals that Ash knew well. First, Ixtab—pronounced "Esh-tawb"—the Mayan goddess of the gallows. Ash had met her only once in Miami, but felt a deep affection for the girl. Ixtab led a tough life. Her gift—if you could call it that at all—was that whenever a person in the world died through violence, Ixtab telepathically traveled to the victim's side to help him find peace in his final moment. Because of this, she drifted in and out of apparent focus constantly, almost as though she were epileptic. Ash was just grateful to see her alive, since the girl had vanished without a trace in Miami.

The second familiar face was Ade, the Zulu thunder god. With Rolfe, Lily, and now Raja all dead, Ade and Ash were the remaining gods from Blackwood, unless they counted Serena, who was a weird, weird chick, and more a harbinger of doom than an actual friend. Tears had pooled in Ash's eyes when she saw the Haitian boy crest the dune—he was hard to miss, since he had a broad-shouldered, muscular body that seemed incongruous with his boyish face. He closed the distance between them in no time at all, and suddenly his arms were wrapped firmly around her. The last time she'd encountered him, he'd been drugged and sedated as the hostage of a crime syndicate in Miami. Not that the circumstances of their reunion now were much better.

When he pulled away, he scanned the group of gods

that was milling around them. "Raja's not here yet?" he asked.

Ash set her lips in a grim line. All she could do was slowly shake her head until he understood. He looked down at his feet. Ash wondered if he felt the same survivor's guilt that she was starting to experience, as her friends dwindled in number around her.

Ixtab pulled Ash aside at one point. "Thanks to my abilities, I've actually made a few out-of-body trips to the Blackwood campus, where the Dark Pantheon is gathered." Ixtab was able to identify some of the evil gods they would be up against too: A Mayan bat demon named Camazotz and a brutal goddess of the dead named Hel from Norse mythology, to name a few. "They're so hot-headed and volatile from having been imprisoned all these years that they've been murdering each other over petty, nonsensical disagreements," she explained.

"Good news for us," Ash said. "The more they diminish their own numbers before we get there, the better."

But that didn't seem to put Ixtab at ease. "Yes and no," she said. "These gods, Ashline . . . They've lost all perspective. Whatever humanity they had before the Cloak locked them away, it's flaked away over the course of time and left something raw and destructive in its place."

Ash didn't even hear Eve come up behind her on the beach. "It's the life tree," Eve said. "The Cloak were wrong. They thought that gods-turned-evil were just flawed models that they could harvest for their tree, and the tree would rehabilitate them over time, correct the flaws, and produce a stronger, more selfless person. But it has the opposite effect." Her eyes went glassy, and Ash could tell she was thinking of her short stay in the leafy prison. "While you're in that tree, you're not just left to your own thoughts—you can feel the darkness of the others in the tree as well, flowing through it like toxic sewage. It scorches you, poisons you. And when you're finally freed, all you can think is: Someone has to pay for what they've done to me."

Eve had never talked about her time in the Cloak prison before, so this was news to Ash. And Eve had only been attached to the tree for a little over a month. She couldn't imagine the kind of venom that the others might have accumulated after being locked away for centuries.

"There's more," Ixtab continued. "While Colt waits for you in a stone tower off the coast, a Celtic goddess has been stewing mutiny among the Dark Pantheon. Colt had promised the safe passage of you and your sister before, but don't expect these gods to honor that. When we head into battle in those woods, you're just as vulnerable as the rest of us."

Epona, Ash thought darkly. She spared the girl's life back in Massachusetts, and now the girl was convincing the hornet's nest to sting her. No surprises there.

Gradually, the sun approached the horizon. The food had been mostly devoured, and the sense of restlessness was palpable. Most of the twelve arrivals were complete strangers to Ash—gods from pantheons ranging from Central America to the Far East. There were, however, two other recognizable faces in the mix: Papa and Rangi. Without access to memories from their previous lives, they clearly didn't recognize Ash and Eve, nor did they, fortunately, remember that Pele had murdered them two lifetimes ago. In fact Rangi and Papa hadn't even arrived together. This is how it's supposed to be, Ash thought. Everyone gets a fresh start.

Ash knew it was time, but suddenly she wondered what sort of solace or motivation to fight she really had to offer these people. While the threat of the Dark Pantheon was very real, "the world is at stake" was such an abstract and broad and almost ridiculous claim for anyone to wrap their mind around. But she needed to say something.

Ash held up her hand and let a small but vibrant stream of sparks shoot from her fingertips into the air. The impromptu fireworks display snagged everyone's attention, and the group of sullen gods formed a ring around her. Wes and Ade smiled at her encouragingly. Eve crossed her arms and waggled her eyebrows at Ash as if to say, *You better make this good, sis.*

"There's always that point in the movies," Ash began slowly, "where the general stands before his troops, or the coach comes into the locker room before his team takes the field for the last time, and he starts motivationally waxing on about how they may be the vastly outnumbered and outgunned underdogs, but that's exactly why they're going to win. It all builds up to this intense emotionally charged climax where everyone cheers with unity as they fill to the brim with a power they weren't even sure they had." Ash blinked and looked to the sand. "Well, I'm not your coach, and I'm not your general, and in full disclosure, I got a B-minus in the last public-speaking course I took." A few people laughed, but it was a choked, tense laughter.

Ash switched on her internal furnace, and fire instantly lapped over her arms, all the way up to her elbows. She held them out for the group to see. "There was a time, even after I learned that I was a one-woman pyrotechnic freak-show, where I thought I could live a normal life if I just retreated to schoolwork and dances and tennis matches, and pretended like this other, ancient world didn't exist. But then I met Colt Halliday, this"—she searched for the word to call him—"this fucking asshole, and the world started to fall apart around me. Friends turned on each other. People I loved dearly were murdered in the most unmentionable, personal ways. Hell follows him like a shadow, and everyone pays for it. Everyone."

Ash gazed to the south, between Ixtab and Serena, in the direction of the Blackwood campus. "As long as Colt Halliday walks the earth, nobody's fireproof. He manipulates everyone around him, and then steps back and watches the chaos. One morning you'll wake up with a knife between your ribs, and while it may not be his hand on the dagger, you'll hear him laughing from the shadows. That's how the douche bag operates. And now he's got a posse of gods, some of whom have spent centuries stewing in a sweaty prison and are about to make up for lost time by torching this world. They'll let the whole planet burn for no better reason than to watch its ashes blow in the wind."

Ash knelt down, scooped up a handful of sand, and let it sift down through her fingers. "As much as the gods we'll be going up against probably deserve to be punished, it makes me sick that anyone has to die. I've seen so much killing in the last few months, all because of Colt's puppeteering, and let me tell you: It doesn't matter whether the person is innocent or guilty, whether it's in rage or in self-defense, whether it's something I witnessed or an act of violence by my own hand—killing is always a vicious, ugly thing. This one girl, who I once might have called a friend, fell from grace, and I watched her personally murder two of my friends in cold blood." Ash flinched as Lily's face popped into her mind, as if the girl had snuck up behind her. But then she pictured Lily as she'd last seen her, as she died, floating in a moat of water, with blood pumping out of her chest. "I really thought I wanted to avenge my friends, but in that final moment, when I put the sharp end of a broken champagne glass through her heart, I felt no happiness or vengeful excitement. It was awful.

"That's why it's with a heavy conscience that I ask you to join me on what could inevitably be a suicide mission. I'm just a stranger to most of you, and I've already asked too much of you—summoning you to this distant beach, luring you away from your family and friends, and placing you into the path of danger. I had little right to do so." Ash took a deep breath. "Think of those people dear to you when you decide whether to join me on the journey into the forest. No one will blame you if you turn around now and go back to the life you left behind. If you pretend you never saw this cataclysm between the gods brewing." Ash pointed south, in the direction of Blackwood. "But sooner or later, if we fail tonight, then those dark gods will come to your town, to destroy your home and the people you love. So either you can fight by my side now, when we still have a chance . . . or you can fight alone then, when it might be too late."

And just like that, Ash gave them the option. Five of the assembled gods turned and walked away, after various levels of hesitation. One even came up to Ash and could barely meet her gaze as she said simply, "I can't," before she turned on her heel and headed back to the parking lot.

When the deserters had departed, ten gods remained on the beach: Ash, Eve, Wes, Ade, Serena, Ixtab, Papa, Rangi, and two new arrivals that Ash had never met before, in this lifetime or in any of her resurrected memories: Sila, the Inuit goddess of the air, and Erebus, the Greek god of the shadows. They both had very personal reasons to fight. Sila's sister, Sedna, an Inuit goddess of marine life, had been tortured by the awful Epona, racked with nightmares for hours at Colt's request. Sedna had survived the ordeal, but was now institutionalized and hadn't uttered a word since. "Even if you stand in front of her," Sila explained, her face hard but her eyes welling with tears, "it's like she stares right through you."

As it turned out, Erebus and Eve already knew each other, which Ash didn't realize until she saw her sister give him a civil clap on the shoulder. The teenage shadow god, along with Eve, had been part of Colt's dark entourage a year ago, when the trickster was still moonlighting as the masked figure Blink. Once Erebus had seen the big picture of Colt's plans, he'd tried to escape . . . and Colt had sent Itzli to "take care" of Erebus's girlfriend as a parting gift. Itzli had crushed the girl—a mortal—with a massive stone from the neck down, so Erebus would be able to recognize her face when he returned to the apartment. Until now, however, Erebus hadn't known where to find the trickster to seek his revenge.

Nightfall landed, and Ash knew it was time to move out. They would strike Colt's Dark Pantheon first, then storm the trickster's stone tower afterward to rescue Ash's parents and Rose . . . that is, if the girl wanted to be saved.

Thanks to Ixtab's visions and her in-depth knowledge of mythology, they had a pretty good idea of some of the gods they were up against out in the wild. However, this didn't put Ash at ease, because she knew that identifying the gods was one thing—but surviving a battle against them was something else altogether.

In the beach parking lot they loaded up into the two jeeps that Wes had rented for the attack. "I hope you opted for the insurance on these," Ash said to Wes, as he handed a pair of keys to her.

"Unfortunately, the insurance only covered 'acts of God' and not 'acts of gods,'" Wes joked.

"Damn these rental companies and their refusal to acknowledge the supernatural." Ash leaned into Wes and pressed her forehead against his collarbone—she had to stand on her tippy toes to accomplish this. "You drive safe, Wesley Towers," she said to him, since they'd each agreed to drive one of the jeeps.

Wes pulled her in close. "We're just driving down the 101," he said softly. "We're not piloting dual space shuttles on a dangerous mission to destroy a globe-killing asteroid." But they both knew that the risks were every bit as high, and that the moment they parted here could be the last moment they shared alive.

Ash couldn't handle the thought of a prolonged good-bye, so she kissed Wes hard on the Adam's apple, then turned and walked to her own car without making eye contact.

She was surprised to find Ixtab in the passenger seat of the jeep, in addition to Ade, Erebus, and Sila, who'd loaded up in the back.

"What?" Ixtab said defensively when she saw the way Ash was looking at her. "Let me guess: You want to know what good my powers will do us out in the field? How the whole 'I see dead people' shtick will help me out there?"

Ash put a hand on Ixtab's shoulder. "You've already done so much. Because of you, we've been able to identify some of the gods we're up against tonight. You've given us a fighting chance. You don't have to do anything else to—"

"Look," Ixtab interrupted. "I may not be able to ignite things, or make earthquakes, or summon the wind, or . . ." She glanced back at Erebus. "Or whatever the hell that guy does with shadows. But humans have fought for centuries with more material means, and that's exactly what I intend to do. Colt's underlings already took one person I love from me." Her weary eyes went somewhere else for a second, and Ash could all but see Aurora's pumping wings reflected in them, the Roman goddess of the dawn taking flight. "I won't let that happen to anyone else while there's still breath left in my body."

Ash nodded. Even if she were stripped of her own fiery abilities, nothing would stop her from marching into battle to avenge any of her friends.

And after all, Ash thought with a wry smile as she started the jeep, even before she'd acquired her own powers, she'd always been able to throw a mean right hook.

"Buckle up, kids," she instructed the four gods in the car. "It's going to be a Wilde ride."

"Really?" Ade groaned. "You went there?"

"Let me get this straight," Sila said, buckling her seat belt nonetheless. "We're headed into a cataclysmic battle between the gods . . . and you're concerned about seat belts?"

Ash looked into the rearview mirror and raised her eyebrows. "Clearly you've never driven with me before." Then she threw the car into drive, slammed her foot down on the gas pedal, and rocketed past the jeep containing Wes, Eve, Papa, and Rangi. Serena stood on the corner, with her cane slung over her shoulder, and in true Serena fashion, shouted, "I'll see you soon, Ashline Wilde," as the jeep flew past her.

How the blind girl knew it was the jeep with Ash in it, Ash would never know.

The drive from Crescent City to the Blackwood Academy campus was only forty miles.

Thirty miles into it, the passengers of Ash's jeep fell into an anxious silence.

Thirty-eight miles into it, they hit the fog.

It started as just a light mist over the narrow road. After another minute, it thickened until the enormous, towering redwood trees that flanked either side of the highway disappeared into a dark, gray cloud. The road glistened with an inch of standing water, even though it hadn't rained. Ash slowed the jeep way down and chanced a look over her shoulder just to make sure that Wes and the others were still following behind them. Wes flashed his headlights reassuringly.

Behind Ash, Sila had tilted her head to the sky. "This isn't right," she said, and sniffed the air. "This fog isn't . . . natural."

Ash had figured as much herself. If one of the Dark Pantheon was behind this, then there was a good chance that the welcoming committee already knew they were coming.

Somewhere in the trees off the passenger side, a large crack resounded from the woods. Before Ash could even see what had made the sound, Ixtab grabbed her arm and shouted, "Watch out!"

Ash slammed on the brakes just as the colossal trunk of a redwood tree came chopping down across the road like a cleaver. It landed just ten feet in front of them, and even at the jeep's diminished speed, Ash had to whip the steering wheel to the side. The jeep hydroplaned side-ways over the slick road before it stopped inches from the fallen tree.

Behind them, Wes's jeep screeched to a halt as well, and Ash stood up and frantically waved for him to turn around. But even as Wes started to put his jeep in reverse, there was another crack, and a second redwood toppled across the road behind them. They were now trapped in a wooden pen, with nowhere to go in the jeeps unless they tried to go off-roading into the forest.

A third crack. This time, through the mist, Ash saw

the tree hammering toward the second jeep. "No!" she screamed over its groaning, splintering trunk.

Wes leaped out of the driver-side door, and at first Ash thought he meant to get out of the way. Instead he stepped right in the path of the falling tree, braced his legs against the asphalt, and extended his massive arms over his head.

Even with his superhuman strength, the Aztec night god staggered backward under the tremendous weight of the tree, and the pavement cracked beneath his feet. The tree's descent stopped only a foot from crushing the jeep and its occupants, who took the opportunity to scramble out onto the road. As soon as Wes was sure everyone was out of harm's way, he growled and then heaved the trunk off to the side.

Everyone was evacuating Ash's jeep when a fourth redwood came crashing down. With no one to catch it this time, it crushed the abandoned jeep just as Ash and her compatriots dove clear. Glass shattered everywhere, littering the road. The tree trunk practically folded the vehicle in half, mangling the steel of the jeep's chassis as though it were Play-Doh.

"It's an ambush," Sila hissed, as if that weren't obvious enough. The five from Ash's car defensively backed up into each other, as the milk-thick mist continued to pulsate around them.

There was a shriek down the road, in Wes's group, and Ash snapped to attention just quick enough to see some sort of man-size creature with batlike wings carrying Rangi up into the mist, its talons fastened around the god's neck. Ash prepared to launch a fireball up at the creature, but dared not, lest she hit Rangi in the process. She could no longer see the creature in the clouds anyway, so she'd be throwing blindly.

Ten seconds later, Rangi's body fell back through the mist and hit the pavement next to Ash with a wet *thuck*. Blood seeped into the rain-slick road, mixing with the gasoline that was leaking out of the jeep.

"Back toward the tree line," Ash barked at her group, trying to urge them off the road and out of the open. There was nothing they could do for the dead Polynesian sky god now.

Before they could properly retreat, the beating wings of the bat creature sounded through the mist, and as he swooped over them, he vomited a fireball down at the mangled jeep. Ash barely had time to leap in front of the vehicle before it ignited. The explosion from the gas tank sent her reeling back, but Ash recovered her footing and held out her arms, shielding her friends from the angry flames. She let her fireproof skin absorb the heat before letting the shield drop altogether.

The remaining eight gods all retreated to the forest, and not a moment too soon: A series of inhuman growls echoed out of the woods on the opposite side of the road, from the direction of Blackwood. At first Ash thought they must be coming from some crazed gods. But the figures that emerged through the mist were far more terrifying.

It was a pack of woodland animals indigenous to the redwoods—coyotes, mountain lions, and black bears—only they were all in various states of postmortem decay. Most of them had lost all but patches of their fur in the decomposition process, leaving behind exposed fat, sinew, and bone, which glistened in the firelight from the exploded jeep. They didn't look friendly, either—they foamed rabidly at the mouths with hunger, and their gnashing teeth looked as sharp as the day they'd died.

Behind them, walking coolly, was a human figure: Hel, the Norse goddess of the underworld, if Ixtab had identified her correctly. She pointed at Ash and the other fleeing gods, and the zombie animals loped after them.

Ade boldly stepped forward and raised his arms, preparing to bowl the creatures over with one of his signature waves of thunder. But before the Zulu thunder god could release a shock wave, a zombie elk came barreling through the mist. It rammed into Ade with its head down and scooped him up with its antlers, carrying him off into the wild.

Not only did the attack of the undead animals force the rest of them deeper into the trees, but their angle of attack divided Ash's squad even farther from Wes and the others. The last thing she wanted to do was to lose sight of her sister and Wes when there were bloodthirsty creatures in pursuit, but she had little choice, so she dashed like hell was on her heels into the mist. The last she saw of Wes, an undead bear was taking a swipe at his head with a bone-breaking swing of its claw. Wes ducked under the bear's right hook, and then countered with one of his own that knocked the bear's lower jaw right off its skull.

Ash made it a solid forty feet into the forest before she heard the quickly approaching padding of paws on dirt. She knew it was only a matter of time before she was outrun by the reanimated animals, so she turned on her heel, switching to the offensive. The outline of a cougar materialized through the mist, coming fast. Ash launched a fireball in its direction, hoping to burn the creature alive.

But the problem with burning the cougar alive was that it was already dead. The fireball exploded across the exposed sinew of its face, but the mountain lion didn't even flinch. It just continued to lope forward, in flames, and Ash couldn't even get out the words "oh, shit" before it pounced and landed on her.

Its claws sank into her shoulders, and the weight of the creature took Ash to the ground like a falling tree. It was all she could do to thrust out her hands and wrap them around the zombie cougar's neck and squeeze. This kept its gnashing teeth inches from her nose. The fiercely putrid smell of burning, rotting flesh threatened to make her vomit, and she tried her best not to scream as its claws dug deeper into her flesh.

Ash's own anger was growing at the thought of dying at

the mercy of a carcass. Hel couldn't fight her own battles, so she summoned carrion to do her bidding instead?

"Fuck this," Ash growled. She kicked off the ground, somersaulting backward with the mountain lion, then launched him by the neck hard at the nearest redwood.

The cougar hit the tree back-first, and its exposed spine snapped in half. Still, with its back and hind legs twisted at a macabre angle, it tried to drag itself forward through the dirt on just its front paws.

Before the fallen creature could crawl its way any farther, Erebus reappeared from the mist, wound up with his right leg and let loose a kick across the cougar's face. Its head snapped off its neck and flew into the mist. "Got to admire its persistence," Erebus said, as the broken, headless corpse on the ground continued to lash out blindly with its claws.

The two of them had been so fixated on the cougar that they didn't hear the other creatures creeping up behind them until a bear stepped on a dry leaf. Ash spun around to find not one but five undead animals surrounding them, with Hel a few paces to their rear. Her nappy, twig-littered hair ran all the way down to her waist, and she flashed them an ugly, taunting smile.

As Ash and Erebus backed into a redwood, not daring to turn their backs on the pack of bears and coyotes that was slowly closing in on them, Erebus whispered to Ash, "Now would be a good time to cast a little light for me."

Ash didn't question Erebus, even though she knew the zombie animals wouldn't fear fire like a living creature might. She just launched a fireball down into the ground in front of them, which erupted in an impromptu bonfire.

The firelight bathed the zombie animals in its red glow, casting long shadows behind them.

Ash watched with morbid delight as Erebus raised his hands . . . and the shadows of the animals came to life.

The silhouettes emerged from the soil, no longer in two dimensions but three, and the distorted, darker versions of the zombie creatures were even larger and more terrifying than their originals.

Hel blanched as she saw the silhouettes turn on her. She didn't even have time to run before the pack of ravenous shadows pounced. Her awful, earsplitting screams only lasted a few seconds before one of the shadow bears ripped out her throat with its teeth.

Instantly the five zombie animals in front of Ash and Erebus crumpled lifelessly to the ground, once more becoming rotting cadavers, as they had been before Hel disturbed their eternal rest.

"Killer shadow puppets?" Ash said, impressed, and toed the black-bear carcass in front of her. "And I really thought I'd seen everything . . ."

Erebus gave her a humble grin and shrugged. "You know what they say about being afraid of your own—"

In a flourish of ugly translucent wings, the red-eyed

bat god—the one Ixtab had identified as Camazotz, a demon of sorts from Mayan mythology—dropped out of the mist and raked his sharp talons across Erebus's throat. The shadow god immediately grasped his neck to cover the wound, but blood just oozed out between his fingers and down onto his T-shirt.

Ash released a vengeful cry and lunged for Camazotz, but without even turning around, the bat god dropped to his hands and bucked out with both of his legs, like a rodeo bull. His feet connected with Ash's stomach, and she tripped over an exposed root as she fell backward.

Ash was on fire by the time she even got to her feet. Camazotz stood between her and Erebus, who was curled up on the forest floor, still applying pressure to his neck. There was less blood pumping out now, which could mean that the demon's claw had missed the boy's jugular . . . or it could just mean that he was already running out of blood. Either way, Erebus was going to need medical attention soon.

Just as Ash stepped forward, preparing to flame broil the bat god, a strange sensation came over her. The corona that had erupted around her started to dim, the flames retracting back into her body against her will. Her lungs felt heavy, and she realized that the air she was breathing in was suddenly devoid of oxygen. Her mouth opened impotently, trying to draw in fresh air, but the burning in her lungs only worsened.

That's when Sila stepped into view from where

she'd been lurking under the cover of mist. Her fingers were curled tight, and she never took her gaze off Ash. "Traitor," Ash rasped. The girl had to be on Colt's payroll, which meant the story she'd told them about her brain-dead sister was probably bullshit, too. At least Ash no longer needed to guess who'd alerted the Dark Pantheon to prepare an ambush for them.

With the Inuit air goddess stealing Ash's oxygen, it was impossible for Ash to tap into her fiery abilities. Camazotz and Sila watched her intently, content to let her asphyxiate. Even as the inky spots blossomed in her sight and Ash began to panic, she noticed a large outline appear in the mist behind the two sinister gods.

Ash staggered to the right, which prompted Sila to laugh. "Moving around won't get you the oxygen that your lungs are so desperately yearning for," the Inuit goddess ribbed her. "The vacuum goes where you go, Pele."

Ash dropped to one knee a few steps later. "Not searching for air," she croaked. "Just moving out of the way."

That's when Ade sent a hard current of thunder into the two standing gods. The blast of thunder bowled both of them over, but the less fortunate Sila collided with a nine-foot-wide redwood headfirst before dropping to the ground.

Camazotz landed closer to Ash. He struggled to his feet with his hands covering his explosively ringing ears, but the concussion from the thunder had discombobulated him. Ash pinned his right wing to the forest floor with an angry drive of her boot, then leaned in close so he could hear her. "I knew another winged god once," she said, referring to Aurora. "I liked her far better than you."

With a fierce twist of the bat god's head, she broke Camazotz's neck, and he slumped back into the dirt.

When Ash finally removed her foot from the dead god's wing, she turned her attention back to Erebus. Ade was kneeling over him and wrapping a section of his own T-shirt around the shadow god's throat. Ixtab had also managed to find her way back to them, and Ash was relieved to see that no gods or undead animals had torn the Mayan girl to shreds.

Erebus was moaning something in a low rasp— Camazotz's claw must have nicked his vocal cords. "I don't think his jugular was hit," Ade said, and Ash felt a wave of relief. "He might sound like a James Bond villain from now on, but he's going to be okay."

"Do you think you can navigate your way with him to the Blackwood campus?" Ash asked Ade, who nodded. This part of the forest was a cell phone dead zone, but Ade would be able to call for help from campus. "I'm hoping it will be god-free since all the bad apples seem to be out here in the woods. But if you come across anyone who shouldn't be there . . ." Ash spread her hands. "Make their ears ring in the afterlife."

With no time to waste, Ade scooped up the fallen god as delicately as he could and hurried off into the mist.

Ash and Ixtab continued through the forest in the direction they hoped would reconnect them with Wes, Eve, and the others. Midnight was fast approaching, and even though Ash had committed to battling it out with the Dark Pantheon first, time was dwindling down to the deadline Colt had given her for meeting him at the lighthouse.

The woods were disconcertingly quiet as Ash and Ixtab walked through the mist. Ash tried to not read into this—Wes and the others weren't about to start shouting and giving away their location to any other demented gods who happened to be lurking nearby. Still, she couldn't keep her imagination from traveling to dark places. The thick mist around them was a blank canvas that was just asking for morbid thoughts to be painted upon it. . . .

A curious sound finally interrupted the silence, quiet at first, but growing louder. It was the sound of a rope swinging rhythmically back and forth. As they traveled toward the noise, a shape appeared through the curtain of steam: a large pendulum of sorts, a thick object swinging from the bottom of the rope.

Once they took several more steps through the trees, Ash recognized it for what it was: The rope was a vine.

The object at the end of it was Papa.

She was dangling upside down by one foot, the vine fastened around her ankle. Her hair swished around her face as the rope listed back and forth. The earth goddess was still alive, but there was a gash across her skull and a growing bruise where she'd been struck with a blunt object. Her eyes squinted in and out of focus at Ash and Ixtab, dulled by whatever concussion she'd been dealt.

Ixtab drew a pocketknife from her jeans and immediately started toward Papa, preparing to cut her down. Ash paused in her tracks, sensing that something was afoot. "Ixtab, wait—" she whispered harshly to the knife-wielding goddess.

There was the creak of a second vine, somewhere in the canopy above. Ash realized the ambush that was happening, but even though she rushed forward to tackle Ixtab to the ground, she didn't reach her in time.

Ixtab never knew what hit her. On the end of a long vine, swinging like a deadly pendulum, a boulder-size clump of thorns slammed into Ixtab. It lifted her up in the air, with the long, Jurassic-size thorns sticking into her like she was a pin cushion. The booby trap finally dumped her unceremoniously against the trunk of a tree. She sat there, slumped like a broken doll against the colossal redwood, multiple stains of red soaking into her tank top.

Ash sprinted for the girl, dodging the pendulum as it made a slower second pass in the opposite direction. Ixtab was wheezing hard with shallow breaths—the brambles must have pierced her lungs.

A figure dropped out of the trees, landing between Ash and her fallen friend. She recognized Tane, the Polynesian forest spirit, both from her visions and from when Colt liberated him from the life tree. He must have also been the one uprooting those redwood trees back on the 101.

Ash thrust out both hands, showering Tane with dual spouts of fire, but his powers were quicker on the draw. A series of barklike plates slid over his entire body, an organic armor that covered him from head to toe. It finished in a helmet with bestial ears and eye slits exposed just enough for Ash to see his green, glowing eyes staring out at her. Most wood might burn or scorch, but Tane's new wooden plating meant that Ash's fire just washed around him innocuously.

Redwood bark. He'd armored himself with redwood bark, one of the most fireproof of all the world's trees.

Sure enough, when Ash finally turned off her internal pilot light, Tane had only suffered a light singe to his bark. He looked down at the black marks on his armor and the steam rising off them as though Ash had just scuffed his favorite sports car. Then he wound back with his arm and backhanded Ash with the hard, spiky edge of his forearm. She tumbled back so far, she nearly wound up back in the path of the swinging bramble ball.

Ash touched the bloody edge of her lip, but stood tall and resolute as Tane strode toward her. "You're not the first plant god to try to kill me," she said, spitting a bloody wad at Tane's feet. "You can join the last one in the compost pile."

"Ignite all you want, Pele," Tane growled. The jovial

spirit of the Tane that Pele had known two hundred years ago was gone, replaced with something inhumane and vicious. "But you can't make a bonfire out of fireproof logs." Tane held up both arms, letting the thorny quills grow longer and sharper out of them. Then he lunged for Ash, preparing to skewer her.

A gunshot resounded through the woods. Tane's body stiffened mid-flight and Ash sidestepped him as he crashed limply down. He landed helmet-first on the bramble pendulum, shuddered, then went still.

At the base of his neck, where the wooden armor was thinnest, a single bullet hole smoked faintly.

Ash looked over toward Ixtab. The girl was still slumped against the tree, but she held a pistol stiffly out in front of her. It must have been concealed in her waistband all this time—she hadn't been kidding when she'd said she intended to fight with more material means.

Once Ixtab was sure that Tane wasn't getting up, her gun arm fell weakly to her side. "Fireproof," she rasped, using her last breath. "But not bulletproof . . ."

Her quaking chest seized after the last word, and though she died looking at Ash, her eyes stared piercingly into an altogether different world.

Ash knelt over the girl and wept. She barely had enough strength to gently close Ixtab's eyes. The Mayan goddess of the gallows had seen enough of this lifetime. Ixtab had spent most of her days comforting others in their final moments and shepherding them into the beyond—it was the blessing and the burden of her powers.

But when the gallows goddess died, who was there to comfort her in her final moment?

Eventually, Papa's moans snapped Ash out of her mourning. Ash picked up the switchblade Ixtab had dropped and used it to saw through the vine. Just as Ash sheered through the last plant fiber, she managed to catch Papa before she could drop headfirst to the dirt.

"Thanks," Papa mumbled dazedly after Ash was sure the woman was lucid enough to stand on her own two feet. Papa's eyes focused and refocused as she recovered from the concussion. She didn't regain her bearings until her gaze fell upon Ixtab's blood-stained body. "I'm sorry," the earth goddess said. "You knew her well?"

"No," Ash replied. "Yet she was still one of the most selfless people I've ever known."

A primitive scream sounded through the mist, followed by the galloping of hooves. Difficult as it was to see through the steamy forest, Ash knew the girl riding toward them on horseback could only be the wretched Epona. As Epona came into view, Ash saw that the insane redhead had a long, sharp-tipped spear cocked back and ready to throw. She aimed the metal javelin at Ash.

Ash was sick of all these games, all this detestable violence. Papa, too, stood her ground with no small amount of contempt.

"This one's for Ixtab and Rangi," Ash said, and let a

single, explosive flare burst from her open palm.

The flare struck the ground just in front of the wild mare and ignited into a crackling fire. The horse, which had been charging like it was in the front line of a Civil War cavalry charge, bucked wildly at the sight of the flames, throwing Epona from the saddle. She flipped over the fire before landing hard on her back.

Epona tried to regain her footing and reach for her fallen spear, but Papa waved her hand at the soil beneath the Celtic goddess. The earth around her liquefied in a matter of seconds, and Epona plunged into the quicksand.

For a moment, Ash thought the girl was going to drown, but Epona's head resurfaced through the muck. Her red hair and freckled cheeks were filthy with mud, and she groped around wildly for the edge of the sand pit with panicked, unsure gasps.

Papa wasn't done with her yet. The earth goddess drew her hands back, and just as quickly as the soil had liquefied, it hardened back into a solid. Epona let out a series of frightened, mousy squeaks, but to no avail—the hard-packed earth locked around her, burying her from the neck down.

The image nearly made Ash laugh. It reminded her of the time she'd encased Colt in rock up to his waist.

While Epona continued her impotent struggle to escape, groaning with exertion, Ash whispered something to Papa, who smiled darkly.

"What's so funny?" Epona snarled, only her head visible above the quicksand. "Are you freaks joking about how you're going to kill me?"

Ash shook her head. "We're not going to kill you, Epona," she said, and waited long enough for Epona's face to soften with hope. "But," Ash continued, and gestured to the now hard-packed soil beneath her feet, "I'm not sure if you've noticed, but you're buried up to your head in the center of a natural valley in the forest floor." She glanced meaningfully up at the sky. "And the forecast tonight calls for rain . . . a lot of it."

There might have been mud coating Epona's face, but Ash was sure that even the girl's freckles must have gone white as she imagined the natural crater filling up, the rains flowing down the slopes and pooling around her head, her mouth and nose slowly disappearing under the rising water level. . . .

"My best advice?" Ash knelt down and slapped the side of Epona's face lightly with her hand. "Drink real fast."

They left Epona, whose fruitless efforts to free herself were accompanied by small, sobbing shrieks. Once they were out of earshot, Papa said to Ash, "The forecast tonight called for clear skies, didn't it?"

"It did," Ash said. "But when your sister's a storm goddess, there's always a chance of rain."

"Speak of the devil," Papa said.

Because they'd stumbled upon Eve in the mist.

Eve was leaning against a redwood, looking a

little bored. At her feet, Ash recognized Tangaroa, the Polynesian sea god, whose body was still convulsing with the electricity Eve had pumped into him. Ash could even see the blackened, festering welt on his chest where the lightning bolt must have struck.

"Like dropping a toaster in a bath tub," Eve said casually.

Tangaroa's eyes rolled back into his head finally, but his body still continued to twitch posthumously.

Not too far away, Ash heard Wes's voice calling for her. Papa opened her mouth, about to summon the night god over to them, but Ash caught her by the elbow. "Listen, Papa," Ash said. "Eve and I need to go take care of something . . . alone. But my noble boyfriend is going to want to tag along. Could you do us a solid and distract him for a few minutes?"

Papa frowned uncertainly, but then nodded. She hurried off into the fog, which was already starting to dissipate now that Tangaroa was dead.

"You ready for this?" Ash asked her sister.

"Yes." Eve's eyes crackled with static electricity. "This was just a warm-up for what I'm going to do to Colt. I brought a little backup plan too, in case we need a distraction. . . ." Eve opened the knapsack that she'd kept on her back, long enough for Ash to see the music box inside.

Hopefully it wouldn't get anyone blown up this time.

Together they headed in the direction of the coast, away from the sound of Wes's voice. It pained her to leave him behind, especially when she couldn't be sure there weren't other gods from the Dark Pantheon lurking in the forest. He'd no doubt be furious that they'd confronted Colt without him, but this final battle was for the Wilde sisters alone.

The walk lasted several miles, until the trees finally thinned, and the swooshing roll of the ocean emerged through the silence. And when they stepped out onto the pebble-strewn beach, it wasn't hard to locate their destination.

A half mile up the coastline, a colossal stone structure rose out of the shallows like a middle finger flipping the bird to the Pacific horizon. Itzli must have had a really good time creating the nightmarish lighthouse, because he'd designed the limestone exterior to look almost like a massive coral reef, complete with jagged rocky fingers that reached off into the night. The sadistic bastard, Ash noted with scorn, must have an artistic streak.

At the lighthouse's impressive summit, backlit by the glow of a fire, a man stood at the edge, staring down the coast in their direction. It was impossible to distinguish any of his features from this far away, but it had to be Colt.

"I think it's time to go break up with our old flame," Eve said to Ash.

Ash nodded in agreement. "And let's not let him down gently. . . ."

As Ash and Eve passed through the entrance into the dark interior of the towering lighthouse, the first thing they noticed was the staircase. Ash illuminated her hand at the same time Eve let an electric luminescence glow around hers, two torches floating in the dark. Thick stone steps spiraled around the inside walls, a helix wrapping around the tapered shell of the tower. They eventually disappeared high above, through an aperture in the ceiling.

Ash immediately started for the stairwell, but Eve caught her by the wrist. Eve opened and closed her mouth several times; whatever she wanted to say, she was fighting tooth and nail not to let it come out. "Look," Eve said once her lips finally cooperated. "Anything could happen up there, so I just wanted you to know . . . shit," Eve said, unable to get it out on the first try. A glossy coating had formed over her eyes, glistening bluish white from her electric torch. "I spent so much of my life being a bitch that sometimes saying something human is like trying to vomit up a bowling ball."

Ash rubbed her sister's arm and smiled wanly. "Lovely image."

"The point is," Eve continued, "I hope you realize that I never ran away from Scarsdale because of you." She gazed up to the roof, where their hostage parents presumably awaited them. "I didn't even run away because of them. I just woke up every morning in my bed and saw what a monster I was gradually becoming. I mean, there's teen angst, but the awful, hurtful things I started to say to everyone, the parties, the drinking, the fights at school . . . I lost control. I walked all over our parents, and then my friends at school, and eventually . . . even my best friend." Her wet eyes fell on Ash. "It was like this out-of-body experience. No matter how much I kept telling myself that I needed to be a better person, my mouth just kept saying the same caustic shit, and my fists just kept on swinging. So I ran. Far away. I did it to find a fresh start, but every time I found myself alone in a bathroom—in rest stops, in hostels, in abandoned apartments where I'd squat—I always ended up looking at myself in the mirror, thinking, 'You used to be such a good kid, Eve. What happened to you?'"

"You may think you've said or done things so terrible that you can't come back to us," Ash said. "But then why have Mom and Dad still spent the last year clinging to every hope that you'd eventually come home? And as for me, I went to hell and back—literally—to find you. We never gave up on you." Ash pointed to the stairs. "So let's go up there, save our parents, kill an unkillable trickster . . . and if we make it out of this alive, I promise we won't have to wait until our next lifetimes to make a fresh start . . . together."

Eve gave a dark, curt laugh. "Be careful how you use the word 'together,' considering there's a psychopath up there trying to blend us into a single brain for the rest of eternity."

It took them a solid three minutes to travel up the spiral staircase. While it was tempting to run to the top to confront the trickster and his hit man, Colt probably wanted them to show up out of breath and too bedraggled to fight.

When Ash climbed the final step and popped up onto the lighthouse's observation deck, it was like walking into a cocktail party full of people she never wanted to see. Colt and Rose stood together at the edge of the platform, looking out over the Pacific Ocean like they were just some happy couple on a Caribbean cruise. Itzli stood guard next to Ash's parents, who lay in a special cell the stone god had constructed for them. There were no sides to it, or bars, like a normal prison—instead the Wildes lay on one slab of stone, while a second, thicker slab that must have weighed at least a few tons loomed several feet over them. It was supported at each corner by four precarious-looking supports, also made of stone. If more than one of the supports gave way, the top slab would make a short drop and crash down on Thomas and Gloria. It looked heavy enough to pulverize bone if that happened.

Colt smiled when he realized they'd arrived. He checked an imaginary watch on his wrist. "Right on time, ladies," he said, then gestured around at the lighthouse. "What do you think of our lighthouse, now that you've had the tour?"

Ash shrugged and cast an unimpressed look at Itzli. "Shoddy workmanship. A three-hundred-foot stone tower, and you don't even install an elevator?" She pointed to the stone booby trap containing her parents. "That canopy bed doesn't look too sturdy either. I mean, seriously guys—are you gods, or are you two boys in a sandbox building castles out of Legos?"

Itzli remained stoic, but Colt laughed gaily at her joke, like they were sharing a friendly bottle of wine over dinner. "I've missed your sense of humor, Pele."

Ash shuddered. In his mind, Colt truly did see the three of them not as individuals, but as fragments of one person. To him, they were all Pele. "You know," she said. "I'm not sure how well you really remember the old Pele, because I've had a chance to relive a few visions of her, and she wasn't exactly a stand-up comedian. She was more along the lines of a—what's the word for it . . . ?

Oh yeah: a crazy bitch who electrocuted and burned her friends alive. All for the sake of some lying, lonely trickster who washed up on her shores."

"You loved me!" Colt screamed. In an instant he switched gears from his grinning trickster-self into crazed, unrestrained malice. He worked so hard to maintain an air of control all the time; Ash had only seen him completely lose it like this twice before. "I gave you the gift of a glimpse into your old memories, let you peer into the looking glass of time so that you'd realize that we loved each other. Deeply. Loyally. Enough so that, yes, you were willing to cremate anyone that got in our way. Yet even after bearing witness to the greatest love story of all time, you still fight this. Why? Why won't you let me fix you? Why won't you just let me love you again? Why won't you let yourself love me back?"

As absolutely insane and illogical as Colt had become, his outburst made him transparent just long enough for Ash to see him for who he truly was: a scared, lonely boy. He might be in the body of a college-aged student, but his brain was struggling with the weight of a few thousand years' worth of memories. Finding Pele again, for him, wasn't just about romance or sex or world domination—she was the only person volatile and unhinged enough to *get* him. To understand all his whack-job idiosyncrasies, to revel in his millennia-long history of conquests and trickery.

To maybe even love him back—the whole him.

After seeing this fractured, almost human component

to his soul, Ash decided to try a tactic she'd almost given up on with him: appealing to his humanity, or at least what little of it that remained. "Colt, as much as the way you've gone about this has been twisted and warped and hurt a whole lot of people, I don't doubt that your love for Pele was very real. And I'm not saying the Cloak were right when they split our soul into three pieces like they did. But that doesn't mean that putting us back together, against our will, is right either. Maybe we were fragments at one point, but those fragments have grown into full souls, different personalities that are too big and too diverse to squeeze back into the one-brain container they originally came in. There's no going back." She took a step toward him. "Love isn't just about fiery, unrestrained passion, or two kindred spirits. It's about choice. It's about choosing to be with that one person whose fire burns so bright in our eyes that the other six billion people in the world don't even feel like an option. You just know."

Colt laughed sardonically and gestured around him, then back in the direction of Blackwood Academy. "Considering all that I've done to get you back, I think it's pretty clear that I've chosen you."

"Yes, but I have to choose you, too!" Ash shot back. "*We* would have to choose you. To choose the life you've somehow already decided for us. But this . . ." She pointed to the stone prison and her parents lying inside it. "This isn't choice. It's coercion."

Her logic fell on deaf ears—Colt's face returned to its normal placid state, and he started talking as though their conversation hadn't taken such a dramatic detour. "In order to reunite Pele, the three of you are going to have to return to the stormy, primordial fire from which you came. Together, you must draw a volcano from these waters. Then, with your minds quiet and your hearts focused, you must bathe in its crater . . . then you will rise from the lava as one."

"Wait, wait, wait." Eve held up a hand. "Your plan to mold us back into Pele . . . is to have us sacrifice ourselves in a volcano? In case you were unaware, one of us—me—is not fireproof like the others."

"There is no healing without pain first." Colt smiled ironically. "Trust me, I would know."

"And if we don't?" Ash asked, even though she already knew the answer. She looked to the stone prison that held her parents. The supports quivered, and Ash could now see that Itzli was actually concentrating on the stones to get them to balance like that. Should his concentration break . . .

"Let's not ask obvious questions, Ashline. Banal conversation is beneath you," Colt said. "But if you need it spelled out: If you two attempt to fight this in any way, if you try to take out either me or my associate with a strong gust of wind, or lightning strike, or explosion, or burst of flames—hell, if you sneeze the wrong way in our direction—the vibrations could easily topple the stones supporting that top slab. It will crush your parents instantly like a boot to an egg. Have you ever seen a juicer squeeze an orange until every last drop drips out the bottom?" He let the image sink in until Ash could visualize the blood seeping out of the stone corners.

Only now did Ash truly see the impossible choice Colt had put before them. In her head she'd envisioned that she and Eve would outsmart the trickster, somehow using their powers to both rescue her parents and prevent Colt from gluing them back into the supergoddess they came from.

But the risks involved were too great, his booby trap too well-conceived, and now they would have to choose: retain their individuality and kill Colt, while almost definitely sacrificing their parents, or submit to Colt's bidding so that he might let their parents live.

To Ash, the choice was a horrible yet obvious one. The only reason that the Wildes were involved in this was because they had had the heart to adopt two orphaned baby girls sixteen years ago and give them a shot at a good life. They had nothing to do with Colt's disgusting quest, yet it was they who might die for it. Her parents were also mortals. They only had this one life on Earth, aside from whatever the afterlife had in store for them. Even though Ash might lose part of her individuality as Pele, at least a piece of her—and of Eve, and Rose—would have a chance of coming back lifetime after lifetime.

When Ash turned to Eve to gauge her reaction, she

saw that her older sister was looking at their parents, who were helpless and still as corpses. There were tears in Eve's eyes again. "I took them for granted," she said, her voice breaking. "I took them for granted when they made so many sacrifices for us. It's about time . . ."

She couldn't get the last part out, but Ash could see the rest of the sentence written in her eyes.

It's about time we make a sacrifice for them.

Ash didn't see any other option. Thomas and Gloria Wilde had taught her everything she knew about family and love, and now Colt would use both of those "weaknesses" against her. Ash and Eve didn't say anything to each other after that; they just both stepped sullenly up to the edge of the lighthouse platform together.

Three hundred feet below, the Pacific waters looked calm, but they wouldn't be for long. Ash held out her hands. Although her abilities had grown in spurts over the last few months, she'd never accomplished anything quite on this scale before. It was going to take all the energy that she had. Even gods weren't without their limitations, were they?

Ash shot a vengeful look over her shoulder at Itzli. "You better concentrate hard on those supports," she told him. "It's going to get a little bumpy, and if anything happens to my parents, it's you who will be bathing in the volcano."

Itzli nodded once.

Ash returned her attention to the waters. When she

reached out, she could feel the sandy sea floor hidden beneath them, then the earth's crust beneath that. She let her consciousness descend down, down until she could feel the geothermal warmth, the molten furnace within the earth. Her fists tightened as she harnessed that power. A single word escaped her lips in a rasp:

"Rise."

The waters had been dark before, except for the moonlight reflecting off them. But now an orange glow pulsated from the depths. It grew brighter as more magma trickled up through the fissure she'd cracked in the earth's crust. Steam rose off the sea until at last the lava piled high enough that it breached the surface.

The molten rock bubbled up in a fierce yellow before it cooled and died to orange, then red, then hardened into rock. But even as that rock hardened, more lava piled up and took its place, slowly forming an anthill-shaped cone.

The base of the volcano kept growing wider, starting the size of an inner tube barely visible from Ash's perch, to the width of a car, then a semitrailer, then a basketball court. All the while the summit continued to rise higher: five feet, ten feet, twenty feet. The fissure on top caved in on itself, forming a crater, and more lava spilled out over its rim.

As it continued to rise, Ash could feel the power surging up in her, and for one out-of-control moment, she wasn't herself. She could feel what it was like to be Pele again, taste it, the devastating, earth-rending power that no one being should wield.

Eve extended her arms. With her hands spinning in small circles, a stormy wind descended upon the rising volcano. The gales twisted and shaped the soft molten rock, smoothing its contours into a gentle slope. Eve, too, seemed to be tapping into a taste of what it was like to be Pele, because now and again blinding lightning bolts would hammer down near the top of the mountain, blowing away sections of rock, only for her winds to smooth the gouges over again.

Rose, too, joined them, sensing the opportunity to use her own gifts. Until this point the volcano's formation had been a fairly fluid process. However, as soon as Rose pointed to the crater, an explosion rocked the summit. The volcano spewed a fiery boulder into the air. The boulder left the crater with such incredible speed that the enormous, burning cannonball sailed up into the sky, penetrating Eve's dark storm clouds. Far off in the distance the boulder finally dropped back through the clouds, but its trajectory had carried it so far away that the tank-size stone looked like a tiny fiery marble as it plunked into the sea.

Ash took her gaze off the process long enough to make sure Itzli was holding the stone prison steady despite the heavy vibrations. In that brief look she also caught Rose's expression illuminated in the flickering firelight, a crazed grin gleaming on her face.

When the volcano had risen nearly to the height of

their stone lighthouse, Ash finally felt the last reserves of her energy dry up. She dropped to one knee and dry-heaved a few times, so exhausted that she felt nauseous. Sweat dripped from her bowed head.

Colt was applauding gleefully. "Good, good! Do you see how coming together makes you that much more powerful?"

"Right," Ash grumbled. "Because raising whole volcanoes out of the ocean is that useful in everyday life. So what now—we just go over there, climb Mount Pele, and go for a dip in the lava?" Her typical defensive sarcasm was still coming out, but it sounded oddly flat and without resonance, since she realized that she was about to possibly vanquish her individuality as she knew it.

Colt nodded. Now that the end was so near, he seemed to be enjoying every word out of her mouth with an intense sexual ecstasy. "Your Pele instincts should take over when the time is right. The three shards of you have always been magnetically drawn back to each other; you just have to give them the right circumstances to merge."

"And what guarantee do we have that this will work?" Eve asked. "Where did you look this up, anyway, Wikipedia?"

"There is an old seer in Hawai'i, a man who can gaze into the future and wander its many branching roads," Colt explained. "Each century he is reborn, just like us. These days he's regarded as a kook, a crazed homeless man who spends his days fishing beer cans out of recycling bins to turn a dime. However, those who stop to listen to him discover that his ravings aren't madness—they're prophecy."

It must be the same man who'd prophesied the destructive touch of the Driftwood Stranger.

And he'd certainly been right about that one.

Ash wanted to stall longer, but she could find no more questions to ask. It would be better to get this over with before her self-preservation instincts took over. She cast one last look at her sleeping parents and wondered, *Will I still feel the same way about you both when I return as Pele? Will I still love you, still be capable of loving you? Or will I look at you as disgusting, expendable mortals and cut ties with you completely?*

Ash stopped in front of Itzli on her way back to the staircase. He was taller than her, but she raised herself up so that her nose nearly touched his. "If my parents aren't here, alive and unscathed, when I get back, we're going to play a little game of rock-lava-lightning." She leaned and whispered into his ear. "And we won't be playing best out of three."

"Attachment is weakness," he said in a hard Spanish-sounding accent—the first time Ash had even heard him speak. "Freedom is strength."

"And evil is cowardice," Ash added before she backed away.

It was time. She turned, heading for the hole in the platform, mentally preparing herself for the short but torturous journey that lay before her: three hundred feet down the stone steps, wading through the water to the offshore volcano, then up to the crater on top, where the lava boiled like a stew in a Crock-Pot. How would it all go down? Would she feel their consciousnesses melding together? Would it be a fluid move into Pele's brain, with her awake the whole time, or would Ashline Wilde have to die first for Pele to rise out of the primordial womb of the volcano? Would her memories—all of their collective memories—transfer over in Pele's rebirth? Or would the last thing she saw be the warm, liquid touch of the lava folding over her body like a blanket before everything went black?

Ash had so many questions, and the five minute journey it was going to take wasn't enough time to come to terms with any of it.

At the top of the spiral staircase, she became aware that only Rose was following her. "Come on, Eve," she started to say.

But when she turned to look at her sister, a fist hit her square in the nose.

Ash's world rocked as the blow hit her face. Hot and sticky blood poured out of her mangled nose, and she dropped to her hands and knees, more out of surprise than from the pain that had erupted where she'd been struck. When the initial daze wore off enough for her to get her bearings, she looked up . . . and saw that the fist that had struck her belonged to Eve.

Eve massaged her knuckles, which had a single brush stroke of Ash's blood smeared across them. "You fucking bitch," Eve seethed, as furious as Ash had ever seen her—and that was saying something. "This is all your fault."

Before Ash could ask what the hell Eve was talking about, Eve picked her up by the front of her shirt with one hand, drew back her other, and then cuffed Ash across the cheekbone.

More flashbulbs burst in Ash's vision, and she

staggered across the platform, so far that she nearly toppled off the edge. As the light cleared from her gaze and she stood on two wobbly legs, she saw that the fight had effectively frozen Itzli, Rose, and Colt, who were all watching in suspended animation. Colt had counted on Eve and Ash fighting back against him and Itzli . . . but he hadn't anticipated the two of them fighting each other.

Of course Ash hadn't anticipated that either, so she could barely raise her arms to defend herself before Eve swung her hand from left to right and a heavy current of air hit Ash from the side. This succeeded in throwing her off-balance, and she tumbled across the stone landing before flopping hard onto her back.

Eve loped toward Ash and knelt down on her shoulders before Ash could pick herself up. Colt was calling out for Eve to stop fighting and embrace her fate, but Eve ignored him. In fact Eve had positioned herself so that her back was now turned to Colt.

"I hate you, Ashline!" Eve screamed with such ferocity that spittle flew into Ash's face. However, even as Eve's teeth were bared in a wolflike snarl, she whispered something audible only to Ash. "That volcanic flesh trick you did back at the museum—how strong is the stone?" Her eyes flickered just briefly to the stone prison and their parents.

That's when Ash figured out exactly what Eve's endgame was.

Instead of answering her, Ash bared her own teeth, and with a banshee wail she shot out both her arms into Eve's chest.

Eve flew up into the air and landed ten feet away on her back. The hit from Ash and the landing had both been incredibly hard, real. This wasn't a theatrical fight where they pulled punches—it had to look completely real; neither of them could hold back.

Colt was clearly about to intervene, so Ash knew the time to hatch their plan was quickly expiring. She circled around so that she set herself up just where she thought Eve might want her to stand, directly between Eve and their parents' stone cell. Ash tried to relax her body for the powerful hit that she knew was about to come next.

Everything happened incredibly fast. Eve expelled a hard gale that lifted Ash off her feet, throwing her backward. Her airborne body slipped right between the narrow gap separating the two stone slabs, so that she came to a stop lying between her two prostrate parents.

Ash let the volcanic flesh armor every inch of her body. It ripped open her clothes in shreds as the layers of igneous rock coated her skin, and what little didn't tear apart soon burst into flames. She knew that the heat must be scorching her parents, but they had worse injuries to worry about.

Itzli snarled, getting ready to drop the slab on Ash and her parents, fed up with this whole ordeal. Colt screamed, "Wait!" but Itzli looked like he was done taking orders from the trickster. The Aztec stone god pulled back his arm to knock the supports free.

He never saw Eve's gale of wind coming. It him in the chest, and with a very effeminate final squeak he flew off the edge of the three-hundred-foot stone lighthouse he'd built.

Without Itzli's concentration to steady them, the supports gave way to gravity, and the three-ton stone slab collapsed. Still flat on her back like a turtle, Ash braced herself and caught the rock with the flats of her forearms and her shins, like the slab was a tabletop and her limbs were its legs. Even with her own body armored with fiery rock, the stone was so heavy that she thought her bones might break. Then she and her parents would all be flat-tened.

Out of the corner of her eye she caught a glimpse of her mother's sleeping face, comatose and distressed from whatever sedative they'd used to keep the two of them under. Her parents had always seemed so strong, viva-cious, and composed, resistant to the wear and tear of middle age. Ash had hardly been aware that they were getting any older at all . . . that is until now.

She had no doubt it was because their two children had both run away—first Eve, then Ash. It didn't matter that Ash had only run away to boarding school, instead of a life of delinquency. It didn't matter that she made occasional phone calls home, or Skyped her mom for an awkward conversation from time to time. Maybe she hadn't cut them completely out of her life like a tumor, the way Eve had, but she'd pushed them away just the same, albeit with a lighter touch.

Eve was right. They had made so many sacrifices for their adopted daughters.

The emotions of all this renewed Ash's strength. With a war cry that could probably be heard as far as Blackwood, she arched her back. She let the steam build up in her limbs as though they were pistons.

And then she hurled the three-ton stone slab off her with so much force that it flew off the side of the tower. Once Ash made sure that her parents truly hadn't been squashed by the slab, she let the volcanic armor soften back into flesh. She stretched her sore arms and legs, and joined Eve at the edge of the lighthouse. Down below they could see the slab, broken into pieces, a shattered stone commandment in the tide. Itzli's body floated face-down in the shallows next to it.

"You're really developing a thing for throwing people off buildings," Ash said.

"My only wish," Eve said, "is that the lighthouse had been taller."

Their parents were safe, but there was still the matter of Colt and Rose. Colt was standing at the edge of the lighthouse, tensed and ready for action. Ash could see in his eyes that he knew he'd lost this round. But Colt was regenerative, just like his powers—you couldn't maim him or cut him out of your life. If he got away now, he'd just find a way back into their existence, again and again, until he finally succeeded.

Colt turned and took a wild leap off the lighthouse, trying to pull the same stunt he had back at RazorWire Laboratories. He would just hit the water below, take the pain, let his body mend itself quickly, and then escape off into the night.

Eve was ready for him though. A massive updraft of tornado-force winds caught him mid-flight, and for a moment his body hung in the air cartoonishly, his limbs windmilling. Then the gust tossed him right back up onto the lighthouse platform. Eve sent a heavy current of lightning through his body to subdue him, and Colt writhed on the stone, his body shuddering with a violent seizure.

Before Ash and Eve could converge on him though, they heard a strange sound: It was the tinkling of a music box.

Rose sat on the edge of the lighthouse platform, cradling the music box that Ash had salvaged from her old home. She must have spotted it poking out of Eve's abandoned knapsack and grabbed for it in a moment of anxiety, hoping that the familiar song would comfort her.

Only this time, when the melody reached a certain point, the gears inside caught. Rose frowned and then wound the key several more times. Again the glockenspiel-like music danced lightly on . . . until it reached the same point in the song. The box must have been damaged when Rose exploded back in Central Park, after hearing it the last time. Now, every time the music snagged on that one note, Rose grew increasingly distressed.

The rumbling of the offshore volcano crescendoed suddenly, and the stone lighthouse bucked hard under their feet. The unexpected earthquake caught Rose by surprise, and the music box slipped out of her grasp.

Ash watched in horrified slow motion as the music box hit the stone platform.

As it bounced over the edge.

As Rose let out a half-sob and reached unsteadily for the familiar toy.

And as she lost her balance and slipped right off the edge with it.

Ash and Eve both cried out, but it was Colt who wailed the loudest. Ash started to take a step toward the lighthouse edge to look down, but the thought of what she might see in the water below was just too much to handle.

Colt rolled onto his side, practically foaming at the mouth as he glowered viciously up at the two remaining Wilde sisters. There was no love left in his eyes. "Look what you've done!" he snarled. "Now I'll have to wait until the next lifetime to put you back together."

"That's what you're worried about?" Ash shrieked at him, wiping the wetness from her face. "A bloody battle between gods, your right-hand man is splattered on the water below, a little girl just accidentally took her own life . . . and you're worried that you'll have to wait another eighty years to get your Frankenbride?" Ash ignited her hands. This was it. This was the final push she needed to end Colt's life, even if it was in cold blood. He had nothing left to defend himself with, and Ash was still ready to rip the heart right out of his chest.

Before she could lunge for him, the rumbling of the volcano deepened even more. Something was wrong. Ash reached out to the volcano with her mind, and she could feel the heat reaching critical mass, feel the pressure building inside it.

And just like that, the crater on top exploded. A salvo of enormous fiery stones rocketed up into the sky, burning bright, burning hard. The dump-truck-size boulders left the earth with such velocity that they punched a hole right through the clouds and continued upward. Eventually, they would reach the top of their arcs and hurtle back to the earth.

Most concerning, when Ash reached out with her mind to the fiery stones, mentally tethered to them by their shared volcanic origins, she could feel the trajectories they would follow.

And as one of them ran out of steam, miles above, she could feel it begin its descent.

Heading down toward the lighthouse.

In that moment she saw exactly what she had to do. Because of his abilities, Colt theoretically could only die if his heart were removed . . . or completely destroyed.

Ash placed her hand on Eve's shoulder and squeezed.

"You're just as strong as I am. Carry Mom and Dad down the stone steps as fast as you can."

Eve was crying again, and Ash could see her own image reflected in her sister's glossy pupils. The two sisters had never looked more alike. "What are you going to do?" Eve asked.

"See this through to the end." Ash wrapped Eve in the tightest hug she could, but released her before Eve could hug her back. They had no time.

Ash dove for Colt, who was crawling his way toward the edge. He, too, seemed to have noticed the comet that had reached the peak of its arc in the sky above them and was heading back toward earth . . . back toward him. Ash caught him by the shoulders and pinned him to the ground. He writhed, struggling to free himself like a worm caught in a bird's beak, but she just clamped her burning hands into his shoulders. Rage had made her stronger than ever, and there was no escaping her now.

"This is what you wanted, isn't it?" Ash screamed into his face. Fire wreathed her head, and she brought her nose down to his. She wanted Colt to experience terror, true terror, in his final moments on earth—even if they were to be her final moments as well. "You and Pele, together until the end?" She pressed her scalding lips to his in an angry, violent kiss. "Well you've got your wish."

When she pulled away, Colt's charred lips healed themselves, and he stared up at her in defiance. "You may have stopped me this lifetime," he says, "but I'll be back. You'll wake up a century from now with no memory of all this, and I'll just charm my way back into your life. You can't out-trick a trickster, Ashline." He let out a crazed laugh.

Ash continued to stare into his eyes. She didn't want him to be the last thing she ever saw, but she also didn't have the courage to watch the fireball come down. The air around them quivered electrically, and she could feel the umbra of the enormous comet coming down to destroy them both. Ash might be fireproof, but that would do nothing to save her from being crushed by the volcanic boulder or the three-hundred-foot fall afterward. This was her death sentence, her burden.

A hand wrapped around the back of her shirt, and in the brief second before she was yanked back, her first crazed thought was that Colt had somehow grown an extra arm.

The phantom hand heaved her backward across the stone platform, and a gust of wind carried her the rest of the way to the stairs. When she finally recovered herself and looked up, she discovered that Eve had replaced her, kneeling on top of Colt. She sent an electric current through his struggling body to immobilize him, then turned back to Ash over her shoulder. "Go!" she cried out to Ash. "Go live your life, and live it better than I did."

"No!" Ash croaked, but almost no sound came out. Above Eve and Colt, the magnificent, catastrophic ball of stone hurtled toward the platform, growing larger by the moment.

"I promise you," Eve yelled over the approaching roar of the comet. "I promise you I'll be a better sister in the next lifetime."

There was no time to say good-bye, because Eve hit her with one last gale that tossed Ash backward down the stairs. She didn't stop rolling until she landed on her unconscious parents, whom Eve had tucked partway down the staircase. And because there was no time left, Ash swallowed her quaking tears, scooped up her parents with all the superhuman strength she had left, and sprinted down the steps.

She only made it halfway down when the fireball hit. The thunderous blast knocked Ash off her feet as the behemoth slammed into the top of the lighthouse. It sheared the platform on top clean off.

With her parents in a heap at her feet, Ash drew herself up protectively over them. She focused on keeping her front side cool, then let a curtain of fire erupt out of her back, which she'd armored once more with igneous stone. As the rock debris from the pulverized platform above showered down on them, the fiery armor acted as a protective shield.

And then it was over. Ash dropped, exhausted and faintly smoking, into a heap beside her parents, who were just starting to stir from the fading sedatives. Even as they blinked and mumbled in unconsciousness, Ash just lay there staring up at the sky through the gaping open jaws of stone where the platform used to be.

Eve was gone. She waited to see some flash of lightning, or some shooting star through the constellations above, one of those mystical signs people always saw in movies to remind them that their dead loved ones were still out there somewhere.

But this wasn't the movies. There was only an unbearable quiet, until Ash's mouth was able to form the one thing she wished she'd had more time to say up top:

"I promise I'll be a better sister next time too."

Ash had been leaning against the trunk of the palm tree for over an hour, watching the one-story house across the street.

She still wasn't sure she could go through with it.

She'd been out on the islands for nearly three weeks now, researching Hawaiian family trees, practically living in the libraries and town halls while she combed through public records. She'd started in Maui, where she'd nearly destroyed the entire island almost two hundred years earlier after she'd summoned Haleakalā to erupt. The culmination of her search had led her here, to a suburb of Honolulu, where a woman named Kalama lived.

If her research was correct—and there was no way to know for sure, since a lot of it was guesswork—Kalama might be a descendant of the baby girl Pele had abandoned two centuries ago, right before the Cloak dragged her away . . . the very child that Pele might have incinerated if the Cloak hadn't stopped her in time. In fact, after nine generations, there were actually more than forty people on the islands who might trace their lineage back to Pele's abandoned love child.

Which meant that Ash had forty great-great-grandchildren—most of them older than her—living and working and raising families on the islands.

The thought of it was almost too weird to handle.

Still, she'd felt compelled to seek one of them out. Maybe it was just plain old curiosity, or maybe she felt some element of remorse for abandoning and almost murdering the child. Maybe she wanted proof that the visions of her previous lives hadn't been strange dreams.

Maybe after all the death and destruction that had sullied Ash's life in the last two months, she just wanted to see that something good had come out of her tumultuous, deadly relationship with Colt Halliday.

But more than anything, Ash was just looking for something to distract her from the palpable void Eve's death had left in her life. Rose's death too, even though she'd barely known the girl. In just a matter of months she'd found a sister she never knew she had and won back another sister who had for years been nothing more than a silhouette in her life.

Then she'd lost both sisters in a single night. Now she was left struggling with the memory of Eve, trying to reconcile all the different facets of her inconsistent personality. Who was the true Eve? The girl who'd started petty, brutal fights at school? The girl who'd run away from home and broken her parents' hearts—broken Ash's heart? Or was she the penitent, selfless girl who'd given her life to save her family that night on the lighthouse?

Now Ash found herself staring at a stranger's house in Honolulu, wondering what comfort could be provided by a distant relative who, other than shared blood, she probably had nothing in common with.

Still, she had to try.

When Ash finally worked up the courage, she crossed the street, marched up the front walkway, and pounded on the door before she could chicken out. While she heard footsteps approaching inside, she held on to the rusted, flaking metal railing for support. It was too late to run now.

When the inner door opened, a girl only a few years older than Ash stood inside, peering out at her through the screen. Even though Ash knew it was a stupid thing to think, she'd pictured Kalama as an uncanny cross between herself and Colt—maybe with the gentle curve of Ash's jawline and the jewel-facet cheekbones that made Colt so handsome.

In reality, as far as Ash could see, Kalama bore absolutely no obvious resemblance to either of her deity ancestors . . . which made sense, since after nine generations Colt and Pele made up only a small percentage of the girl's ancestral blood.

"Can I help you?" the girl asked, squinting at Ash.

Ash looked away in embarrassment, suddenly realizing she'd been intensely gawking at the girl's face. "Are you . . . Kalama?" Ash managed to stammer out. The girl nodded, so Ash went on. "I'm Ashline Wilde, from New York. I was doing research on my family ancestry for a summer project, and part of my assignment was to track down a member of my extended family that I'd never met. According to my research, you and I are . . . distant cousins." Mostly lies, but enough of the truth that Ash wouldn't feel bad.

At first the girl continued to squint, so Ash wondered if the story she'd concocted was too transparent or ridiculous . . . but then the girl broke out into a wide grin, the kind of real, deep smile that Ash wasn't sure she'd learn to do again.

"Well, aloha then, cousin," Kalama said. She popped open the screen door and held it open, a gesture to invite Ash inside. It was only when Kalama turned in profile that Ash caught a detail she'd missed, studying her through the screen door.

Kalama was pregnant.

Very pregnant in fact—from the size of her baby bump, she looked like she might go into labor if she sneezed too hard.

Ash smiled and pointed to Kalama's belly. "My research was pretty extensive, but it didn't pull that up. Congratulations."

Kalama chuckled and clasped her hands over the bump. "You came here expecting just to meet a distant cousin, and within a minute you find out you're going to be a distant aunt to a baby girl as well. It's a two-for-one deal."

A few minutes later Ash was sitting out on the small patio overlooking Kalama's backyard, which was overgrown and turning a crispy yellow. Hawai'i was going through something of a dry summer—it had only rained twice in the entirety of Ash's visit.

These days Ash prayed for rain. Prayed for storms, and lightning, and the roll of thunder. Prayed for echoes from the thunderclouds to remind her that Eve was somewhere out there in the cosmic expanse, watching over her little sister.

Kalama emerged from the house holding a pitcher of iced tea and two glasses. "Is this your first time to Hawai'i?" she asked Ash as she poured the iced tea.

Ash nodded. "I feel a bit embarrassed that I'm only revisiting my heritage now. My parents adopted me from Tahiti, but from what little I know about my past, my roots also lie here."

"And does being here stir those roots in you?" Kalama handed her a glass, on which condensation was already starting to form. "Does being here feel like home?"

Ash thought carefully about this, because it was something she'd wondered herself. Walking the beach at night when the libraries and town halls had closed. Climbing

Kīlauea, then Haleakalā, up the volcanoes that Pele had given rise to. Standing ankle-deep in the crystalline pool beneath Waimoku Falls, where she'd consummated her love with Colt Halliday two centuries ago. All that, and she'd expected it to stir in her some sense of belonging, something buried in her heart or her memories. "No," Ash finally answered. "I wanted to, but . . . Honestly, no place feels like home right now. I guess I'm just adrift."

Kalama gave her an exaggerated mock frown. "I believe that's a very serious medical condition called being a teenager."

Ash had come there to pick Kalama's brain, to find out all about her and what sort of ancestors she and Colt could have given birth to, for better or worse . . . yet, in her easygoing and gently prodding manner, Kalama somehow turned the entire conversation to Ash and her past. Thirty minutes later Ash had spilled a detailed account of life growing up as a Polynesian girl in New York, her volatile relationship with Eve, and her transfer to Blackwood Academy. Even though she was omitting the supernatural elements, and just about everything from the last two months, it felt good to just tell a real story for once.

In fact as Ash waxed on about life in Scarsdale and her parents, she felt this profound sense of relief. While she was happy to be done with cults of evil gods, and bloodthirsty god-hunting millionaires, and especially Colt Halliday, she'd been harboring this secret fear that when all that bad stuff was over, it would be impossible to return to a normal life. More than anything, she feared that living among mortals again would feel boring and trivial by contrast. Sure, she wouldn't have to endure the harsh agonies of watching her loved ones die violently anymore, but there was an excitement to her life when she was fighting for something, when the fate of the world hung on her shoulders.

It turned out to be just the opposite, however. She had more longing than ever to return to Scarsdale and accept the challenge of resuming her old life. Ash hadn't had the smoothest childhood. But she'd been so busy running from the ways her upbringing hadn't fulfilled her that she'd never appreciated the ways that it had.

Ash finally managed to steer the conversation back to Kalama. "Now that I've practically vomited up my personal history to you," Ash said, "do I know you well enough to ask about the baby's father?"

Kalama gestured to the patio seat next to Ash, and for the first time she noticed the five-by-seven framed picture sitting in the seat. In the picture, a handsome Hawaiian boy in a naval uniform stared out. Even though the photograph was static, Ash got the impression that the boy had the same chipper personality as Kalama and probably had struggled not to smile for the picture.

"Don't worry, he's still with us," Kalama assured Ash when her expression clouded with panic. "He's just overseas for another eight months. And then alternating years after that," she admitted grudgingly.

"It must be hard," Ash said, "living half your life without someone." Strangely, even though she didn't want to feel sympathy for him, her mind gravitated to Colt, inheriting all his old memories, then spending two decades away from his beloved.

"Everyone says that." Kalama stared thoughtfully at the lemon that was floating in her iced tea. "But picture the man you love. Now ask yourself: Would you rather live half your life with him? Or all of it without him, with someone else instead? When you look at it that way, the choice is much easier than you think."

This time it was Wes's face that blossomed into Ash's mind, the image surfacing and then dissolving like a drop of ink in water.

Eventually the conversation wound down, and Ash didn't want to drag it out—she'd barged her way into the girl's life as it was. And for better or worse she'd gotten what she'd come for: Something good had come out of her multi-lifetime affair with Colt. Not just Kalama, but the husband who could think lovingly about his wife and child while he was overseas. And the child who would hopefully grow up to find that love too, and the same for all the generations that would follow.

After Kalama had walked Ash out of the house, the two of them shared a hug so tight that Ash almost forgot they were still basically total strangers, despite their shared blood. Where the swell of Kalama's belly pressed into Ash's stomach, she felt a crackling electricity—the power of possibility.

"I forgot to ask if you'd picked out any names," Ash said.

Kalama laughed tersely. "Oh, we've got a laundry list of them. But it's hard to pick something out for a person you've never met, you know? We can't even decide whether we want to choose an English name or something more traditional. My husband's even pickier than I am." She shook her head at the space next to her, as though he were standing right by her side, preparing to argue.

Ash cleared her throat. "Well, I'm sort of the outsider in these parts, but I have spent a lot of the last few weeks looking through names and looking up their translations to see what they meant. I came across one girl's name that made me smile: Ualani." Ash paused, then added: "It means 'rain from heaven.'"

Kalama's eyes lit up. She seemed like she was actually considering it. "Ualani . . . ," she repeated. "It's beautiful. Kind of a funny image though. You always think of heaven as this sunny place with immaculate, island weather." She shrugged. "But then again, heaven is a very personal thing. I'm sure it rains in someone's heaven."

Ash lifted her eyes to the sky, where the beginnings of gray clouds were finally starting to coalesce. "It does in mine," she said.

Six hours later Ash sat on the beach as the rain hammered down on her. She'd discarded her soaked towel and was resting in the sand, hugging her knees to her chest and staring out at the Pacific. Only a few brave beachgoers remained, mostly surfers who probably figured they were here to get wet regardless. The rest of the tourists had fled when the storm failed to relent after ten minutes.

She'd done what she'd come here to do, and tomorrow she'd return to New York, to try to put her life back together. There were decisions to be made. For starters, should she return to Blackwood Academy in the fall, or give life at Scarsdale High a second chance? But the biggest adjustment was going to be the relationship with her parents.

When they'd woken from their sedated, nightmare-plagued state in the shattered stone lighthouse, Ash had struggled to fabricate a story that would explain how they'd both lost consciousness in Scarsdale and woken up on the California coast thirty-six hours later. In the end she decided the easiest solution was just to tell them the truth.

All of it.

Sure, they might have thought she was high at first as she launched into her story about Colt, and the gods of Blackwood Academy, and the bicoastal saga that had unfolded from California to Miami to Boston and back again. But when they watched as their daughter spontaneously combusted into a volcanic-plated fire monster, right in front of their eyes, the rest of the wild story must have been a little easier to swallow.

The supernatural stuff was a breeze to explain. It was trying to explain what happened to Eve that nearly snapped Ash in two. She'd grappled with whether she should write Eve completely out of the story, or at least the final chapter of it. Was it better for her parents to think that their daughter was somewhere still out there, alive, riding her motorcycle from town to town, but always having to wonder why she wouldn't come home? Or was it better for them in the long term to know that their daughter had loved them, had sacrificed everything so they could live . . . but had died in the process?

There was no end to the crying when Ash told them. They wanted to lay their daughter to rest, but there was nothing left to bury but her memory and a room full of stuff she'd outgrown at home, items that really no longer had anything to do with the girl who'd climbed to the top of that lighthouse and given her life for her family.

Or maybe those items had everything to do with her.

She heard the footsteps in the wet sand, but didn't know they belonged to Wes until he dropped down behind her and wrapped his arms tightly around her waist. She'd recognize those biceps anywhere.

"You know," Wes said, leaning his big, square chin down on her shoulder, "it's cheating to hold a wet T-shirt contest when you're the only contestant."

Ash laughed despite herself. She leaned back and craned her head around to kiss him. Kisses between them these last few weeks on the islands were partially for pleasure, yes, but also to put off all the questions they'd yet to answer about their future. Would he come back with her to Scarsdale? Would he follow her to school in the fall, or return to the lifestyle he'd abandoned in Miami? And would their love for each other flourish without the death and cataclysm to hold it back . . . or would it feel strange and foreign now that things had quieted down?

It was sort of like meeting somebody in a loud nightclub, Ash realized. You hear only the tinniest edges of their voices over their music, see the sultry, uninhibited side of them with their faces shrouded in darkness and laser lights. Then at the end of the night you step out under the streetlamps, and without the noise to drown each other out, you think: So that's what he looks like, what he sounds like.

Even if it would take some time to readjust to the silence, even if they didn't know whether the future might separate them, Ash realized that she felt the same way Kalama did: Given the choice between half her time with him or none of it at all, the decision for now felt easy.

Ash didn't realize she'd been sitting silent the whole time until Wes said, "I can't see your face from back here, but even the back of your head looks pensive." Ash elbowed him in the ribs, and Wes faked a wheeze. "What? You have a very sexy back side to your skull.

Some men are boob guys, and others are butt guys, but I'm a skull guy through and—"

Ash spun around and flattened him into the sand, pressing her whole body to his with another kiss. Once she pulled away, she let her dripping hair drape around him like a weeping willow. "Sometimes I think you run your mouth just so I'll kiss you to shut you up."

He smirked. "Am I that transparent?"

Ash rolled to the side of him, and they lay there, backs coated in sand, letting the rain paint their faces. It was dying to a drizzle, so at least they weren't drowning in it.

"I . . . ," Ash started finally. "I want to feel this sense of victory, this sense of closure. But I just keep thinking: This is only really a temporary victory, isn't it?" Wes went to interrupt her with some optimistic bullshit, but she just talked right over him. "Colt's dead, but in eighty, ninety years, all of us will be reincarnated again, and that bastard will be the only one to remember any of this. He'll be able to walk right up to me, pretending to be a stranger, and I'll be none the wiser. What if he works his way back into my life? What if he does succeed in melding my sisters and me back into one goddess? What if I fall for the guy and I let him? Just the thought of him touching me like that, as lovers . . ." Ash shuddered.

"Hey." Wes rolled onto his side, propped up on his Herculean elbow. "You've got a chance for a fresh start here. Yeah, Colt's got a few cards stacked against you for when you come back next time around. But he started with the upper hand this time too, and look how it turned out for him." Wes gently tapped the side of her temple, then let his hand linger there. "You've got tools up here that are far more powerful than lighting things on fire. The truth is, you have a whole lifetime to enjoy now, and if you don't because you're constantly worrying about the future, then Colt will have taken the present from you too. Then what would be the point of all this?"

He was right, of course. And if she was going to forge a new life, then there was no better time than sharing a beautiful Hawaiian beach at sunset, in a rainstorm, with the goofy but charming Mexican boy she was falling for all over again.

She cocked an eyebrow and traced her fingers seductively along his arm, from his wrist up to his elbow. "Remember that night in Miami? On the beach, as we waded half-naked in the Atlantic Ocean, and I heated the water to make us our own private steam room . . . ?" Where her fingers went, the rain evaporated off his skin in small puffs of mist.

He inched closer to her. "I hope that's a rhetorical question. I'll never forget that night."

It had been the last carefree moment they'd shared until now. Everything descended into hell after that. But if they could just find their way back to that little bubble of steam, that pocket of serenity . . .

"I was just thinking," Ash went on, "that now would be a very good time to see how the Pacific Ocean compares." Her eyes darted playfully down the beach to the waterline.

He cupped his hands around her face. "I hear the water's just right here," he offered. "I hear . . . that it's paradise."

She jumped to her feet, and before he could even rise next to her, she was tossing off articles of clothing haphazardly into the sand, leaving a trail down to the water. Her sandals, her shirt, her jeans, until she was down to only her bikini. She splashed in up to her knees and then dove into the Pacific with a graceful dolphin arc.

Wes was hot on her heels, deceptively fast for his size, and just as he surfaced, he threw his arms around her and lifted her up out of the water. He let her linger up there so she could look down at him for once. Her hips pressed into his bare chest, and he slowly lowered her so that the contours of her curvaceous body slipped down the hard angles of his.

The steam started to rise out of the water, enveloping them in a fine, warm mist. "Just pretend for old time's sake," he said, "that there's no world outside. It's just you and me floating in our own private cloud."

"For old time's sake," she agreed, and pressed her lips to his.

The cloud slowly enshrouded them, and to any remaining bystanders on the beach they might have looked like two teenage spirits, deeply in love, vanishing into the great abyss.

REUNITED

Johanna sat at the bar, a near-empty bottle in her hand. The rest of her fellow crew members— all men—were scattered around the bar. Most of them were playing darts or hitting on the few local women who were unlucky enough to stumble into this pub on this night. The women came for a drink and maybe a little attention; what they discovered instead were a lot of sex-starved sailors with wandering eyes and hands.

Those men had learned better than to sit next to Johanna.

After all, she was Joaquin's girl.

The bartender continued to polish a glass in front of her, eyeing her, but she kept her gaze on the old, broken holo-screen, which flickered with age. The three-dimensional image showed a torn-up field and a gaggle of rugby players wrestling for a ball. Johanna had no idea of the rules of the game, but the barkeep had confused her Polynesian roots for New Zealander and become convinced that she was originally from the island, even after she had assured him that she had grown up in Toronto, and she was on shore just for the night, before the crew left port tomorrow.

She felt the stranger looming behind her before he even had a chance to say anything. His shadow spilled over her like an oil slick, blocking the light from the dingy electric lantern overhead.

Johanna didn't even give him a chance to draw first blood. "Oh, come on," she said, over her shoulder, without even looking at him. "You should know that you're supposed to think of the pickup line, *then* walk over. Not the other way around. What is this, amateur hour?"

Still, he said nothing, but from his shadow she could see that he was gesturing with his hands. "Are you listening to a word I'm saying?" she started to say, swiveling around on her barstool.

She stopped when she saw the stranger. He was a strikingly handsome man, with a dark, even tan, and hair cropped close to his skull. Either he came from a life of hard, manual labor, or he was just naturally built, because his forearms were like small logs. She could tell that his T-shirt concealed some hard, toned lines as well.

But it wasn't the man's beauty that stopped her midsentence. It was the fact that he was gesturing wildly with his hands, alternating between signs and then touching his throat.

The man was a mute.

"I am so sorry," Johanna said. She clamped a mortified hand down over her forehead. "If I'd known you couldn't speak . . ."

Then the stranger's hands fell back to his sides, and a devious grin spread across his face. "There's nothing wrong with my vocal cords. I just wanted to see you squirm."

Johanna crossed her arms. "Wow, this must be a new record for me," she said. "You've only put two sentences together, and I already hate your guts."

The stranger nodded back toward the door. "Want me to give it a second try? I'm sure if I worked really hard, I could have made you hate me in one sentence."

"Great. Think of one and come back tomorrow. I'll be here." Johanna spun back to face the counter.

The stranger slid onto the barstool next to her. "Here's the thing. I fully acknowledge that I've blown whatever remote chances with you I thought I had, before I awkwardly approached you from behind and inconveniently found myself speechless. I assume, from the calluses on your hands and from the surly coworkers of yours who have invaded this bar, that you probably work on the boat that pulled into port this morning, and that romancing you is futile when you'll just set sail again tomorrow. Your general standoffishness tells me that you're either not looking for romance or you've got a boyfriend, and the fact that a room full of horny, sex-starved sailors are keeping their distance from you like you're radioactive suggests that it's probably the latter. So," he said, and propped up his head on his beefy fist, peering at her profile. "Think of this like a trade: I buy you a drink, in return for you enduring a conversation with me so I can save face. Everybody wins."

Johanna finally gave him the courtesy of eye contact. "That doesn't buy you much time. I drink very fast."

"Fortunately, I talk very fast." The stranger held up two fingers to the bartender, already assuming she'd agreed to his terms.

Johanna pushed away her empty bottle and accepted the fresh beer from the bartender. "You know, some say persistence is a virtue. I say that persistence can get you killed."

"You'd be surprised what I'm impervious to," the stranger replied. He took a sip of his beer to cover a smile.

When he turned back to her, he could see something in her eyes as she peered at him. She'd shucked the whole standoffish act, replaced it with curiosity . . . and if he wasn't mistaken, the first symptoms of déjà vu. "What's your name, stranger?" she asked.

"Colton Halliday," he said, and held out his bottle to toast her. "Call me Colt, though."

"Colt?" She giggled in a way that was disproportionately feminine for a roughneck deckhand. "Are you a man or a horse?"

This time it was his turn to itch with déjà vu. "Some would say neither," he said.

She rubbed her eyes wearily. "I'm sorry, I . . . I was just overcome with this weird sensation. Have we met before?" She studied him, taking in the hard lines of his cheekbones, the disconcerting flawlessness of his skin. He was beautiful to be sure, but there was something surreal to the perfection. He was like one of those computer-generated people she'd seen in old films, where they were so immaculately animated that they looked too real to be real.

There was a flash of concern on his face, and he shrank back in his seat under the scrutiny of her gaze. "I assure you," he said finally, "that if we had met before, there is no way I could have forgotten you."

This visibly relaxed Johanna, who loosened up a bit with a mocking smile. "And I guess there's no way I could have forgotten your over-the-top, pitiable charm."

But despite their rough start, she played right into his hands: She indulged him in conversation, a real con-versation, while they both nursed their beers. She talked about growing up in Canada, adopted as a newborn from a Micronesian orphanage, and about tracking down her long-lost sister twenty years later, who she had been sepa-rated from when she was too young to remember. Colt told her about his own life, also as an orphan—raised through foster care in the American southwest before he was emancipated at age sixteen. Taking on what odd jobs he could find, enough to pay his way as he traveled the world. He talked about certain elements of his life in great detail, and shrouded others in vague statements.

Colt noticed how Johanna wasn't racing to finish her beer. And if he had any doubts that she was enjoying his company, they were erased the moment she signaled for the bartender to bring them two more.

Tell me now, he thought with a mental smirk, *that persistence doesn't pay off.*

His entire existence, his mission in life—for the last five hundred years—had hinged upon unflagging persistence.

And it was about to pay off.

He could see her eyes growing cloudier the more she drank. She was laughing more frequently, relaxing her posture, even touching his knee once or twice during their conversation. She didn't even look disapproving when his eyes took the liberty of roaming her body once or twice.

Little did she realize he knew every inch of her body very well.

Eventually, while she was in the middle of a story about a bar fight in a Taiwanese port, Colt interrupted her: "Hey, do you want to get some fresh air? Step outside and go for a walk?" She raised an eyebrow at him, so he continued innocently, "You only get to spend so much time on land, it seems a shame to spend most of it cooped up inside a dingy bar."

Johanna's eyes flicked to the other sailors, perhaps

weighing the consequences of following Colt outside. But then she chugged the remainder of her beer, set it down hard on the bar, and took Colt by the hand. He led her through the front door, and as the eyes of the other sailors followed her with surprise and warning, she offered them a wan smile back that said, *I've got this under control.*

Outside the bar she took the lead, but she only made it three steps before she felt Colt resist. With a masculine but graceful confidence, he spun her back to face him. Before she knew it, she was in his arms, sandwiched between his chest and the brick wall of the bar.

Still, he paused just shy of kissing her. "What about your boyfriend?" he whispered, like it mattered to him at all.

Johanna let her lips trace a line along his jaw before whispering back: "What boyfriend?"

Colt tried to lead her back in the direction of the motel room where he was staying, but Johanna laughed mischievously and dragged him toward the freight ship, *Renaissance*, that was docked nearby.

For the next ten minutes Colt lost himself in a cloud of desire and excitement, barely aware of his surroundings as Johanna led him onto the *Renaissance*, then through a labyrinth of shipping crates. They seemed to be moving away from the crew's quarters, which made sense if she bunked with her supposed boyfriend. Instead she stopped at a blue shipping crate on the port side of the ship, looking off to the western horizon, where the dusk sun was just finally plunging into the ocean. He didn't have time to enjoy the view, however, as Johanna heaved open the rusty, squeaky door of the shipping crate.

"It's my little oasis," she explained, then stepped into the dark interior. "My quiet haven on the ship to escape the rest of the crew." Her face slowly slipped beneath the cover of shadows as she backed inside with a playful smile. "Follow if you dare."

Colt did join her, closing the door behind them so there was just a crack of dusk light casting a line against the steel walls. In the corner, a new, fiery light blossomed, revealing Johanna standing in front of an old-fashioned lantern. He didn't see any matches, and he realized with a thrill what this meant:

She's come into her powers.

The rest of the shipping crate was sparsely decorated for an "oasis"—just a small nightstand in the corner with three books on it, and a quilt and some lumpy pillows spread out on the floor.

He wasn't here to critique her interior decorating though. "Lie down," she told him, nodding to the quilt.

He did as she said, feeling the hard metal floor of the crate press unforgivingly through the thin quilt. But pain, especially for him, was nothing in pursuit of a dream that had been postponed for the better part of a century now.

Johanna kneeled over him seductively. Her fingers slipped inside his button-down shirt, and with a harsh rip the buttons popped free, exposing his chest. She ran one hand over his bare skin, and he closed his eyes in ecstasy, taking in the smell of her. "How hot do you like it?" she whispered to him, her breath warm against his hear.

"Very," he groaned back, his eyes still closed.

Then he felt the heat. His eyes shot open. Her hand, now pressing hard against his chest, had ignited in a wreath of fire, searing a deep, red burn into his flesh. He screamed, despite himself, and jerked back, trying to get out from under her.

She knelt down on him hard though, locking him in place. She pulled her hand away, and even as he struggled to conceal his chest with his shirt, she watched as the molten handprint began to fill in, then lighten, then disappear altogether, as skin fused back over it.

When the healing was done, she nodded, pensively staring at the scar-less flesh, not looking surprised at all. "I just needed to be sure," she said, matter-of-factly.

Something snapped around his ankle. Johanna's other hand, which had disappeared behind her, had fastened a metal shackle just above his foot. She backed off to admire her handiwork, while he reached down for the restraint. The shackle—which had been concealed beneath the quilt—was snug around his ankle, like it had been molded just for him. The other end of the thick chain was bolted to the shipping crate floor.

He sprang to his feet and lunged toward Johanna, but the metal leash stopped him, his fingernails swiping just inches from her unconcerned face.

"Why are you doing this?" he said, trying to muster innocent confusion as best he could, but he was starting to panic. "Johanna, is this some sort of game?"

Johanna rolled her eyes and leaned against the inside of the crate. "Here's the deal," she said. "I'm going to stand here and say absolutely nothing until you drop the ignorance act."

"Johanna, I don't understand!" he cried out. For minutes he pleaded with her, begged her to let him go, saying he'd do anything, pay her anything.

Johanna just yawned into her hand. Her eyes never left him. They were cold and bored.

Eventually, he saw that his ruse was going nowhere. So he conceded defeat the only way he knew how. "So," he said. "How much do you remember? All of it? Some of it? Has it bled in through your dreams?"

Johanna shook her head. "I remember none of it," she said, with complete honesty.

"Then how—"

She waved for him to be silent, then pulled up a small stool, still out of his reach. "To answer that," she said as she sat down, "we have to go back seventy years . . . to when Ashline Wilde was still a teenager."

He flinched when he heard the name. Another nail driving into his coffin.

"Put yourself in her shoes," Johanna said, then corrected herself. "In my shoes, I suppose. You, Colt Halliday, are finally dead, and I want to start living my life like you never existed. But in the back of my mind I know the awful future that's in store for my next lifetime: I'll return remembering nothing, and you, who remember everything, will seek me out. The dance begins again, and sooner or later, you'll win. Maybe not this lifetime. Maybe not the next. But eventually you'll get to me.

"Now," Johanna went on, and this part seemed to excite her. "If I know I won't remember anything when I'm reborn, then my next best bet is to reach out to her—to me—to warn me. But that won't work either. The old me, Ashline, has to die before the new me, Johanna, is born. I don't know who the future me will be adopted by, or where, or what her name will be, so there's really no way to leave a message for her, is there?" Johanna left a pregnant pause. "Unless . . . unless I leave that warning someplace public. Someplace very public."

Colt's eyes widened as he realized what she was getting at, but she'd waited too long to let him finish the story for her.

"What if," Johanna continued, "I wrote down my whole story—starting from when I first discovered my volcanic abilities, my identity as Pele, through your fateful arrival in my life . . . and documented all of your treachery, and eventually, your death? And what if, rather than filing that story as nonfiction—because who would ever believe that, really?—I published it as fiction. And what if"—Johanna accented the final "if" triumphantly—"a girl named Johanna, raised in a culture that's not her own, one day decides to start reading stories about her heritage, about someone just like her. She finds the book that Ashline wrote and realizes that the girl described in the books has all the same fiery powers that she's just discovered herself. It could be coincidence, it could be fiction, but then again . . . maybe it's not."

"Johanna—" Colt tried to interject, but as much as Johanna was curious to hear whatever bullshit he'd try to manipulate her with, she was too proud to let him interrupt her story.

"Sure enough, when I did some research, I found Eve and Rose—the new Eve and Rose, that is, living under new names, with new families. I found others from the stories too." Johanna pointed through the open slit in the crate doors. "That's why I took a job that allowed me to travel so much. I've been slowly finding all the people from the last story. Enlightening them. Letting them know that they're not alone. But there was still one person, one god, I needed to meet to know with absolute certainty that everything Ash had written down was real, a person that in all my travels, I'd never met. . . ." She smiled grimly at him. "Until tonight."

"I didn't mean you any harm," Colt pleaded with her, sounding like a little boy who'd been caught shoplifting candy. "I wasn't going to try to mold you back into Pele, you have to believe me! I just . . . I just couldn't stay away from you. The attraction was too strong."

Johanna shook her head. "All you had to do was leave

me and my sisters alone. To learn your lesson. But you tracked me down anyway. And you tried to feed me lies from the moment you introduced yourself in that bar. The only thing you were too stupid and arrogant to lie about was your name. Of course, even if you'd changed your name, I still would have recognized you. Names can always change, but flesh—" She pointed to his bare chest, where she'd burned him. "Flesh never lies."

Johanna—the girl he once knew as Ashline, and before that as Lucille, and before that as Pele, and in the many lifetimes their paths had crossed throughout history—opened the door to the shipping crate but lingered in the entrance. "I warned you that persistence can be deadly, Colt. Fortunately—or maybe unfortunately—for you, I'm not going to kill you. But I am going to leave you someplace where you'll never harm me or my sisters again."

Colt came at her hard this time, sprinting toward her and the door. Maybe he thought he could pull hard enough that his restraint would snap clean off the floor, but she'd welded it herself, with her own fingers. The chain held fast, and she could hear his ankle break. He howled and dropped to the floor, and came at her on his hands and knees, like an animal. Spittle flew from his mouth.

Johanna looked down upon him now with pity, as his extended fingers clawed at the toes of her work boots. "I'm not going to sugarcoat it for you," she said. "If you're truly invulnerable the way the books say you are, then I guess that means you won't asphyxiate or drown in this container the way a human would. The bad news: Eternity in here is going to be very boring . . . and very wet. That's why I've been kind enough to leave you a present." She nodded back toward the nightstand. "I recommend you read it as quickly as you can while that lamp still has fuel left."

With that, Johanna stepped outside the container and slammed the door shut, muffling Colt's bellowing inside. She wrenched the lever handle closed, and then with her torch-hot fingers she welded the steel seam closed.

Johanna camped out outside the entrance of the crate for an hour, staring off into the night sky. She heard Colt struggling for a long time. She wouldn't put it past him to try to break his own foot again to pry it free of the shackle. Ironically, his regenerative abilities probably healed him too fast for that to work, and even if it did, escape was futile.

Eventually, Colt stopped screaming and pounding at the inside of the crate. Even his chain had stopped rattling, so he must have been lying still on the quilt.

Shortly thereafter, the *Renaissance* blared its horn and pulled out of the dock. It took several hours after that for Johanna to completely lose sight of the New Zealand coast, at which point she knew she was far enough out to sea for what needed to happen next. She pointed her finger up in the air and fired a single firework, a flare that burst into a million fireflies at the peak of its journey.

Joaquin was there in under a minute. She heard his lumbering footsteps on the stacked shipping crates before he even said anything. Still, she waited for him to come up behind her, draping his elephantine arms over her shoulders as affectionately as a giant his size could.

"It's done?" Joaquin asked.

She nodded. "He came, just like Ashline anticipated he would."

He spun her around and held her out at arm's length. "And you're positive you want to follow through with this?"

Johanna considered this for just a moment. She walked over to the shipping crate and ran her hands over the metal doors. If this were just about her, just about revenge, she might have talked herself out of it.

But Ashline and Evelyn Wilde had stopped Colt the last time, not out of malice, but for the love of their families.

Now Johanna had loved ones to protect too.

"Thousands of years' worth of accumulated wisdom and memories," she said, and she half-hoped Colt could hear her inside. "And all he had to do was learn from one mistake." With that, she tapped twice on the shipping crate door and stepped away.

Joaquin lifted his head to the night sky. As the moonlight bathed over him, his eyes turned an inky black. His already rippling muscles swelled.

He walked over to the side of the shipping crate, pressed two hands and his shoulder against the metal wall. Drew in a deep breath.

And he pushed the shipping crate off the edge of the boat, into the water.

Johanna and Joaquin sat together with their legs dangling off the boat, watching as the *Renaissance* left the sinking container behind. The dark Pacific waters swallowed it before it even reached the end of the boat.

"You know, there's a silver lining to Colt Halliday's story," Johanna said.

Joaquin slipped his hand through her hair and planted a kiss on the top of her head. "And what's that, love?"

"If Colt hadn't done all those awful things to get Pele back, Ashline would have never written that story . . . and I would have never found you again." She smiled, and the moonlight illuminated the tears of nostalgic joy in her eyes. Her hands cupped the side of his face, and her eyes were a hundred years deep as she peered into his. "Some loves are too small for just one lifetime, Wesley Towers."

Inside the shipping crate, Colt slammed against the wall, then the ceiling, as the container fell off the side of the ship. There was a tremendous *whoosh* as it hit the ocean and sank beneath the surface, at which point the crate's rotation slowed. Meanwhile, water slowly trickled through the seams around the doors.

Two minutes and an eternity later the crate struck

the seafloor, and Colt's world was righted again. He had to untangle himself from the chain, which had coiled around his leg like a metal boa constrictor while the container spun.

Miraculously, the antique lantern hadn't smashed during his prison's descent or been doused by the water, although from the dimming light he could tell it was almost out of fuel. He picked it up and started with some trepidation toward the corner where the "gift" Johanna had left for him floated in the rising ankle-deep water.

The three books were tied together with a red bow. His trembling fingers managed to unknot it on the third try, and he held up the book on top.

The title read: *Wildefire*.

He flipped to the soggy first page. The flickering light of the lantern illuminated the words in a vengeful crimson only long enough for him to read the very first sentence, before the lamp consumed the last of the kerosene and immersed Colt's underwater prison in darkness for good.

"Ashline Wilde," the book began, "was a human mood ring."

Acknowledgments

Let me begin by saying that all young-adult authors, myself included, are neurotic, emotionally unstable worry-warts prone to extended periods of paralyzing self-doubt and angst—which is, I suppose, why we are so well-qualified to write from a teenage perspective.

On outward appearance, when you see us at book signings or author events, we may seem cool as a cucumber (an expression that I've never entirely understood, since most cucumbers that I've encountered have been room temperature at best). But in the three years since I entered the tumultuous world of publishing, I have yet to meet an author—debut or established, contemporary or fantasy, human or cucumber—who hasn't developed Chicken Little syndrome in the weeks surrounding the launch of his or her latest book. This anxiety ultimately boils down to one question: Who on earth is going to read this book?

This goes doubly so for series authors, who after years of avoiding basic arithmetic, decide to dabble in the black magic that is calculus with nonsensical equations that look like:

If x people read my first book,

And only y% of those readers pick up the sequel,

And only $1/z$ of *those* readers bother with the third one,

Then how many marshmallows can I fit in my mouth at once?

But sooner or later you have to stop worrying about who's not reading your book, and focus on the readers who have, and are, and will. Which is why I'd like to thank just a handful of the readers who have made this experience so rewarding, particularly Rachel Clarke, Cindy Thomas, Alexandra Cenni, Kari Olson, and everyone who has stuck with Ashline Wilde until the bitter end. Every tweet, message, e-mail, review, and carrier pigeon you've sent my way has gone neither unnoticed nor unappreciated.

To my favorite bookstore owner, Peter Glassman. If I could build a pillow fort and live inside one bookstore in this world, it would be Books of Wonder.

To my new editor, Kristin Ostby. It's a somewhat thankless job to seize the reins of a trilogy on the third and final installment. Somehow, in the course of one summer, you were able to absorb all three books and still dazzle me with incisive, contemplative insight into my characters that had never occurred to me before—and I've lived with these characters for four years now. Your fresh perspectives have made me a better storyteller, and for that, I thank you.

To my former editor, Courtney Bongiolatti. I have

missed your wit and wisdom these last few months. But more than anything, I missed the opportunity to gloat when the Giants didn't make the playoffs.

To Bernard Ozarowski and Lili Corn, for your hospitality in letting me crash with you and your seven hundred cats in the Lower East Side whenever I have an author event in New York City.

To Steve Dicheck, who you would think is my publicist based solely on the number of times he has whipped out his iPhone to show random strangers the eBook of *Wildefire*.

To Lydia Finn, who you would think is my publicist because she, in fact, is.

To Justin Chanda, Mary Kole, Laura Antonacci, Colin Riley, and all the hardworking bookworms at Simon & Schuster, Simon & Schuster Canada, and Andrea Brown Literary Agency who have given me the experience of a lifetime.

To Mom, Dad, Erin, Kelsey, Ray, and Victoria, for continually putting up with me even though my adolescence has clearly spilled over into my late twenties.

At the time that I'm writing this, it's been exactly 997 days since I got a phone call from New York that changed my life. I only hope that the next 997 days make for a formidable sequel.